SONG
of the
RED CLOAK

CHANTEL ACEVEDO

SONG OF THE RED CLOAK

CHANTEL ACEVEDO

ALSO BY CHANTEL ACEVEDO

LOVE AND GHOST LETTERS

"*Love and Ghost Letters* is enchanting; a heartfelt story. It tells
volumes about the intimate life and loves of a family in pre-
Castro Cuba. Along the way, it captures, beautifully, the
atmosphere and emotions of a time which, both Cuban
Americans and many an American reader, will find both
reminiscent and fulfilling. A great debut."

-Oscar Hijuelos, author of *The Mambo Kings Play
Songs of Love*

"Acevedo, a first-generation Cuban-American, shapes each of
her characters with clear-eyed reverence, guiding their steps in
measured, lyrical prose that is often breath-taking, exquisite."
--A. Manette Ansay, author of *Vinegar Hill,* an Oprah Book
Club Selection

For Orlando and Penelope, *s'agapo*

CHANTEL ACEVEDO

I wish to tune my quivering lyre
To deeds of fame and notes of fire;
To echo, from its rising swell,
How heroes fought and nations fell.

"Translation From Anacreon," Lord Byron

Prologue

It began with a pair of infants, both just a few days old. In each house, a young woman held her baby against her chest while her husband poured wine over the baby's face. They watched the children carefully, their limbs tense, the womens' hands gripping their husbands' forearms.

One child cried. He howled for hours, and his tall, fair-haired mother wept with him. "Tell no one," his father said, looking away from the baby in disgust.

Meanwhile, in another house, a dark-haired mother peered into the face of her son. He did not cry when the wine splashed over his cheeks, mouth and nose, but opened his small eyes wide and looked at his parents curiously. This baby had passed the first test of his life, the ritual of the wine bath.

"There will be countless tests to follow, a lifetime of tests, but what a way to start!'" the father said. Already, the small boy was proving his strength.

6

"What a fine Spartan you will make," the mother said, swiping at her eyes to dry them.

But an old man burst upon the scene. His arms and legs were laced with thick purple veins. His long, silvery hair and beard lashed the air as he ran through the palace gates, claiming he'd been to the sibyl. "It has been prophesied. One Spartan prince will betray the other. If such a thing were to come to pass, the Sparta that we know would be destroyed. So spoke the sibyl. The ephors have decided. There can be only one prince." He was an ephor, one of five advisers to the kings. His hands, wrinkled and claw-like, reached for the baby.

The mother cried out, clutching her child. Her husband said nothing, could not look his wife in the eyes. When he pulled the infant away from her, she scratched him, screamed until she gagged, begging, "Not my baby," over and over.

"Enough! Be courageous. This is what it means to be a Spartan woman," he said to her, but his voice was not angry.

"Then I shall not be one!" she shouted, crumpling to the floor.

That night both new fathers sat in council with the ephors. Their wives' grievous cries still rang in their ears. The gods had been consulted. As they spoke, debating the ways to appease the gods and avert the disastrous prophecy, a single, lean dog had crept up behind one of the men, and nudged him with his snout.

"Ares sends a messenger," the other new father had said, pointing at the gaunt, sniffling dog. "Ephors, bear witness. His son has been chosen by the gods, not mine. Not mine."

Afterwards, the man that had been selected scaled a great height, then stood overlooking a gorge. His entire body trembled as he held the wiggling baby. He'd faced Persian battalions in the past, fierce, merciless soldiers, but he'd never shook this way.

"Our fate is set in stone," he told the child, but even his voice quivered as he spoke to his tiny son, the one he was about to destroy for the sake of Sparta. The gorge was dark and deep. He could see the peaks of jagged rock below him. Whimpering now, on the verge of his first real cry, the baby kicked his plump legs.

"For Sparta," he said. Then he said it again, "For Sparta," more loudly. His voice echoed into the night, bouncing in the canyons beneath him. He took one last, long look at his son. He extended his arms before him. The child hovered over the edge of the mountain, his father's strong hands beneath him. They trembled together, father and son.

1

The cloak was made of heavy wool and dyed a deep, blood red. Galen weighed it in his hands, felt the itch of the fabric on his palms. He unfurled it with a fierce whip. The cloak snapped out, caught the stiff breeze coming off the Mediterranean, and then floated gently down.

He draped the cloth on his shoulders, just as he heard a girl's voice, low but urgent, saying, "Please, Galen. Please," again and again. Ignoring her made him feel a little sick, the way he felt when he jumped off the top of a high place. He fumbled with the cloak's bronze hook and eye clasp at his neck. It pressed against his throat, making it hard to swallow. He wished the girl would stop pleading. Her voice caught. She was crying, and now, his eyes stung too.

By the gods, the cloak was heavy. Yet he felt so oddly cold. It was as if…it was…

"It's time! Move it now, you rotten beetle!"

"Okay. All right, all right. I'm up," Galen grumbled, and pushed away the sole of a sandal that was being pressed forcefully to his cheek. He was groggy from sleep, and the dream muddled him a bit. He wondered about the girl, the one who'd said his name in the dream, but she faded from his mind the moment Feodoras, his master, bent low over him. Galen could smell his hot, rancid breath, and it was worse than even the latrines that had been dug downwind of the agoge, the school for Spartan boys where Galen lived and worked as a helot, a slave in the Greek city-state of Sparta.

Feodoras growled, his lip curling back to reveal a blackened front tooth. Though Galen had known Feodoras for sixteen years, his whole life, he'd never seen him smile. "Come again?" Feodoras asked and his voice dropped to a dangerous volume, the kind that usually preceded a punch.

"Sir," Galen corrected himself, on his feet now. "I'm up, sir."

"You slept through dinner preparations, Galenos," Feodoras said, twisting a willow switch in his hands. Galen couldn't help but wince. The thrashing was coming.

In the kitchen, the other helots had spent hours turning the bony goat Galen had picked up at the market earlier that morning into a meal. The thing was pitiful, not worth the half-drachma he gave the goat-herder for it. But that was the idea. To bring home one of the fatter goats would have been a mistake. The students of the agoge were meant to go hungry. The boys would be soldiers one day in the finest army the world had ever seen. They entered the agoge at age seven, staying there until seventeen, when they joined the army at last. They trained to be tough, to resist the pangs of hunger, the ache of a wound. Those lean years spent away from the warm hearths of home sharpened the young Spartans, making them battle-strong and heartless. Most of the boys at the agoge stole food from helots and each other to round out their meals. The students were supposed to be punished if they got caught, but the truth was, their teachers often ignored the practice.

That morning, the little goat that would be stew had eyed Galen as if it might love him, as if it thought it had been spared. Galen looked away. There was no use in making friends with dinner. The goatherd, a white-haired helot named Brygus, put a rope around the goat's neck. Galen often sought out Brygus when it came time to buy meat for the agoge. His deals were fair, usually, and he never said a word, which Galen liked. He hated idle talk more than anything. But there was another reason Galen went to Brygus.

A girl about Galen's age often accompanied the goatherd. Galen had never spoken to her, though he sometimes imagined taking hold of her hand, leading her to a shady spot under a pomegranate tree, sharing some bread with her, learning her name. They were temporary flights of fancy for Galen, ridiculous fantasies of what free men and women did. His mind would wander this way during boring tasks—like sweeping the stone floors of the kitchen, or polishing the mosaic tiles in the dining hall, the ones arranged into a picture of Hercules tearing a lion in two. He would be concentrating on work when thoughts of the girl seeped in, distracting him.

That morning, Galen had watched as the girl knelt down beside the goat and kissed its head. "Have a good death, small one," she whispered, and when she stood, she met Galen's eyes, narrowing them as if in challenge. Hers were mottled, green eyes, the color of leaves in late summer. Her dark eyebrows were heavy, but shapely, and her hair, a deep brown, was often braided in three thick ropes down her back, reminding Galen of a stand of trees. He sometimes wondered whether a nymph, those spirits of the woods and seas, had a hand in making her.

"Thanks," Galen said, and she rolled her eyes and returned to Brygus' side. This was the problem with growing up in a school for boys. Galen had never had a real

11

conversation with a girl. To him, they were mysteries as deep and turbulent as the River Eurotas.

When Galen pulled hard on the rope around the goat's neck, its legs stiffened, and it fell on its side, as if dead. It must have guessed Galen's intentions. He carried the unconscious goat the rest of the way, and before long, Galen smelled like the creature—musky and rotten, as if it had died long ago. He carried the pathetic beast a mile up a steep, rocky hill to get to the city center and the agoge facilities. No wonder he'd fallen asleep soon afterwards.

Galen had meant to help with the killing and skinning, the separating of flesh from bone, the plucking out of stinky organs with a wooden spoon. He'd missed, too, the sacrifice to Ares, the god of war and the agoge's patron. A cave outside the agoge served as Ares' temple, and at every meal, a bit of blood was poured at Ares' altar, then sawdust was scattered over the sacrifice to keep the wild dogs away.

Galen had slept through all of the preparations for dinner, and now, Feodoras, smelling like goat himself, his apron splattered with still sticky blood, gripped the willow switch tightly. How could Galen *not* wince? Feodoras had never backed away from an opportunity to strike Galen, even when Galen was little and such an act should have shamed Feodoras.

But Galen wasn't a child anymore. He was nearly as tall as Feodoras, though not as thick. In the last year, hard work had filled out Galen's arms and legs in a way that turned the heads of young women in the market. But his nose had been broken three times in wrestling matches against the agoge students, and it had developed a small bump. There was a scar that cut through his left eyebrow, the result of a spear training session. His dark hair was shaved nearly to his scalp. All helots, even the women, were made to wear their hair this way. And though a kitchen girl had once told him "Could I write, I'd compose a poem about you," Galen, who had sputtered at her sudden compliment and run away, hated his reflection when he

12

came upon it. What he did value in himself was that he could take a punch without falling. These days, when Feodoras hit him, Galen would stumble a bit, feel his brain rattle in his skull, and recover quickly.

This time, Feodoras came after him with the switch. Galen ducked under Feodoras' first strike, but stumbled over a clay water vessel on the floor, so Feodoras managed to lash him once, twice, across the face, slashing against his eye. Galen cupped his hands over his eye and ran.

"That's for being useless," Feodoras yelled after him. "I'd give you another, but you've got worse coming!"

Galen ran until he was behind the far western wall of the agoge. He thought he'd gone blind for a moment, felt the panic rising in his chest, then the blessed relief of his eyesight coming back. It had only been a reaction to the pain. But what pain! It sent pulsing shocks into Galen's head, so hurtful, that he felt he would never be able to compose another thought, to think of anything but the agony he was feeling.

When he'd recovered a bit, Galen pulled a ragged piece of cloth from inside his chiton, walked to the crooked little stream that ran past the agoge, and wet the cloth, which he used to nurse his eye. Bent over, wringing the cloth, Galen didn't notice that a cloaked figure approached him. The man was as tall as a Persian. Only the tip of his fine nose peeked out from the darkness of his hood. He bent down before Galen, surprising him. Galen scrambled backwards.

"Who are you?" he asked, his hurt eye still closed.

The hooded man didn't answer, but gripped Galen's arm, twisting it to take a look at his tattoo, where the word "captive," λίσκομαι, had been inked before Galen could remember. It was the permanent mark of all helots and prisoners.

"Let me go," Galen said, struggling to get away. But the hooded man's grip was strong and painful.

"Who hurt you?" the man asked.

13

"My master," Galen answered.

"We outnumber them eight to one, boy," the man said. "We could own all of Sparta. Bring low our captors. The Eurotas will run red with Spartan blood for once, instead of ours." The man smelled of incense, and it made Galen's stinging eye water.

"Rebellion," Galen whispered, and the hooded man nodded.

The man cupped Galen's chin in a gnarled hand, and peered into Galen's face. The sun burned high behind the man, casting his own face in shadow, so that Galen could not see him in return. "The one you call master is not long for the world, boy. Remember this moment," the man said, releasing Galen roughly.

Galen's imagination caught fire at once. The possibilities presented themselves like a flood—to sit at the assembly, to own one's land, to travel across Greece like a free man, to fight in a war, to wear a red cloak. "Who are you?" Galen asked again.

"You need not know my name. The viper is coming. Be ready," the man said, and walked away, disappearing in the bright glare of midday.

2

As soon as the strange, hooded man was out of sight, Galen ran to the cave behind the agoge, Ares' simple temple, and entered.

Galen could feel his arms trembling. *Rebellion,* he thought. Then: *viper.* What had the hooded man meant about that? Galen's mind was too restless to try to figure it out. It latched onto the idea of a slave revolt and wouldn't let go. Sooner or later, Galen knew, he wouldn't be able to stop himself from striking back at Feodoras, whose punches didn't hurt the way they used to. Tears didn't come to Galen's dark eyes anymore, the way they had when he was a child. Now, when Feodoras hit him, all Galen saw were images of his master on the ground, Galen's fingers wrapped around the man's throat. These violent pictures in Galen's head always came fast, like thunderstorms at night, lightning striking the Parnon Mountains to the east, Mount Taygetos to the west,

15

illuminating the whole countryside for an instant before it all went back to black.

Galen saw himself facing Feodoras, a spear in his hands, an army of helots at his back...

Galen shook his head. There was no army of helots, nor was there likely going to be one. Most of the helots he knew were content to go about their lives, working their trades. After all, helots weren't the kinds of slaves kept in shackles. They did the work that Spartans would not do—the farming, the smithwork, the hunting—and so they moved about Sparta freely enough, as long as they knew when to bow before a Spartan, or answer a Spartan's call, or die for one of them, if the need arose. But maybe Galen had perceived the world around him incorrectly. Maybe other helots were as angry as he was. Galen shut his eyes to steady himself, because he was seeing it again, Feodoras at the end of his spear...

The temple smelled like fresh blood, and Galen took deep, full breaths of it. He never had enough to eat, and the iron taste in his mouth was oddly satisfying. His eye still burned, and he pressed his palm against it. What did Feodoras mean about something worse coming Galen's way? What could be worse than this life? Death? That was no punishment.

He looked around the unrefined temple where he now found himself. On a wooden bench stood a figure of Ares cast in bronze. It was small and rough looking. Galen had never touched such a sacred object, but now, his fingers were tingling to do so. Next to the figure was a scrap of red wool, a torn bit of Spartan cloak. Nestor, the agoge supervisor, once told a wonderful story about the cloth during dinner. He'd said it belonged to King Leonidas, the one who'd fought off thousands of Persians at Thermopylae with only three hundred Spartans behind him. They'd all died in the battle, but what a death! Leonidas' men had been brought home, dead on their broad shields. The king himself had been torn to pieces by the Persians, but his red cloak came back, to be divided among the

16

temples. The cloth was considered sacred, but Galen held it anyway and rubbed his fingers against the scratchy material.

Galen thought, quite frequently, that if he weren't a helot, he could be a Spartan soldier. He could throw a spear so that it flew straight and with great force. He could wrestle other boys to the ground, slamming their heads to the packed earth so hard their eyes crossed. On foot, Galen could outrun even the great Nestor, leaving the man wheezing a few paces behind him.

Galen crushed the bit of fabric in the palm of his hand. What choice did a helot have anyway? They weren't free. Though helots were born in Sparta, they had no rights of citizenship. Helots couldn't vote, or attend the Spartan schools, leave the city if they so wanted, or ever dream of wearing the warriors' red cloak. Still, Galen did dream it, every night since before he could remember, and so vividly, that he could close his eyes in the daylight and feel the weight of the cloak on his shoulders, as if it was really there.

Once more, Galen indulged in the pleasure of imagining himself wrapped in red, his foot pressed tightly against Feodoras' bulging voice box…

The truth was, Galen daydreamed often. In the summer, the singer came to the agoge to share his songs. He usually sang about great kings and heroes. Sometimes, he told a story featuring shades, the spirits of those who had died, and how they visited the living. When Galen was little, he'd pretend his parents would come to him from the underworld. He imagined they were shimmering ghosts, who wiped his brow and filled in the gaps of his life, those days when they'd lived, and Galen had had a mother and father, people he had absolutely no memory of. Then Feodoras would come and knock him aside, cutting short his daydream, reminding him he was an orphan and a helot.

"Blast," Galen said aloud, and felt his throat get tight. It wasn't wise to blame the gods, but what else could he do? Who was it that had fashioned his destiny as a helot rather than a true son of Sparta? Galen would have liked to blame Dionysus, the god of wine. At night, Feodoras drank until he fell asleep where he sat. In the morning, he reeked of sour grapes.

Galen's eyes settled on the bronze figure of Ares, the god of war and bloodshed. He was the one the Spartans most loved. During war, all of Sparta took up the cry, "We don't need walls to protect our city! Ares and the men of Sparta are all the walls we need!" Galen considered how dogs were Ares' special creatures, and how he had never met a dog that could tolerate him. On Galen's left leg was a crescent shaped scar from a wolfish hound he had had the misfortune to meet when he was twelve, and carrying a load of firewood down to the agoge. The creature had clamped onto Galen's calf, letting go only after he pounded it with a log and cracked its skull. On his right hand was another scar, given to him by a small, yapping yellow puppy at the palace during Galen's first visit there when he was seven.

It's Ares, Galen decided. He was the one to blame for his destiny. Galen took the bronze figure off the wooden bench and wrapped his fingers around the small head. The neck was delicately shaped. It would be so easy to snap it off, to behead a god. But then what? How soon would Galen be riddled with disease? Or speared through in a freak agoge training session? His hands shook because he didn't want to put the figure down. He wanted to destroy it. Just one twist. One simple motion.

"Don't," Galen heard at the mouth of the cave, and his heart leapt.

"Hey, Nikolas," Galen said, trying to sound as if he hadn't nearly been startled to death. Ares slipped from his hands and fell to the ground.

"You shouldn't be here," Galen's friend Nikolas said, his eyes widening when he saw the figure of Ares at Galen's feet. "And you definitely shouldn't touch this." Nikolas lifted the bronze statuette tenderly, placing it on the wooden bench.

In his hand was a piece of dried meat, which he laid on the ground as a sacrifice, and covered it with sawdust.

"You could have eaten that," Galen said to him, but Nikolas shrugged.

"There are more important things than hunger," Nikolas said.

"Like saving me from a god bent on revenge?"

"Yep," Nikolas answered, closing his eyes before the altar.

Galen hated it when Nikolas went religious on him. But Nikolas was a good Spartan son, as spiritual as they came. They were trained to be that way in the agoge. If a war was to be fought, the sibyl was consulted. Even if the enemy was at the city limits, the soldiers did not lift a shield or sword without the consent of the gods. Galen thought such customs were unproductive and futile, but he would never say so to Nikolas, who stood now, his head bowed, honoring Ares.

Galen slipped out of the cave to give his friend privacy. Outside, the sun was beginning to set. Galen was due back at the agoge for dinner service within the hour. How he hated it, carrying food to the student tables. He'd stand with the other helots at the back of the mess hall, his mouth watering, waiting for them all to finish. Only when they cleared the hall were helots allowed to eat their own meals, usually made up of the organs of whatever animal they had prepared. Galen was particularly fond of creamy brain meat toasted over an open flame, but he knew a good bit of shank or a plate of ribs was tastier.

Galen heard Nikolas mumbling now, and guessed he was at his prayers, surely asking Ares for strength, for a warrior's heart. *Pointless requests*, thought Galen, who knew of no one kinder than Nikolas, the Eurypontid prince. The prince couldn't throw a spear or javelin as far as Nestor would like, and when he managed a good toss, he missed the mark by a wide margin. Nikolas had never beaten anyone but Galen at a wrestling match, and that was because Galen let him win. Nikolas couldn't creep up behind anyone. His lanky frame was made for making noise, somehow.

Galen had even heard it said that the Eurypontid prince was "pretty." He'd had to stop himself from lunging at the helot who'd said it. It was true Nikolas had a head of glossy, dark curls, a fine, shapely nose, and a long, casual stride. All the girls in Sparta seemed to be in love with him, and Nikolas, an incurable romantic, was in love with all of them. But the prince also had a clever mind. More than once, both Nikolas and Galen had gotten in trouble at the agoge for staging pranks. Most recently, after Nestor had left the dining hall for a few moments to use the outhouse, Nikolas got the entire agoge to rearrange the tables, the artwork, even weaponry on the walls, so that the hall was a reversed image of its former self. All the students had helped at Nikolas' urging, persuasive as he was, and when Nestor returned, they contained their snickers at the man's initial confusion at finding himself at the front of the room, when surely, it was once the back.

The fact that Galen was a slave, and Nikolas was a prince, helped them pull off those pranks. If they were caught whispering in doorways, Nikolas would sometimes pretend he was giving Galen an order, and Galen, a skilled liar, would drop his head the way helots were taught to do, dog-like, and say, "Yes, Your Highness." So it was that no one suspected that what the two actually had been discussing was where to move the outhouse. Later, Galen in the helot quarters and Nikolas in the dormitory would hear the splash of a helot or student falling into the exposed outhouse hole, and both boys would bite their fists to keep from laughing out loud.

There were other benefits to their unusual friendship. Galen reported to Nikolas the rumors that circulated among the helots and farmers. If there were fears about the fall harvest, or anxieties regarding taxes, or gossip about the senators, Galen was sure to hear them, and these he related to the prince. So it was that Spartans found Nikolas to be exceedingly aware of the problems of his people, and quick to respond when he could. Similarly, Nikolas made up easy jobs for Galen to do in the palace, or around the agoge, on days when the helots were gathered for lectures, or punishments, or backbreaking work like bridge building.

There had been talk of sending Galen away, to parcel him out to a farm, in order to discourage the prince from associating with someone so low-born, but Queen Isaura herself, Nikolas' mother, forbade it, explaining that it was good for a Spartan prince to know the minds of all persons living in Sparta, not only the sons of senators. So it was that Galen and Nikolas' friendship was allowed to thrive. When he'd heard what the Queen had said, Galen formed an instant fondness for her, though she'd only treated him with a distant air.

Suddenly, Galen remembered the hooded man and his talk of rebellion. "We outnumber them," he'd said, and the pictures in Galen's mind flashed again, differently this time, with images of Nikolas and Queen Isaura facing an angry, helot mob. Galen pushed the worry from his mind.

Nikolas gave the final blessing at last and Galen stepped back inside the temple. They sat on the ground together. Nikolas' eyes were red-rimmed. He dragged the back of his hand across his nose before speaking. "I heard something troubling about you," Nikolas said.

Galen thought of the hooded man again. "I didn't. I wouldn't know--" he started to say.

"I overheard Feodoras talking with Nestor. He was apologizing about tonight's meal. Said it was going to be awful and he blamed it on you," Nikolas said.

"Me?" Galen shook his head, relief sweeping over him. So Nikolas hadn't heard any rumors about a slave revolt. This was about Feodoras. The flashes were going off in Galen's head again, and he saw himself sweeping Feodoras' legs out from under him with the broad side of a sword.

"Can't you be obedient? Even a little?" Nikolas asked.

"His Highness disapproves?" Galen returned.

"Nestor is right. I shouldn't befriend a helot. You're a bad influence," Nikolas said, grinning.

"I know it. I'm a terrible human being," Galen said.

"Terrible human being," Nikolas echoed, "But a good kid." He laughed, then rubbed his face tiredly.

They joked this way all the time, repeating what the rest of Sparta whispered about their friendship—that it was odd. That it was worse than odd. That a future king of Sparta dishonored his country by allowing a slave into his personal life. If Galen had been a girl, public opinion might have been different. Kings had the right to their mistresses, and a helot girl's body was not her own. The public could understand the prince occasionally satisfying his desires with a helot girl. After all, only very old women worked on the agoge grounds, and they were of no interest to the students. Every once in a while, a student was caught with a girl in the barracks. They were punished, of course, though there was no real shame in it. But a real friendship with a helot? One based on mutual respect? That was troubling.

Galen watched as Nikolas' brow furrowed in thought, his left hand flattening the sawdust around him. "You and Prince Acayo should go bond over taxes and betrothals and tedious meetings. It would do you a world of good," Galen said, trying to lighten the suddenly somber mood.

"Acayo," Nikolas said, shaking his head. "You say his name and I am instantly bored."

Unique in all of Greece, Sparta had two royal lines—the Eurypontids and the Agiads. Officially, both houses ruled at once, consulting one another on decisions. The truth was, only one royal house held the favor of the people and the assembly. For the moment, Nikolas' family, the Eurypontids, were firmly in charge of things. But recent events in Persia had complicated

22

matters. Nikolas' father, Leandros, had been killed in battle. Queen Isaura was so beloved by the Spartan people that the senate did not name a new king. Rather, they promised to bide their time until Nikolas turned eighteen, and could rule.

For the most part, Galen thought it all a good system. Typically, one of the kings worked out well, and the other was completely worthless.

Prince Acayo, for example, who attended the agoge, too, was good with a spear, and a fair wrestler, but he was careless. Last year, during a lesson on rappelling off a cliff face, Acayo forgot to tie his rope before climbing down. The look on his face when he realized how fast he was falling was one of Galen's most treasured memories. Unfortunately, a shelf protruding out of the rock stopped him too soon. Acayo only twisted his ankle. He'd heard Galen laughing, roaring really, and Acayo was especially rotten to him after that, getting in cheap ear twists and elbow digs during wrestling training when Galen served as a sparring partner for the agoge students.

There were rumors about the princes. Their births, within days of one another, were thought a bad omen. But Spartans were a superstitious lot, and Galen ignored the chatter, as did Nikolas.

"I would be careful insulting the Agiad prince, if I were you," Galen teased. "Saw Acayo practicing with a new short sword this morning. Corinthian, by the looks of it." Galen paused, tugged on his sandal then added: "You know, one's sword is for more than just admiring one's reflection. Mark that."

Nikolas grabbed a handful of sawdust and threw it at Galen. But it was a half-hearted throw. Both boys went quiet for a moment, as a pack of dogs howled in the distance. Galen's skin erupted in bumps at the sound.

"Hounds will be the death of me," Galen muttered.

"Not dogs," Nikolas said.

"What are you talking about?"

23

"The Crypteia. Nestor says I have to join the hunt this year," Nikolas said. Galen felt out of breath, as if he'd been kicked in the gut.

They were silent for a while. Galen's mind turned over the word "Crypteia" again and again. It was an annual event, one that sent every helot into hiding. At the end of their training, students of the agoge participated in the Crypteia, during which skilled, unarmed boys were required to kill a helot in cold blood. They slipped through the night like wolves, leaving dead slaves behind. If the boy was caught, or if he failed to kill a slave, he was given a whipping in public, one that either killed him, or left him bedridden for days. But usually, there was no evidence left behind, not even a single footprint. The families of the dead helots could not ask for compensation for their loss, nor could they take revenge. The truth was, no one cared if helots lived or died.

The Crypteia was a test of manhood. A boy's first kill was supposed to be a glorious moment.

"What say does Nestor have in this? Don't the ephors assign the rules of the Crypteia? Isn't it their job?" Galen asked. As far as he understood it, the advisors to the kings, the old and wizened ephors, determined the Crypteia. They depended on a sibyl, a female seer, who would analyze the stars first, then, a bull's sacrifice would be made. The animal's intestines would be read for an omen. After all of that, the date and the rules of the Crypteia would be announced.

"That's how it usually goes," Nikolas said, "but we haven't had a Spartan sibyl in years. Anyway, it doesn't matter. Nestor announced the Crypteia this year, and when it comes to the agoge, Nestor's in charge."

"Nestor's lost his mind!" Galen shouted, and then lowered his voice to say, "You're too young for the Crypteia." Nikolas was sixteen, Galen's age, and still two years away from this particular rite.

"Nestor says we're ready," Nikolas said. "The war with Persia requires soldiers. The sooner we get past this rite, the sooner we prove we can fight in the war."

The war. It had been going on longer than Galen had been alive. Earlier that week, a Spartan troop of two hundred had left for the frontline at Salamis. They formed a barricade of red-cloaked warriors surrounding the Persian city walls, blocking access to farmland, and hence, food. But Persia controlled the sea, mighty ships, and a massive army, and so the war seemed as if it would never end.

"When is the test?" Galen asked.

"Tonight." Nikolas' face was pale. His hands shook a little.

Galen sat up tall, gathered strength for them both, and said, "We'll do it together, Nikolas. We can catch one of the helot herders before dawn." Even as he said it, Galen's stomach started to turn. *This is how a Spartan talks*, he thought, disgusted with himself.

Nikolas shook his head. "If they find you helping me, you'll be executed."

"The other students always work in groups," Galen said. "They form death squads, Nikolas. You know they do. You can use my help."

Nikolas' left foot tapped the ground so fast it raised a little dust cloud around them. "You can't go out tonight. Stay inside. Hide if you can," he said.

"I'm not hiding," Galen said, his pride punctured. "They kill grown helot men," he argued, "Never someone my age. They…"

"It's Acayo," Nikolas managed at last. "He plans on making you his kill. I overheard him earlier today."

Ah, thought Galen, *there it is*. This was the "worse thing coming" Feodoras had mentioned. Acayo! What a fool. What could he do? Annoy Galen to death? Acayo had some skill, but

Galen could outmatch him. Still, if Acayo had help…"I can take that idiot, Acayo," Galen said, but Nikolas frowned.

"He's the Agiad heir. You can't 'take' him. You can't TOUCH him, you know that. King Morfeo could have you put to death."

"We spar all the time."

"It isn't the same. Helots are fair game during the Crypteia. You aren't supposed to fight back." Nikolas put his elbows on his knees and cradled his head in his hands.

"You think the helots killed in the Crypteia each year don't fight back, Nikolas? Even a lamb struggles against the knife when it is slaughtered," Galen said. Sometimes, Galen wondered how Nikolas could be so thick.

"Even so," Nikolas said, trailing off, staring at his hands.

Galen knew what his friend was thinking. Nikolas was worried about Galen, of course, but he was thinking too about what it would be like to kill someone. Galen had plenty of practice with animals. It was easy enough to slide a knife across the throat of a lamb, or to twist a rabbit's small head in his hand. But a person?

"Listen, Nikolas, one of the herders will be simple," Galen said, but wasn't really so sure. If they failed, if they injured the helot without delivering a fatal blow, then the helot would surely say there were two of them. Everyone knew Nikolas and Galen were friends, though their friendship confused all of Sparta. If they were caught tonight, Galen would be implicated for sure.

There was also this worry: Nikolas couldn't fail, and especially not if Acayo succeeded. Already, the Spartans were sizing up the two princes, deciding who would be the man they followed in a few years. Queen Isaura held sway over the populace for the time being, and they favored Nikolas, too. But Greek politics changed swiftly, like sea winds, and the people were watching Nikolas closely now that Sparta was losing the war. Galen heard them at the markets, the old women and men, wondering whether Nikolas would grow up to be like his father, whether he would be the one to end the Persian War. Being flogged publically would ruin Nikolas' political reputation. They would have to make a clean kill, for Nikolas' sake and for Sparta, not that Galen cared about Sparta.

Still, Galen thought that if the helot begged, if he looked Galen in the eye, if it was someone he knew, he was not sure he could do it. And Nikolas didn't have the iron stomach for it. He was made of more tender stuff, that one. It would have to be Galen.

Tonight, Galen thought, *I become a murderer*.

"Pray with me?" Nikolas asked, and Galen suppressed a groan. He bowed before the Ares figurine and listened as Nikolas made their case.

"Great Ares, son of Zeus, heed our cause. Make our hands strong. Make our feet swift. And may our victim know the pleasures of the Asphodel Meadows in the underworld."

Nikolas dropped another hunk of dried meat onto the floor of the temple. Galen scattered the sawdust, all the while thinking of what Nikolas had prayed for. The Asphodel Meadows were the only hope of slaves and common Greeks in the underworld. The Elysian Fields were for heroes and kings. Then there were the burning, monster-filled lands of Tartarus, where murderers and traitors went. *After tonight, it'll be Tartarus for me*, Galen thought bitterly.

They left the cave together, walking into the fresh air. Galen scanned the agoge yard as he always did, wary of Feodoras, or other Spartans that might make demands on him. The yard was empty, save for a figure that cast a long shadow, heading off in the direction of the palace. He was tall. He wore a hood.

"Where is your mother, Her Highness?" Galen asked abruptly.

27

Nikolas faced his friend, a puzzled look in his eyes. "In the palace, I suppose. I haven't visited home in a few weeks. Why?"

"No reason," Galen said. Thankfully, the bell began to ring for the helots in the kitchen, so Galen took his leave of Nikolas, afraid of being late to Feodoras' call to muster, not wanting another lash from that willow switch. It wouldn't be right if his victim saw him bruised and bloodied.

It was said the dead could launch curses at the living from Hades. That was the last thing Galen wanted to deal with. Life was cruel enough already without even more hard luck.

3

Nestor scheduled spear training late that afternoon, before dinner. Galen, hearing the announcement, sighed with pleasure. Here was a thing to take his mind off the Crypteia. In general, no helots were given weapons instruction, but serving an agoge had its advantages. The students needed someone to train against, and who better than a helot opponent? Since a helot's life held little value, the students could fight without holding back. Luckily for Galen, he'd picked up some wrestling skills, and was especially good with a spear.

The only problem? The helots in the agoge were not given a shield or a breastplate to go with the spear. These required lots of bronze and iron, which made them expensive equipment. A spear was cheaper—it was made of ash, with only an iron point shaped like a leaf on one end, and a bronze butt at the other. The bronze end was called a "lizard-killer" because it was thrust into the ground when a soldier was at rest, and sometimes, that movement skewered a hapless reptile.

So, Galen improvised. He learned to block an opponent's thrust with a swipe of his leg or arm. A few times, he'd gotten a bloody gash for his efforts, like the one that had left the scar across his eyebrow. But he was good, and took special joy in disarming students. Prince Acayo in particular. That afternoon, Nestor paired Galen up with Timios, the son of a senator and a good friend to Nikolas and Galen. The sun was just starting to set, casting a warm glow on the boys, their weapons shimmering in the light.

"On guard!" Nestor called, and the two boys hefted their spears. These were six feet long, and used in savage thrusts meant to impale enemies. Spears were only thrown as a last measure, and then, the Spartan soldier would draw a short sword. Timios trembled behind his enormous shield. These were made big enough to use as a stretcher, and Timios, who was small to begin with, disappeared behind it.

"Come on!" Galen shouted, bouncing on the balls of his feet.

"Strike hard, Timios!" Nestor yelled from the sidelines.

Timios peeked out from behind his shield, took two tentative steps forward, and attempted an underhand thrust of the spear. Galen sidestepped the move, and for good measure, swept Timios' left leg out from under him, so that the boy crashed to the ground, his helmet rattling.

Nestor clapped so loudly Galen's ears rang. "Boys!" he called. "You saw him? Man to man, offense is your best defense!" Nestor shook Galen's shoulder, "Would that you were one of us, boy," he said warmly, and Galen felt his stomach burn with pride, as if someone had lit a fire in his belly. Then, Nestor drew his fingers to his lips, whistled piercingly, and gestured for Acayo to step forward.

Acayo wore a bronze breastplate with intricate designs, as well as a brass helmet that had been polished to burn like the sun and bore a crest of crisp, red feathers along the top. *No expense spared*, Galen thought. His face was completely obscured, but there was no mistaking the Agiad prince. Acayo was tall and wiry, and he walked with a slowness of purpose that was a little intimidating. Nothing ever seemed to faze him. In the distance, Galen spotted Nikolas, who used equipment borrowed from the agoge, like everyone else. Before he died, King Leandros had demanded that his son train with gear no better than the other students had. "A king is no more important than a farmer, or a priestess, or anyone," Nikolas had told Galen, repeating his father's wisdom. That's what Galen liked about the Eurypontids—they didn't hold themselves above other Spartans.

Acayo drew a skinny finger across his neck before approaching Galen. His friends, the sons of assemblymen all, slapped his back and laughed. It made Galen nervous. Their laughter scared him more than Acayo's little gesture. This wasn't about spear training. They would band together for the Crypteia to assure their success. It was cheating, of course, but who was Galen to develop a sense of fairness now? Nikolas and he were going to cheat, too. Anyhow, Galen didn't want a pack of nearly trained Spartans after him tonight.

Perhaps if I can injure Acayo now... he thought.

"On guard!" Nestor commanded, and the two boys faced off, spears hoisted at their ribs. Acayo moved with the first thrust, one that Galen dodged expertly. Galen faked an underhand thrust, which Acayo tried to block, then switched to an overhand move, that struck the prince on the side of his helmet, leaving a dent in the expensive brass, and making a clanging sound that hushed the crowd. Typically, the helots went easy on the princes. The game, they all understood suddenly, had changed in this match.

Galen was breathing hard. This was risky, he knew. To engage the prince at full effort was to invite vengeance later.

But he hoped to exhaust him enough to keep Acayo in bed tonight for the Crypteia.

Acayo adjusted his helmet. His fingers touched the dent, and a low, awful growl escaped the prince's lips. He charged, the spear point aiming directly for Galen's chest. Galen waited until the last moment, then slid to the ground, wrapping his hands around the shaft of Acayo's spear, and driving the point into the earth alongside him, effectively twisting the spear out of Acayo's hands.

The students cheered, and Galen, flat on his back but holding two spears now, risked a gloating moment, looking Acayo in the eye and raising an eyebrow. So it was that Galen didn't notice Acayo raising his foot and driving it into his groin.

The pain was blinding. The cheers turned to boos. And Galen heard, as if through a fog, Nestor calling off the practice. The old teacher knelt by Galen, patted his back, and said, "Shake it off, boy. Best not be late for the next meals preparation or Feodoras will do you worse."

Nikolas was at his side next. He helped Galen sit up, groaning as he went. "You'll never have children now," Nikolas said, laughing a little.

"Thanks a lot."

"What were you doing, egging on Acayo like that?"

"Trying to keep him home tonight," Galen said, and Nikolas' smile faded.

"I'm afraid you just made things worse."

Galen nodded. "It was a good move, though, wasn't it? That slide to the ground?"

Nikolas laughed again. "You'd be dangerous with a shield, Galen. When it's my turn at battle, I'm keeping you close by."

Galen felt it again, that warmth in his stomach. A helot's greatest hope for glory was to serve a Spartan during war. He'd get to carry light arms, maybe even get involved in skirmishes every once in a while. And with no one but Nikolas

32

to answer to, Galen would feel more like a free man than at the agoge, under Feodoras' thumb.

"I can walk," Galen said, rising to his feet.

"Can you fight?" Nikolas asked, his eyes glimmering. He drove the lizard-killer tip into the ground and faced Galen.

Galen picked up his fallen spear. He spun it over his head. "Anytime, Your Highness," he said, and settled into a fighting stance.

Nikolas drew his helmet down and crouched behind the shield. "Give it your best," he shouted, his voice muffled and tinny sounding.

Galen didn't need to be asked twice. He drove forward with a blow to Nikolas' breastplate that sent him tumbling. But Nikolas was up fast, mimicking Galen's moves like a shadow. Soon, they'd both picked up speed and strength so that the sound of bronze clashing with bronze rang in the air, and they forgot, for a moment, that they were fated to kill an innocent man that night.

4

Galen's stomach was still growling. He picked at his dirty chiton, splattered with grease and dried bits of food. For a moment, he considered putting a sizeable crumb in his mouth, then, thought better of it. At dinner the bowl of stew had looked surprisingly full when Feodoras handed it to him. Only later did Galen realize it had been a trick. One of the goat's hooves was at the bottom of the bowl, displacing the liquid. *A shame*, thought Galen, *the stew was pretty good*. His chiton was another shame. Galen only had two. They were made of coarse wool, and dyed the color of the earth. Chitons were short, grazing the wearer's mid-thigh, and had no sleeves. Normally, chitons were fastened at the shoulders with buckles, but Galen's chiton was tied at the shoulder with ragged cords. Another cord, dingy with age, gathered his chiton at the waist. Most of the boys in the agoge wore red chitons, and about the city-state, dark colors, like purple and blue, had become

34

fashionable. Galen poured a bit of water from a jug onto a corner of his chiton, and he used the wet cloth to rub at the stains on his chest and stomach. *Good enough*, he thought, then his belly rumbled again.

He started to dig at the soft earth next to his cot, and thought about what was going to happen soon. The helot that Nikolas and Galen took on tonight wouldn't go down easy. Helots didn't train like Spartans, but that didn't mean they laid about either. Hard work and hard living made them strong, strong enough that during the big battles, some helots got to fight side by side with the Spartan career soldiers. Galen was broad shouldered, and Nikolas was taller than almost anyone in the agoge. But it was stupid to think that size insured victory. Galen thought of Timios, a year behind Nikolas, who was small-boned and came up only to Galen's chin. Yet he was fast, like a rabbit. He couldn't handle a spear, but during wrestling matches, no one could beat Timios, who managed to snake his skinny arms around his opponent's necks every time, choking him.

The Crypteia required that the agoge students be unarmed, but Galen swiped a kitchen knife. It was illegal, of course, for a helot to carry a weapon, but Galen was not taking any chances tonight. There were wild dogs out there, and more than a few boys prowling the night, eager to prove their strength. Galen wouldn't go to Hades without a fight.

It was bothering him more than he let on to Nikolas. As a helot, Galen had never had to think about warfare, about taking a human life. Killing people was not his business. That was for the Spartan soldiers to worry about. No, Galen's concern was staying alive. Galen tried not to think about the person Nikolas and he would target that night, but he couldn't help it. He wondered if the helot might have a family. Maybe he was tucking one of his children in to bed. Maybe the helot prayed each night for a long life. And Galen and Nikolas were going to end it.

Galen's throat ached, and he swallowed hard. Finally, his fingers brushed up against what he was looking for, and it was a welcome distraction. Galen brought up the preserved egg, brushed ash off its surface, and cracked it open. The shell was blackened, but curious snowflake shapes had developed on it, as if etched. It was a beautiful transformation, and Galen was not sure how it happened. Whenever he found a duck's nest, Galen would take an egg or two, roll it in ash from the ovens, a bit of mud, and some salt, and bury it. In a few weeks' time, the egg was preserved, and could stay in the dirt for as long as necessary. The egg smelled rotten, but tasted delicate. It was as good a backup as Galen had ever found for lean food days. The egg slid down his throat, and his belly stopped rumbling. Galen needed all the strength he could get for tonight.

During the dinner service earlier, Galen had kept his eyes on Acayo, watching the prince as he ate. Acayo's mouth was open and slick, and he dribbled stew on his tunic. Galen had never been to the Agiad palace, but he couldn't imagine that Acayo's father, King Morfeo, would be pleased with his piggish manners. His mother, Queen Cyteria, had died earlier in the year of a coughing sickness. They'd all gone to her tomb the day she was buried to make a lamb sacrifice at the site, ensuring the queen's safe passage to the underworld. Her tomb did not bear her name, as was the custom when a Spartan woman died. Only if she passed during childbirth was her name etched in stone. As for Spartan men, their names were preserved only if they died in battle. Death from old age, or sickness merited no memorial. That afternoon was the first and last time Galen felt pity for Acayo, who stood at his mother's tomb stoically, though his jaw clenched and unclenched again and again. The tomb, called a *tholos*, was shaped like a beehive and held many bodies. One day, Acayo would be laid to rest inside the hive, too. *But I will be burned*, Galen had thought bitterly.

36

King Leandros had had no burial, as his body was lost to the Persians, but the old customs were followed. Men on horses announced the king's death in all the corners of Sparta, and the women banged iron pots in the streets. It was a grievous clamor, one accompanied by sullen faces. Because there was no body to prepare or bury, people gathered near the Eurotas River, where a great pyre was built. One of Leandros' shields was placed atop it, as well as a cloak, wreathed in olive leaves. Galen had been allowed to watch beside Nikolas. They were twelve years old then, grown enough to know that while the Spartans mourned their king, they were also watching Leandros' heir for auspicious signs of the future. For ten days after the funeral, the Eurypontid palace gates had been draped in long cloths dyed a deep purple. Within the walls of the palace, artisans worked hard at sculpting a statue of Leandros.

Galen had been to the palace a few times, starting with his first visit at age seven. He'd been selected by Queen Isaura to serve as Nikolas' escort to the agoge. That first time, Galen walked to the palace alone, stepped barefoot into the main chamber and bowed before the Eurypontid Queen. She was from Ithaca, an island of western Greece. Her foreign birth was hard to ignore. Aside from her accent, Queen Isaura did not wear the shortened chitons most Spartan women wore, meant to expose the shapeliness of a Spartan woman's legs. Spartan girls were trained in agoge-like schools, where they learned to fight and dance, and so their bodies, which they showed off in chitons that were short and open along the sides, were muscular and strong. Queen Isaura wore long, embroidered gowns instead, and all anyone saw of her body were her pale arms and the tops of her feet. Her chiton was bound at the waist with a rope of finely woven gold. Another thing about Spartan girls— they were known all over Greece for marrying after their twentieth birthday, and not at fourteen as girls did everywhere else. When King Leandros married Queen Isaura of Ithaca, she

37

was eighteen—a young bride by Spartan standards, and an old maid in the rest of Greece.

On that first visit to the palace, Queen Isaura surprised Galen in many ways. Kneeling before her, he felt her cool hands on his shoulders. Her touch was so soft thinking of it made Galen want to cry. She placed a finger under his chin to lift his face, and when he met her eyes, Galen saw they were gold-flecked. "Galenos," she whispered in his ear, and he felt like he was being named for the first time. "Watch over my son," she said, and Galen nodded. She could have asked him to drown himself in the Mediterranean, to cross over to Hades to retrieve a shade, to do anything and Galen would have agreed, so happy was he to be in her warm presence.

But after that day, the Queen had not looked directly at Galen again. When he accompanied Nikolas to the palace, she would speak *at* him, the way other Spartans did, instead of *to* him. Often, Galen noticed that the Queen's hands trembled at the sight of him, and he wondered if the Queen found him so distasteful that she itched to strike him, the way Feodoras did. It was true that she'd defended Nikolas' friendship with Galen, but Galen wondered more than once if it was a political gesture, a way of proving to the Spartans that the Eurypontids cared about everyone who lived in the city-state, regardless of class.

Presently Galen finished his egg and crushed the shell, burying the fragments. Feodoras did not know about the duck eggs, or the small jug of wine Galen had fermenting on the other side of his cot. It tasted awful, as Galen was no expert winemaker, but it was strong enough to fight back the cold in the winter with one sip, and a good way to cleanse wounds when he got hurt sparring, or at the hands of Feodoras.

Slipping the kitchen knife into his chiton, Galen waited for Nikolas' signal. They had agreed on a dog's bark in honor of Ares. Galen listened for Nikolas' poor impersonation of a dog—three successive woofs. It came just as Feodoras headed down to the latrines. The other helots were asleep, snoring in their cots, and Galen was free to get out unnoticed. He sent a silent prayer to Zeus and headed out into the dark.

Galen wended his way towards the barracks, bent over and keeping to the shadows. His hands went numb and cold, and he knew it was from fear and not the coolness of the night. A snapping sound up ahead froze him in place. His eyes adjusted a bit. The shadows lightened. Another cracking noise, this time closer, had Galen running at full tilt. He turned a corner and plowed into Nikolas, and they both fell to the ground.

"Something's following me," Galen said.

"Me, too. From that direction," Nikolas said, pointing to where Galen had been standing.

"It was coming from…" Galen started to say, then stopped. It was Nikolas he'd heard. Galen began to laugh, and by the gods, it felt good.

"What? What?" Nikolas asked confusedly, but then his mouth began to twitch, too as he realized the mistake. The happy moment was snuffed out quickly, however, by the task before them. Nikolas looked up at the stars for a moment then said, "Do you remember my first night here, Galen?"

Galen nodded. Nikolas' enrollment in the agoge was scandalous. Traditionally, the royals were excused from attendance. They had private tutors to teach them how to kill, how to lead, the proper dances for the festivals, and other requirements of Spartan manhood. But Nikolas had demanded he attend at the age of seven, embarrassing his father, King Leandros, by running into the assembly during a session, and yelling, "I'm joining the agoge, father!" His father had stomped towards his son, and laid him out with a backhand to the cheek.

"Only men may enter the assembly," King Leandros had said to Nikolas, and then resumed the meeting of the statesmen.

Nikolas told Galen that story during the prince's first night at the agoge.

"It was the only night I have ever slept in a proper room, in the barracks," Galen said, but did not add that it had been terrible to sleep without a breeze, feeling as if he'd been buried alive. He shared a tent with two other helots. But on Nikolas' first night, Galen was allowed the privilege of sleeping in the barracks only because the young prince did not want Galen to go, and because Nikolas' crying bothered Nestor, who'd never taught a prince before.

Nikolas nodded, taking his eyes off the sky. "I remember you asked me, 'Why do you want to be here?'"

"You told me, 'To prove to my father I can,'" Galen said softly, his memory of that day vivid still. He remembered, too, how Acayo joined the agoge shortly afterwards. Ashamed by the apparent courage of the Eurypontids, and not wanting to lag behind in Spartan popularity, King Morfeo and Queen Cyteria enrolled Acayo themselves. He cried through most of that first month, and the helots in the kitchens spent a lot of time laughing at the pampered prince, taking turns impersonating him when Feodoras was not around.

Nikolas cracked his knuckles twice, his eyes closed as if in prayer. "I am not sure I can make my father proud tonight," Nikolas said gruffly.

Galen didn't respond, unsure of what might be helpful to say. But when Nikolas turned towards the path that led down a steep slope, to where the helots slept and worked, Galen followed.

5

They headed north of the agoge, away from the city center and toward the helot shepherding fields. The city of Sparta spread out over the side of a mountain, and so the ground was always sloping. There were swells of earth, and then, flat places. The shepherds had their sheep and goats graze on rugged land, where thick tufts of grass kept the animals fat. These places were well away from the city's bustle and the trample of carts and feet.

Galen concentrated on keeping invisible by running alongside low walls, ducking into barns, and finally, on the outskirts of the city, keeping close to gurgling streams, whose sound might mask the noises they made as they went along. Nikolas kept cracking his knuckles, and Galen was about to turn around and whisper, "Knock it off," when they both heard a piercing cry.

"There's the first victim," Galen said grimly.

"Yes, but that's no man," Nikolas said, and ran off in the direction of the sound.

"Wait!" Galen yelled, but Nikolas was gone. *There go the dumb heroics*, Galen thought. When it came to girls, the prince was an easy mark. Once, Nikolas had helped a pretty, redheaded girl he came across in the market. She'd gotten her foot stuck in some kind of rodent's hole in the ground. Nikolas rushed over, grabbed hold of her bare ankle, and yanked the girl free. Then he stared at her, his mouth open, as if he'd never seen a girl before. That's when her father smacked him over the head with his sandal. If the man had known he'd just hit the Eurypontid prince he would have fallen to his knees in supplication, right there and then. Nikolas just said, "Sorry," his eyes still glazed over, and backed away.

Twice, Nikolas had been caught with a Spartan girl in his barracks. As punishment, Nestor had made the prince carry heavy stones back and forth across the agoge's yard for an entire week. Spartan men, even the married ones, did not live with their wives while they were in the army. And yet all Spartan men were expected to find wives shortly after leaving the agoge. Bachelors were often ridiculed and considered untrustworthy. The army barracks were south of the city, and the men got a monthly leave to visit their families. Affection for wives and children was considered a personal weakness, and a liability on the field. What man would fight to the death if his mind were on his wife?

But now was not the time for romantic rescues. Galen tried hard to catch up with Nikolas, who swooped under low tree branches, scattered an enormous ant mound, and pressed on, through mud and brambles. Closer, they heard the girl shouting, "No! Don't touch me!" and Nikolas sped up. He went around an enormous boulder, his hand grazing the rock. By the time Galen got around it, Nikolas was gone from sight.

The girl quieted. Galen stopped to examine his arms and legs that were bleeding from cuts and scrapes. A few long

minutes passed. Galen began to pick his way in the general
direction into which Nikolas had disappeared. His senses were
alert, and Galen found himself jumping at shadows here and
there. A half-moon lit the mountainside in a bluish light.

Overhead, an owl hooted. Another answered. Then
another, and Galen remembered that owls weren't social
creatures. They didn't travel in flocks. Another low hoot
sounded, this one close behind Galen. He swiveled and saw
him, Acayo, smiling.

No, owls don't work in teams, thought Galen. *But
bullies do.*

A boy dropped down from a tree branch, landing on his
feet with a thud. He turned his head as he straightened to his
full height and his neck made a loud cracking sound. It was
Brutus, one of Acayo's crowd, and the largest boy in the agoge.
If someone were going to have an easy time killing Galen, it
would be Brutus.

A laurel tree to Galen's left shook, and another boy
came out from behind it. It was Linus, a skinny kid who
laughed too much. Mostly at anything Acayo said.

"Did you manage it?" Acayo asked Linus, and Linus
grinned. The top of Linus' head was bleeding a little. A red
trickle made its way down his temple and into his ear. Linus
didn't seem to notice.

"She'll keep him busy," Linus said, though he was
laughing through it so the words sounded mangled.

Acayo's features relaxed. He turned to Galen. "Ah,
where *did* that puny prince run off to?"

"I'm looking at him," Galen said. Acayo's nose
twitched. *They've done something to Nikolas*, Galen thought.
The screaming girl was a trap.

"You should be honored," Acayo said. "The name of
my first kill might actually be remembered, sung by the singers
or something." Brutus and Linus closed in behind Galen, and
he could feel Brutus' hot breath on his head.

"What will the song say?" Galen taunted. "That the mighty Acayo bored the helot Galen to death?" He knew Acayo didn't know when to quit talking and start hitting. Galen counted on it actually, buying time in the hopes that Nikolas was okay, that he'd come back.

But Brutus trapped Galen's head in his thick arms, his hand cupping Galen's chin. It wouldn't take much. A swift turn and Galen's neck would snap. Galen's hands were free, so he started pounding Brutus on the side of his face. Brutus grunted, but didn't let go. Linus tried to grab Galen's arms unsuccessfully. So, instead, Linus kicked the back of Galen's knees, and his legs gave out so that he dangled in Brutus' headlock. Galen reached for the knife in his chiton, then paused, his mind racing three steps ahead of him. If Galen injured one of the agoge students, he'd have to run for it. *West, deep into Messenia is my best bet*, he thought. *Perhaps the Spartans won't look for me there. Perhaps…*

"Wait," Acayo said, and Brutus loosened his hold a little. "He's my kill, remember? Wait for your prince in Hades, helot. He'll be joining you soon."

Acayo stood close, his nose nearly touching Galen's, who fought the urge to spit on Acayo's face. *He'll make a mistake*, Galen told himself. He had to be ready for that, ready to run.

"I can do it quick, Acayo. You won't have to get your hands dirty at all," Brutus said.

Acayo's features tightened. His pride pricked him. "Must I repeat myself? He's my kill. Let him go, Brutus," Acayo said.

There it was. Acayo's first error. The moment Brutus' hands were off him, Galen rammed his shoulder into Acayo, who fell onto his back with a dull thump. Galen ran into the dark woods, the kitchen knife in his hand.

The ground sloped upward, and here and there, dark caves peppered the hillside. Acayo, Brutus and Linus weren't far behind Galen, and he could hear their voices. Galen sped up, trying to put distance between him and them.

"There's a broken branch here," Galen heard Brutus say. "He went this way." They were tracking him now. The ephors, the five advisors to the Spartan kings, always called the Crypteia "the hunt," and it was true. Galen was like an animal now. It was only a matter of time before he couldn't run anymore, before one of the hunters reached him.

"Footprints! Ha!" Galen heard Acayo shouting in the distance. He glanced at his muddy feet and cursed his stupidity. *Calm down, Galen*, he told himself, and stopped to look around. There was a cave to his right. He could hide in there. Galen approached the cave's mouth, and stopped just shy of entering. He heard the distinct snore of a bear. It was a grumbling sort of sound, oddly soothing. Then, he had it. An idea. Galen used the knife to cut out a bit of fabric from his chiton and left it near the cave. He made clear footprints leading up to the cave, then, gingerly, he stepped aside and climbed a nearby tree.

Acayo, Brutus, and Linus crashed through the brush moments later. Acayo halted the others in silence. They all bent low to the ground, examining the earth. "There," Acayo whispered, having spotted the fabric and the footprints.

"The helot fool's in the cave," Linus said, chuckling. The three of them stood tall now, proud of themselves.

They walked into the cave as Acayo called, "Come out, Galen."

Galen shook so much in the tree that the limbs shivered along with him. The silence unnerved him, made him want to keep running all the way to Messenia. Then he heard it, a thunderous roar, so loud he felt it in his belly, felt the vibrations of it in the tree bark, and he imagined its being heard throughout Sparta. Acayo, Brutus and Linus ran out of the cave a moment later, scattering, and confusing the bear that lumbered out behind them. It shook its massive head, still dazed from sleep.

Its black nose flared. The bear caught a scent. Then it roared again, trudging off in Acayo's direction.

Galen waited for the bear to disappear into the thick of the woods before climbing down. He was so shaky he could hardly walk straight. His cot back at the agoge called to him. But he knew that was not safe either, not tonight. Besides, Nikolas was out there still.

Only the gods knew what Acayo and his gang had done to him.

6

Galen headed east, towards the boulder where he had last seen Nikolas, and sent a thankful prayer to Artemis, the goddess of the hunt. The architects always carved bears onto her temples to symbolize her strength, and Galen hoped that Artemis was on his side tonight.

He found Nikolas on his knees in a clearing, pounding his fist into the chest of an old man. A girl was on the ground by him, her long, brown hair covering her face. She rocked to and fro.

He did it, Galen thought. *Nikolas actually killed someone with his bare hands.* The shock of it threw Galen, made him nauseous. The Nikolas that Galen knew could never bring himself to murder. Is this what the agoge did? Turn good people into monsters?

Galen walked over to Nikolas. The girl caught a glimpse of Galen, and her moist eyes met his. Galen knew her.

She was the one with the goatherd that morning, the girl he thought about so often. In fact, she'd been creeping into Galen's thoughts all day. How different she looked now. Her cheeks were red, and marked by long scratches. Her own fingernails did that, Galen guessed. She had bitten her lip. There was the distinct mark of a handprint on her throat. Someone else did that to her, Galen knew, and he felt a burning sensation in his chest, as if he might be capable of murder after all.

Nikolas was still beating the old man's chest. With every blow, the man's body jumped a little. It was Brygus he was hitting. The goatherd's eyes were open, but there wasn't life in them.

"Stop, Nikolas," Galen said, but Nikolas didn't hear. "He's dead enough, Nikolas. You have already killed him."

Nikolas froze. He rested his hand on Brygus' chest but did not look up at Galen.

"I wouldn't…I'd never…" Nikolas muttered, then stopped. The unwillingness to end a life was not something a Spartan was supposed to admit. "I didn't kill him," he said at last. "I am trying to bring him back, like Nestor did that one time."

Galen remembered the day one of the senators came to inspect the agoge. He was elderly, and had collapsed in the mess hall. Nestor had pounded the man's chest, three or four times, loud enough that everyone present turned to look at the source of the hollow, thumping sound. Miraculously, the ancient assemblyman woke, coughing.

"It isn't working," Galen said, and Nikolas nodded, giving up at last.

The girl crept over to Brygus on her hands and knees. "It was an honorable death, Uncle," she said to him, closing his eyes with her fingertips.

"I am sorry," Nikolas said to her. "I tried."

She ignored Nikolas and began arranging Brygus' limbs. His legs had been bent in awkward angles. Now, the girl straightened them along with Brygus' arms, and the old goatherd looked like he was sleeping.

Galen heard a low hum and looked around, thinking that maybe it was Acayo and his cronies, signaling to each other again. But no. The sound came from the girl. The humming became a bit louder, blending into words that Galen had a hard time understanding. *What a beautiful voice*, he thought. The song was a dirge, a death song, that at least he could guess.

Nikolas and Galen stood there for a moment, watching her sing. She sang without faltering, without crying. She was steady. Galen wished he understood everything she was saying. He caught some words, here and there, like "sleep" and "forgiveness" and "Father Zeus." But much of it was lost to Galen.

"She's speaking an old dialect, I think," Nikolas said, as if he knew Galen was wondering about the girl's origins.

"What is she saying?" Galen asked. The students of the agoge learned all the Greek dialects as part of their training. Helots had no lessons, save for ones related to their trades.

"Uncle, your troubles are gone. Sleep Uncle. May Father Zeus look kindly on your shade. Remember me, Uncle, in the afterlife," Nikolas translated.

"She grieves like a Spartan," Galen said, meaning that the girl did not cry, or tear her clothes, or pull her hair out, the way women did in other parts of Greece. For Spartans, death was an honor, especially death in battle.

Nikolas nodded, and Galen noticed he was swallowing hard. There was a small cut over his left eye, and the skin beneath the eye was purpling. The girl sang as she gathered leaves off an olive tree nearby.

Nikolas and Galen walked towards the body. They leant over it. Galen had never seen a human's death so close up. Already, the color had left Brygus' face. Every so often, the skin on his hands seemed to twitch, as if he was alive. Animals were the same after they'd been slaughtered. They moved a little in death. *Terrifying*, Galen thought.

"What happened?" he asked after a while.

"Linus," Nikolas said. "When I got here, he had the girl pinned up against the tree. Her chiton hitched up. It looked like he was trying to, to…" Uncomfortable, Nikolas stopped, searching for the right word.

"I get it," Galen said, the heat building in his chest again at the thought of Linus' hands on the girl, who was now arranging the leaves she'd gathered in an intricate design all over Brygus' body.

"So, the goatherd and I arrived at the same time. I think Linus expected me, though, because he started laughing," Nikolas said.

"It was a trap. Acayo, Brutus and Linus were following us. They wanted to separate us to get at me," Galen explained, the pieces falling together now. "They knew if you heard a girl cry out…"

"I would lose my head," Nikolas said, cutting Galen off. His ears turned bright red. "Are you all right?" Nikolas asked after a moment, and Galen nodded.

He didn't want to compete with Nikolas over this girl, but he couldn't help the surge of jealousy he now felt. Except…

"She's working with them, then?" Galen asked, wary of the girl suddenly.

"I don't think so. She looked so furious at Linus," Nikolas said. "The goatherd tried to pry Linus off her, but Linus shoved him away. Then, the old man grabbed his chest and fell down. Died of fear, I suppose," Nikolas explained.

"And Linus?"

"We wrestled a bit. Then a funny thing happened. A thick branch of the olive tree cracked above him and knocked him on his ass. A bough that solid wouldn't fall so easily, would it?" Nikolas asked, pointing to the heavy limb on the ground. Galen could see the break from where he stood. It was clean, as if someone had cut through it with an axe.

"Strange," Galen said. It explained Linus' wound when he and the others had surrounded Galen.

"Linus looked fit to murder me," Nikolas said, "but he heard an owl hooting, and he bolted out of here."

"That was their signal," Galen said. "They ganged up on me downhill." Galen was about to tell Nikolas the story about Brutus' headlock and the bear, when he noticed the girl was no longer singing. She stood by Brygus' body with her arms stretched to the sky and muttered something Galen didn't understand. Galen looked at Nikolas, and he shrugged his shoulders.

The sky was lightening, its blackness fading in the first hints of dawn. That's when they saw it. The olive tree, the one that had shed its limb, was bending slowly, its trunk flexible, its slender branches dangling forward, until the entire tree looked like it was bowing. Bowing right over Brygus. There was a creaking sound, and the olive tree straightened.

Nikolas fell to his knees right away, muttering to Ares and Zeus. "The work of the gods," he said. Then he reached up, grabbed Galen's chiton, and pulled him roughly to his knees, too. "Pray," Nikolas growled, annoyed at Galen's poor religious observance.

But Galen was not thinking about the gods at the moment. He was busy looking at the girl with her flushed face, her chest heaving because she couldn't catch her breath, and her fingers twitching. Around her feet, little olive leaves fluttered, as if they were caught in a swirling wind. Then they settled over her toes and in the dirt. But there wasn't a breeze to be felt. There hadn't been one all night.

When the girl looked up at Galen, he averted his eyes. Galen was no coward, but this girl, he was convinced, made that tree bend, made that branch fall on Linus, and now, standing at

51

the edge of a forest that might be at her command, Galen felt genuine fear. What if she wasn't just a girl Linus had found at the moment, suiting his purposes? What if she wasn't a victim after all? What if this strange creature had been part of Acayo's plot?

The girl walked over, extended her hands to Nikolas and he took them. *There it was*, thought Galen, *that look in the prince's eyes.* It was a look that offered the world—his princedom, all of Sparta—for a chance to hold this girl's hands forever. Galen couldn't compete with that. Already, Nikolas had one-upped him, had rescued her. And he was a prince to boot. *Why does fate always frown upon me,* Galen thought miserably.

Nikolas stood, and the girl knelt before him. "Your Highness," she said. "I am in your debt."

Her voice was thick and intoxicating, too. Galen caught a glimpse of something on the skin of her thigh, hidden by her chiton. In the dim light, it looked like a drawing, a blue-green curlicue peeking out, like the tail of a lizard. He'd heard that the Persians drew on their bodies with needles and ink. How curious to find a drawing like that on the girl. Suddenly, Galen wished to see the rest of the design, to trace it with his fingers…

Galen shook his head to clear the thought. This evening was turning out to be more dangerous than he had expected.

"How do you know who I am?" Nikolas asked.

The girl didn't answer right away. She was looking at Galen, her head turned to the side, her sad eyes unblinking. When she turned her glance towards Nikolas, Galen felt as if he'd just been robbed of something precious.

"I know a prince when I see one," she said.

Nikolas tugged on the girl's hands and she rose to her feet. "I'm sorry about your uncle," Nikolas said.

"Me too," Galen jumped in. He was surprised at his own lack of control, and immediately wanted to punch himself for sounding so desperate. *This girl is a witch, or a siren, or*

52

some other creature, he thought. *She's tempting us, tricking us. Nikolas and I need to get away fast,* Galen thought, his mind whirling.

"Your name?" Nikolas asked.

"Zoi," she said, and Galen heard it then, the sound of a breeze through the leaves of the forest behind them, but not the sensation of wind.

"Zoi," Nikolas repeated, more sigh than word. "What will you do now?" Nikolas asked, recovering himself for a moment. "Without Brygus, I mean."

"She's a helot. Her master will figure it out," Galen said

"Galenos!" Nikolas reprimanded, pushing Galen lightly.

Galen returned the shove, with more force. "What? We owe her nothing. Besides, I think her being here, on this night, is suspicious."

At this, Zoi's pretty green eyes darkened somehow. *Could eye color change like that?* wondered Galen. Again, came the sound of wind rushing, but no cool puff of air on Galen's skin. Who *was* this girl?

"My uncle was killed tonight and you intend to blame me?" Zoi asked, turning her eyes fully on Galen. "You're as ridiculous as you look. And I am no helot," she added with a look of disgust.

"There is nothing wrong with being a helot!" Galen shouted, and Zoi's mouth tightened. Feodoras' beatings hurt a lot less than the superior look she had just given him.

"She is perioikoi," Nikolas said, and Zoi nodded tersely. "It means she's a foreigner. It means she's free," he clarified. Zoi tossed her hair back, and the mass of it, loosened from this morning's braids, fell away from her face and down her back, to lick at her hips.

Of course, thought Galen. *Her hair.* His own hair was allowed to grow only a few fingers widths before Feodoras had a barber shave it all away. As for free Spartan men, they wore their hair and beards long, and braided it, or tied it all back with

53

string or metal bands. Nikolas' own brown curls scraped his shoulders and his beard grew in sparse patches that embarrassed the prince. Why hadn't Galen considered this basic mark of slavery when he first saw Zoi? Had he been *that* besotted by her appearance? Angry with himself now, Galen blurted, "Your Uncle was a helot."

"This does not make me one, too," Zoi answered.

"Perioikoi or helot, you aren't a citizen of Sparta. Never will be," Galen shot back, wanting to pierce her pride. "You're an outsider, a nobody, and without Brygus to take care of you, you'll be wishing you were a helot. A girl like you alone in Sparta? You think Linus will be the last to come after you like he did? I feel sorry for you," Galen spat at Zoi, whose eyes darkened further. As for Galen, he felt deflated and annoyed. This was not how he imagined his first conversation with this girl would go.

"Galenos!" Nikolas yelled again, and that's when the olive tree began to shake, as if it were intent on lifting its roots out of the ground, walking on over, and stomping on them. *Zoi is doing it again*, Galen thought, *bringing the tree to life*.

"What *are* you?" he asked Zoi.

"I'm a nobody, remember?" she said, then, closed her eyes, as if she was trying very hard to restrain herself. When she opened them again, Zoi looked more settled. The tree no longer moved. "Thank you, Your Highness," she said to Nikolas, and bowed low again. She stopped for a moment over Brygus' body, covered her mouth with the back of her hand, and ran off into a cluster of thatched homes in the distance.

7

They left Brygus' body and headed back to the agoge.
The dawn was still about an hour away, but Galen knew there
would be no more hunting tonight, not after what they'd seen.
A breeze stirred in Zoi's wake, and the leaves rustled.

"She is charming, isn't she?" Nikolas asked, squinting
as if he might make out Zoi's form in the distance.

"Charming? She's dangerous, Nikolas. Did you see
what she did to that tree?"

"She's most beautiful," Nikolas said. He stooped to
pick up a tuft of dandelion greens and tossed a few of the leaves
in his mouth. "She spoke what sounded like an old Spartan
dialect at first," Nikolas said mid-chew. "But then she uttered
something I didn't understand. Where could she be from?"
Nikolas began pacing, circling Galen. Every now and then he'd
pause and look in the direction Zoi had gone.

"Nikolas, listen. I don't trust her. She did something to
that tree," Galen said.

"That was an intervention of the gods," Nikolas said, waving his hand. "Where is the nearest temple to Aphrodite? I'd like to make an offering to her."

The goddess of love, Galen thought, *of course.* He was sure of it now—Zoi was not just a girl, not just a goatherd's niece. She was a witch of some kind. A temptress. A siren. Galen had heard the singer's songs about a hero who'd tied himself to the mast of a great ship in order to keep from being lured by sirens intent on destroying him. He remembered stories about mermaids that enticed sailors to drown. And Galen had overheard two female helots talk about strong medicines that bound a man to a woman. There was no doubt about it—Zoi had cast some sort of spell on Nikolas.

"Open your eyes, Nikolas. Zoi isn't what she pretends to be," Galen said.

Nikolas laughed and said, "Oh."

"Oh what?"

"You found her charming, too."

"No, I found her terrifying. Powerful." Galen saw it again in his mind's eye, the girl's cheeks blooming with color, her eyes shut tight in concentration, the olive tree bent as if it had been softened by fire.

"Perhaps she's a goddess in disguise," Nikolas said, and his mouth fell into a lazy smile.

"You're hopeless," Galen said, walking on ahead of Nikolas. He couldn't understand Nikolas. Didn't he have senses? How had Zoi confounded him so easily? Galen considered Zoi's dappled eyes, her long hair, and the way a few strands had floated in the air as if the rest of her were about to take flight. There was that tattoo, a blue tendril snaking out from underneath her chiton. Galen rubbed his upper arm and thought of his own tattoo, wholly different from the design Galen had glimpsed on Zoi's skin.

56

Galen was far ahead of Nikolas now. Before them, the sun was breaking the horizon. Apollo and his chariot were beginning the race across the sky, the bringing forth of day. In the morning, Nestor would gather the sleepy agoge students and assess their success or failure. The students themselves reported the helot deaths they'd caused, and so the Crypteia depended on the honesty of each student. Every year, there was at least one boy who, when called upon to answer the question, "How fared your hunt?" would respond, "I've failed, Nestor." The moment always sent ripples through the mess hall. The boys would cast down their eyes. The failed student would be led away for his public penalty.

This year would be no different. In reality, very many students failed the Crypteia. Murdering a man without a weapon took immeasurable skill, and certainly, not all agoge students were up to that task. How many actually admitted the failure was a different story. *Nikolas is fool enough to do it, though*, thought Galen.

"Galen," Nikolas called out, running to catch up.

"If you want to talk about Zoi some more, you can forget it," Galen said, noticing, for the first time, that saying her name aloud made his stomach flutter.

"No. I just wanted to say, to promise, well...I won't cry out," Nikolas said suddenly, and Galen knew he was talking about the public flogging he'd receive for failing during the Crypteia.

"Of course you won't," Galen said, though he wasn't convinced. He'd seen many whippings, both of agoge students and helots, and there was not a man alive that could keep silent when the lash struck his back. Most times, the sound of the whip as it whistled in the air prompted the first scream, even before it had drawn blood.

"After the healers take care of my flayed back, the senators will be forced to choose a new king. They won't want someone like me to lead them," Nikolas said and kicked a small rock in his path. The stone skittered away from them.

"You don't have to tell Nestor the truth. You can make up a story. No one will question the word of the Eurypontid prince," Galen said.

"I couldn't do that."

"Sure you could. You cheated tonight, didn't you? You brought me along."

"I wasn't going to let you help me murder anyone, Galen, you must know that," Nikolas said. "A Spartan must be a man of his word."

Galen did not say what he was thinking, that Spartans were also cold-blooded. That they valued warfare above anything else. That they were superstitious to the point of lunacy. That for all their talk of strength, the Spartans and all of Greece were losing the war against Persia, and that, under all their noses, there were helots coming together in the dark of night, plotting rebellion.

Galen hadn't seen the hooded man who spoke of rebellion again. Galen had told no one, not even Nikolas, about the encounter. In the morning, his eye felt better, and he wondered whether he'd imagined the hooded man, if he had not been a hallucination brought on by the pain in his eye.

Yet that evening, as Galen had been slurping the meager stew he'd been given for dinner, he had overheard something in the kitchen. Galen had listened as one of the cooks, a woman named Maira, spoke to the oldest helot in the agoge, an ancient man named Lasus, who wore a grubby cloth around his head, covering his left ear, which he'd lost long ago for reasons he would not reveal. Maira was saying something about a viper, about the Parnon's foothills east of Sparta where the Rock of the Sibyl lay.

"A viper?" Galen had asked, intruding on the whispering pair. Maira and Lasus had turned their dark eyes on him. Maira's mouth twitched a little and her brow furrowed.

"No one has said such a thing," Lasus had said in his wizened, raspy voice, and Galen knew to back away and to keep his mouth shut.

It must be a rebellion, Galen had thought to himself. Part of him had longed to join, to find the hooded man, to get his hands on a weapon and free himself for good. But Galen's thoughts invariably turned to Nikolas, to the Queen, and the urge to rise up dampened in him. The royals would be the first targets in a full-scale revolt, he knew.

Still, Galen did not tell Nikolas about what he'd heard.

Keeping the secret bothered him, the way a nagging pain did. But when he imagined telling Nikolas, his thoughts led to an inevitable conclusion—the rebels would figure out who'd exposed them, and Galen would be as good as dead. There was this, too: Galen *wanted* to revolt, *wanted* to be free of this helotry, desired nothing more than to take a knife and carve out the tattoo on his arm.

Now, Galen watched Nikolas as he took the lead. His narrow back would be brutalized under the whip. Nikolas, who was so loyal, and good, and true…Galen's chest ached thinking about it.

At the agoge, Galen and Nikolas parted. The sun was out, and the world was cast in a soft, rosy light. From his cot, where he tried to snag a little sleep before Feodoras' call to muster, Galen saw Acayo, Brutus and Linus, limping towards their barracks. *So the bear didn't eat them, after all*, Galen thought glumly. He was too exhausted to worry about Acayo's vengeance, which was surely coming. Galen slung his arm over his eyes to block out the light, and just as his mind turned to Zoi, her lips parting in his imagination as if she were about to say something, he fell asleep.

8

Feodoras sent Galen out a few hours later to purchase olives and some milk. The drachmas jangled in a pouch inside his chiton. All of Sparta was awake now, and as Galen trudged down the hill upon which the agoge sat, he noticed the effects of the Crypteia at once. Along the river Eurotas, women were washing the winding sheets that would be used to wrap the dead. They worked in grim silence, having adopted Spartan attitudes about death. There would be no rending of clothes among the helot widows. No keening songs. No tears in public.

Up and over a small hill Galen trudged, wondering which of the agoge students had killed a helot last night. There were sixteen students Nikolas' age and older, sixteen young men who had taken part in the hunt. That was a fair number, enough to affect, in some way, nearly every helot that lived near the agoge. Galen walked into the market, which was quieter than usual. The helots there gave Galen a wide berth. They knew he worked in the agoge, and their rage was focused on the school, on the young men who would be their masters. They associated Galen with the place, and so, with the murders. An old woman perched on the lip of a well raised her hands and moved her fingers in an intricate gesture, her eyes fixed on Galen's face. He knew a curse when he saw one. Galen promised to make an offering of tonight's dinner to Zeus.

Out of the corner of his eye, he spotted a man carrying the limp form of a young boy in his arms. The child was no more than ten. His hair was matted in dried, black blood. The boy's father walked slowly, as if each step were calculated, concentrated upon, as if he might fall to the ground at any moment and die, too. Galen found he could not take a full, satisfying breath.

Galen came into the shade of a wooden house, away from the fierce sunlight. *Only a child*, thought Galen, and looked away from the man and the dead boy. There were few agoge students capable of such a shameful act. Acayo was the first name to come to Galen's mind. Guilt wrapped itself around Galen's thoughts like a blanket. *I escaped Acayo, Brutus and Linus,* he thought, *and that child may have paid the price.*

A single sob cracked the silence, piercing Galen's heart. It came from the east. Several helots turned towards it, paused, then went on their way. Yet there was a tension in the way the helots were going about their business, a tautness in their faces that had something to do with grief, and a lot to do with anger. *This is how slave revolts begin*, Galen thought.

A cool hand on his shoulder drew Galen out of himself.

"It is not your fault," Zoi said, her hand dropping back to her side.

Galen caught his breath. She'd braided her hair and twisted it around her head like a crown. The place on his shoulder where she'd touched him was cold. "So you can read minds, too?" he asked, leaning back against a wall and crossing his arms. He wanted to seem relaxed around her. He didn't want her to know that his heart was pounding and his lungs ached.

"No, I cannot read minds," Zoi said. That's when Galen noticed the winding sheet folded in her arms.

"For Brygus," Galen said, laying two fingers on the cloth.

Zoi's eyes watered a little, and Galen felt himself softening towards her. "They're digging a pit grave north of here, for all the dead," she whispered.

"How many?"

"I heard it was twelve," she said, "including my uncle."

Not all sixteen, then, Galen thought, eager to relay the information to Nikolas. Perhaps, if Nikolas knew that not he alone had failed, he'd play the game the other students did—lying to Nestor to save their hides.

"You and the prince played no role in this," Zoi said and held Galen's gaze.

"How can you be sure? For all you know, we killed all those people." *What am I doing?* Galen thought. *Do I want her to fear me?* He watched how she studied him, how her eyes raked his face, and then his body, as if the answer to his question would appear on his skin.

"I simply know. Prince Nikolas is kind beyond measure," Zoi said, and Galen's heart faltered at the compliment, paid only to Nikolas.

"I'm sorry I yelled at you last night," Galen said.

"I know that, too." Zoi gripped the winding sheet close to her body.

"Will you need help with that?" Galen asked. "With Brygus, I mean?"

Zoi's face tightened, and Galen prayed to the gods that she not cry. "No," she said, after a moment. Then: "You, also, are kind, Galenos."

"Galen."

"Galen, then. Be well," she said, and stepped out from under the shade of the house. Galen watched her go, the curly, blue drawing on her thigh peeking out from under her chiton. He'd meant to ask her about it, about the tree that seemed to move with the force of her will. Perhaps she'd confide in him. Perhaps she didn't think a helot was so beneath her after all.

Zoi turned around, many feet away from Galen. "It will be terrible for him, won't it?" Zoi called. "The whipping, I mean." Galen could see her wet cheeks, even from this distance. He nodded, watched Zoi exhale deeply, her mouth a small O. Suddenly, he smelled honeysuckle in the air. Zoi took off running, the winding sheet trailing its end behind her, like a veil caught in the breeze.

Galen served dinner that afternoon, as he usually did, carrying heavy wooden trays with the night's meal piled on them from table to table. He'd been thinking of Zoi all afternoon. Strangely, the spot where she'd touched his shoulder remained cold, even when he'd been in the kitchen, standing before the ovens. It felt very nearly like having a drop of water sitting on his skin, one he could not wipe away or warm. It was a distracting sensation, and added to the general agitation in his mind concerning the girl.

So it was that Galen didn't realize he'd reached Acayo's table until it was too late. He caught Acayo's eyes for a moment, and felt a different kind of chill at the sight of Acayo's smile, which came upon his face slowly, as if he were imagining something wonderful. It was a malicious smile, one Galen had seen on Acayo's face before, usually before he pounced on a younger student and beat him mercilessly. Someone pushed the wooden tray off Galen's shoulder, and behind him, the pieces of roasted lamb lay on the ground. The students who'd not yet been served groaned. Feodoras thundered towards him.

Up stood Acayo at Galen's side, whispering, "That's for the bear." Galen felt a sharp pain in his side, but dared not give Acayo the satisfaction of looking down. "And this," Acayo said, twisting his hand near Galen's ribs so that Galen had to bite his lip to keep from crying out, "is a message for your princeling. Make sure you repeat it precisely: Sparta shall have one king in the end."

9

Acayo sat down just as Feodoras arrived on the scene. Galen chanced it, took his eyes off of Feodoras to watch in horror as a spot of blood began to bloom on his chiton, just between his lower ribs. Weapons were not allowed in the agoge, except for training purposes, and Acayo now sat with both hands on the table, folded together as if in prayer. The dagger he'd used, Galen imagined, was tucked away somewhere.

Galen's vision doubled. Now there were two Acayos, chatting, their mouths moving up and down. Two Feodorases yelled at him, but Galen couldn't make out the sound. His stomach turned. Nausea swept over him as the pain in his wound sharpened. Galen felt dizzy. He was sure he would fall down. He closed his eyes and an old memory came to him of a time long ago, when he'd made his way up the jagged cliffs of Mount Taygetos, where it was said Spartan parents disposed of

65

weak newborns—ones sick at birth—by tossing them over the cliff face. Galen was only nine the day he climbed Taygetos. Feodoras had struck him with a heated pan for picking a bushel of olives that were not yet ripe. He'd pressed the red-hot iron onto Galen's back. Galen had smelled his skin burning; heard a hissing sound beneath his own screams. Then he ran, all the way to Mount Taygetos, his lungs aching as he climbed, intent on throwing himself over the edge. But when he looked down, expecting to see a thousand tiny corpses, Galen saw nothing but rocks jutting out of the ground like teeth, and beyond that, a meadow. He couldn't bring himself to get any closer to the edge. It felt as if a pair of strong hands was holding him back. The truth was, the idea of jumping was so frightening that Galen froze. He stood there a long time, so long, that when he got back to the agoge, Feodoras locked him in the cellar for the night for "running off."

This was a memory Galen would have rather not had lingering in his brain. It was one of many. He opened his eyes and, thankfully, the double vision was gone. But the pain blazed just beneath his ribs, and his knees felt weak.

Nikolas rose to his feet at the other end of the mess hall. Galen willed him to sit, to keep out of it, to avoid drawing enemies to himself, not now when he needed friends, not now when he might be facing the cruel whip for his failed hunt. Galen watched as another boy rose with Nikolas, said something to him, and pushed him into his seat. *Thank you, Timios*, thought Galen, grateful for the younger student's wisdom.

Feodoras trembled with rage. "Pick up the food," he said through gritted teeth, then his eyes fell on Galen's wound. The blood was spreading now, and Galen could no longer stand up straight. Feodoras laughed low, putting his hand on Acayo's shoulder, tenderly, the way a father might. Ignoring Galen who was crouched now, trying to pick up the lambs' meat with

66

shaking fingers, Feodoras called out to Nestor, "Perhaps it is time to reckon the work of the hunt, Nestor?"

Nestor, a round-bellied man who'd gained fame for his role in the battle at the Lydian border against Persia, had just taken a monstrous bite out of some bread. He mumbled and nodded vigorously at Feodoras, saying with a full mouth, "Yes, let's begin. Prince Acayo of the Agiads, how fared your hunt?"

Galen watched from the floor in the corner of the agoge. His vision was undulating now. Maira, the cook he'd heard talking about rebellion, had tried to help him to his feet, but Galen had waved her away. His injury was serious, he knew. It was quite likely this would kill him. Galen thought of Hades, he thought of Zoi and the cold patch on his shoulder. Under his breath, he prayed to Zeus for a few more moments of life, long enough, he hoped, to learn whether Nikolas would be spared.

"Let others boast," Acayo began formally, and Galen pressed his fist hard against his wound, moaning as he did so. "Know this, friends of the agoge, that the son of Morfeo, King of the Agiads, sent a helot man twice his size to Hades shortly after dusk. The body was devoured by a bear, which I watched from a distance. May my success in the Crypteia be an offering to Artemis, the bear-leader," he said and looked at Galen. "And to Ares."

The room exploded in applause, and Nestor rose, brushing crumbs off his beard and belly, to clap so loudly the sound rang in Galen's ears. Galen thought again of the dead boy in his father's arms, the gruesome gash on his small head, caused, certainly, by a heavy stone. How ridiculous to believe that Acayo could hurt a man twice his size. Sparta was already a cruel state. A Sparta led by Acayo would be unimaginably coldblooded.

"Well. Well," Nestor said. "Prince Nikolas of the Eurypontids, how fared your hunt."

Galen watched as Nikolas rose unsteadily. The boys at his table looked up at him, their eyes wide. They'd clapped and whistled when Nestor uttered the Eurypontid name, as if they were rooting for their favorite athlete at the Olympic games.

"Let others boast," Nikolas began, and Galen knew these were honest words, not the false humility of the formal bragging that characterized Acayo's speech. "I have…" Nikolas hesitated. He took a deep breath, which made him seem taller suddenly, but before he could speak, he was interrupted by an earsplitting wail.

Zoi, her chiton ragged and torn, her face muddied and streaked with tears, stumbled into the mess hall. Two helots from the kitchens were behind her, grabbing at her arms to keep her from entering.

"I shall speak!" Zoi yelled. "I demand justice!" She paused to sob into her hands, and her back rose and fell. When she lifted her face, Galen saw that her eyes looked wild and bloodshot. "My uncle," she said, pointing at Nikolas who watched her with his mouth open. "My uncle, who saved me from a lion when I was a child, who bore the scars on his arms from that terrible battle, a man such as that, you dare murder?"

"I, I…" Nikolas stuttered, taking a few steps towards Zoi.

"Do not speak!" she screamed. "I demand justice," she repeated, then crumpled to the floor, like an empty chiton tossed aside.

"Well," Nestor said, chuckling. "Now we know how fared Prince Nikolas. A lion-killer, eh?" Nestor began to clap, and others followed. When the clapping died down, Nestor spoke again, "But you aren't supposed to be caught, young prince." He wagged a thick finger at Nikolas and it was clear nothing would come of that particular broken rule. "Get rid of her," Nestor said, and one of the helots rushed over to Zoi.

Galen had been watching in terror. *What is she doing?* he asked himself, and then it became clear. Zoi had just saved Nikolas from the whip. When Nestor gave the command to do away with Zoi, Galen groaned loudly. He tried to stand, but his legs were like water. Zoi looked up from where she lay prone on the ground, and her eyes met with Galen's for a moment before she looked away.

The helot tried to lift Zoi, but he could not. "She's as heavy as a boulder," he said, and another helot joined him. Together they tugged at her arms, and she allowed her head to loll to the side, her eyes closed, as if she were dead. Maira joined the cause, and the three helots pulled and grunted to lift the girl. Still, she could not be moved.

"Remove her!" Nestor roared.

"Galenos!" Feodoras yelled, and motioned for Galen to help. He staggered to his feet, found them working, and kept his fist, warm and slick now, pressed close to his wound.

Galen approached Zoi cautiously, he leaned over and the room spun a little. Black spots quivered before his eyes. "Thank you for saving Nikolas. Acayo has killed me, see for yourself," he whispered into her hair. Galen's wound pulsed. His stomach was sticky with blood. "But you can defend yourself. I know you can, Zoi," Galen said. He took hold of her hand, which was cold like the blade of a knife first thing in the morning. That's when she opened her eyes. She slid her free hand into the opening on the side of Galen's chiton, nudged his own fist away from the wound, and flattened her palm against it.

His vision was the first to clear, then his legs strengthened, and finally, the pain in his side diminished until it was gone altogether. When Galen gasped, Zoi uttered a short, "Shh," then stood at last. She stared at Nestor and he returned the stare, silently, until he pounded the table before him with his fist, breaking the gaze.

The entire agoge was sizing up Zoi. Some students stood, craning their necks to get a better look at her. Others looked from Nikolas to Zoi, back and forth. Galen wondered if anyone had noticed what she'd done to him. Zoi hid her bloodied hand in the folds of her chiton. She had shushed

Galen, had wanted to keep her gifts secret. *A gift*, thought Galen. *That's exactly what it is.* The tingling sensation in his side was like a drug, blurring the doubts and fears Galen had about Zoi, diminishing his skepticism. He'd wanted to protect her from Nestor's rage moments ago. Galen knew he'd do anything to keep Zoi safe. And for now, that meant, keeping her gift private. Noting that several eyes were on him, too, Galen feigned weakness by leaning against a pillar behind him.

"This girl demands justice," Nikolas said suddenly, and the attention turned to him. "And so she shall be taken to the palace, to my mother, Queen Isaura of the Eurypontids, who has always longed for a daughter."

"Your Highness, that isn't necess..." Zoi began.

"She has broken the laws of the agoge, a hundred laws broken, by coming here!" Nestor said, flustered by Nikolas' sudden command of the room and by the strange girl's daring.

"Well you know, my father, King Leandros, is four years dead, and the Queen is lonesome. The niece of a lion-killer will make good company. Besides, if I murdered this girl's uncle, then I owe her payment, lest the dead man's shade curse all of Sparta," Nikolas said. He'd spoken as if to Zoi alone, never once looking away from her. Galen, who held her arm still, felt her shiver. "For the Eurypontids *are* Sparta, and my actions belong to all of you," Nikolas finished.

At his table, Acayo was chewing the inside of his mouth, staring out a window.

Zoi knelt. "My thanks, Your Highness," she said, then asked, "Who will be my escort?"

"Galenos and I," Nikolas answered, and the students in the room rustled a little. Few of them had been to the palace.

"Then Maira shall go as well," Nestor added, to which Nikolas nodded in agreement.

The helots who'd tried to lift Zoi stepped away at last, leaving her alone at the door to the mess hall. They watched her in fear. She'd been as rooted to the ground as an ancient

70

oak moments ago, but now she moved airily, seemingly as light as a girl of her slight build should be. Maira stood off to the side, waiting. Galen peeled away from the pillar he'd been leaning on. Nikolas left his place at the table, his food still sitting there, and joined them.

Composed again, Nestor called out, "Brutus, son of Melandro, how fared your hunt?"

Galen, Nikolas, and Zoi, did not linger long enough to hear his answer.

10

Galen rushed ahead of Nikolas and Zoi and went straight to the place where he kept his things in order to change into a clean chiton. He paused for a moment to touch the wool, wet with his blood. The fogginess was lifting from his mind, and his doubts about Zoi began to form again. When Galen caught up with the others, they were halfway down the hill, headed towards the palace.

They walked together in the falling light of dusk, with Maira trailing behind them. At first, none of them spoke. Galen could not keep his hand off his side, the place Zoi had healed with a touch. The skin there was smooth, smoother than it had been before. And it was cool, though not uncomfortably so.

Galen longed to ask Zoi many questions, but each time, the words stuck in his mouth. The silence among them was oppressive. It was Maira who broke it at last, crying out, "Ay!

My foot!" falling to the ground to examine her toe. A jagged splinter had pierced the web of skin between her toes. Nikolas and Galen helped her rise and hop towards a nearby well, where Maira sat down to tend her injury.

"Give me a moment, young ones," Maira said, and Galen, Nikolas, and Zoi obliged, seating themselves apart from the woman, who huffed as she tried picking out the splinter.

Galen was about to speak when he glanced at Nikolas. The look on Nikolas' face, the way his mouth was set in a tight line, stopped Galen's speech.

"You should not have done that," Nikolas said to Zoi.

"What? Saved your hide?"

"Lied. Dishonored the agoge," Nikolas said.

Zoi folded her arms and tucked her legs closer to her body, as if shielding herself. "Having that brute Nestor make mince meat out of your back is no honor," she said. "I've watched boys under the whip."

"As have I," Nikolas interrupted.

"And there's no grace there. No honor. Only brutality."

"The flogging is only a test for us. Not a punishment, really. We all must undergo it at eighteen anyway, to prove our resistance to pain."

"You aren't eighteen yet," Zoi said.

Galen wanted desperately to side with Zoi, to lend his voice to her argument. He'd seen how boys were made to grip a wooden pole, how Nestor, or one of the older students, would set about the grim work of the lash, how, after a while, the boy's back was nothing more than raw flesh, how the ground beneath his feet would blacken with blood. Yet, part of Galen understood Nikolas' perspective, too. The violence of the agoge was vital training, not punishment. Boys in the agoge faced a lifetime of warfare. They would never know the peace of a homestead, but rather, would live out their lives in soldier's mess halls, with only occasional visits with their wives and children to lighten their existence. The Spartan force's renown began at the agoge. No other Greek city trained its boys that way. When foreigners asked why Spartan women were the only females in all of Greece allowed to speak their minds, the answer was always the same: because Spartan women gave birth to real men.

"Your interference was shameful," Nikolas said at last. He did not look at Zoi as he spoke.

Zoi became still, unnaturally so, thought Galen. She closed her eyes, and Galen felt a rumbling in the ground, a slight tremor, as if horses had just run past. The sensation faded. She opened her eyes and laid her hand over Nikolas'. "Then why didn't you tell Nestor the truth?"

Nikolas gripped Zoi's hand, saying, "Because it would have meant your death. I suppose what I should say is thank you, and leave it at that." For an instant, Galen thought Nikolas might kiss her fingers, and his chest burned at the thought. But Nikolas released Zoi's hand right away, his cheeks red.

"You don't owe me anything," Zoi said. "In fact, I was hoping you'd let me go altogether. It's not that I don't think the palace will be wonderful, but I'd rather not..."

"You'll be safe there," Nikolas said.

"Palace life just isn't for me," Zoi went on, clasping her hands together as if pleading.

"And you did save me from the whip, after all," Nikolas went on.

"And you saved my life," Galen added.

Nikolas' eyes widened, falling on Galen. "Forgive me, Galen. I saw you stumbling, but didn't know it was that bad. What happened?"

"Acayo," Galen said. "But it's all right now. Zoi healed it." He'd relay Acayo's message later, when he and Nikolas were alone. Galen lifted his chiton to reveal the smooth, hairless skin that had grown over the wound. He had not yet dared to look at it, and found himself in awe of Zoi's work.

Galen poked the new skin with his finger. *Yes, very cold,* he thought.

"What are you?" Nikolas asked slowly, leaning closer to Zoi, as if he might find the answer in her face.

Zoi shook her head, and began to fiddle with a twig she'd found.

"We must know," Nikolas said, his hand stopping her own. The twig fell to the ground.

Again they touch, thought Galen, feeling a curious thing then, the urge to strike Nikolas, to stop him from laying a hand on her again. He tamped down the feeling guiltily.

"Let's just say I have interesting parents," she said.

Nikolas sucked in air noisily. "A daughter of a god. Or goddess then. Which one is it? Apollo? He's known for his healing powers. Or Asclepius, who went among the Argonauts?"

"Don't assume anything," Zoi said. "I don't wish to displease you, Your Highness."

Galen watched with interest. Somehow, he didn't think one of the gods was involved in Zoi's making. There was a darker edge to her that Nikolas was missing, a temper that broiled beneath her lovely surface. How easily she'd feigned wild grief at the agoge. How naturally lying came to her. The strange rituals she'd performed at Brygus' death were directed at no god that Galen knew.

"You put on quite a show back there," Galen said.

"I always thought they should let women perform in the theater," Nikolas added, his smile lop-sided. He was behaving like a puppy, eager to please.

"My grief for my uncle is real, though this outward show of it," Zoi said, lifting her torn chiton, "is not my style."

"Did he really save you from a lion?" Galen asked.

"He did. Brygus found me when I was four. My mother and I were hunting in the woods surrounding Messenia when I got separated from her. I spent two days alone there, drinking only water from a stream I stayed close to. On the third morning, a lioness pounced on me, knocking me down. Brygus had been searching for a lost goat when he heard my yell, and struck the lion with a heavy rock, dazing it, and driving his knife into its throat. He got a gash as wide as my hand on his forearm for his troubles," she said, holding up her hand to show the size of Brygus' wound. "Hurting Brygus was that lion's last act."

"So, Brygus wasn't really your uncle? That's why you're considered periokoi, not a helot?" Galen asked and Zoi nodded. "What about your mother? Where did she go?"

"Never saw her again." Zoi picked up the twig once more and snapped it in half. Galen felt a sudden closeness to Zoi. Neither one of them had been mothered for very long.

"Your father?"

"That's complicated, Galen."

"Tell me," he said, feeling bolder now.

A loud whistle jolted Galen. Maira was standing by the well, her fingers in her mouth, as she let out another high-pitched trill. "All better now! To the palace!" she yelled at them.

Zoi went to stand, but Galen held her down by the hem of her chiton. "Wait. One more question," he whispered.

She twisted at the waist and Galen lost the grip on her tunic. "There's nothing else you need to know," she said. "For now." Zoi tried to stand, and a flash of blue ink on her thigh revealed more of the curly design he'd noticed before. It was like a tail, the pattern of it intricate and reptilian. *Snakelike*, he thought.

A sudden, unprocessed idea came to Galen then. He'd meant to ask about the coolness of her skin, whether his healed wound would ever warm up. Instead, he leaned in close to her and murmured, "I want to know about the viper," hoping that it was low enough for Nikolas not to have heard.

Zoi quivered. Color had drained from her cheeks. She stumbled to her feet.

"Are you unwell, Zoi?" Nikolas asked, helping her to stand straight.

"Yes, Your Highness," she said. "I haven't eaten all day."

Nikolas led Zoi to the well where Maira stood. He drew a cup of cool water for her, and held it to her lips. A foolish smile formed on Nikolas' face.

Galen felt a chill, and it had nothing and everything to do with the cold spot near his ribs. *She's part of the rebellion*, he thought, and the idea filled him with dread and exhilaration, both at the same time. A revolt with a powerful creature such as Zoi involved could be successful. Perhaps the helots might achieve freedom, after all. Galen watched Nikolas produce a square of linen from inside his chiton, watched as his friend wiped a few drops of water off of Zoi's chin. Nikolas was rapt. The linen square trembled in his hand.

Even from where he stood, Galen could see the tail end of the viper markings on Zoi's leg. Could the snake be a symbol of the helot rebellion brewing in the dark corners of Sparta? Galen watched as Zoi looked up at Nikolas, saw how she batted her eyes at him. He remembered the act she'd put on at the agoge, realizing that Zoi had probably not saved Nikolas from the whip out of any sense of kindness. No, there was a plan in place to upend the Spartan order, and Zoi had discovered a weakness worth exploiting—a prince who fell in love easily, and who believed in the goodwill of others.

Galen followed Nikolas and Zoi some paces behind, with the helot Maira at his side. *The helots in their place, as it should be*, Galen thought bitterly. Had Maira noticed Zoi's serpentine tattoo? Could Galen broach the subject with the old woman? He cleared his throat.

"Maira, I have a question for you," Galen began, under his breath.

"About?" Maira was limping a bit. She kept her eyes on her left foot.

"The viper."

Maira stopped walking, jutting out her arm so that it smacked Galen's chest, halting him, too. "Give 'em some room to talk," she said, indicating Nikolas and Zoi. "The prince needs his privacy, eh?"

"Yes, of course. Privacy," Galen said, catching on.

Once Nikolas and Zoi were further down the road, Maira lowered her arm, and began walking again, more slowly now.

"Did you know Sparta has been without a sibyl for ten years now?" Maira asked.

"Ten? That long? How have the ephors advised the kings?" Galen asked. It was unthinkable. The ephors always consulted the sibyl, the woman they kept isolated in the Sanctuary of Artemis Orthia, a temple a few leagues from the village of Limnai, at the base of Mount Parnon. They called the place the Rock of the Sibyl. It was said the seer was insane. Growing up, Galen had heard stories about children who'd wandered too close to the sibyl's home and been devoured by her. It was probably just a story, something told to naughty children to keep them in line.

"The ephors make the voyage out to Delphi now, to see the oracle there."

"That's a long way," Galen said.

"Inconvenient, that's certain. The real mystery is where the Spartan sibyl went," Maira said, her voice low now. "It's said she cast a prophecy about us helots. She saw us rising up, led by a woman in the form of a viper, given Poseidon's grace and protection. The sibyl disappeared like that," Maira said, snapping her fingers, "soon after she had her vision."

"How do you know about it?" Galen asked, thinking about Zoi and the patterns on her leg.

"Even the ephors have helots to serve 'em. And we helots, like anyone else, have eyes and ears, don't we, Galen?"

"And so a rebellion is forming? An army of helots?"

"Something like that," Maira said, glancing behind her.

"What are you waiting for?"

"The viper. And Poseidon's sign."

"What's the sign?" Galen asked.

Maira rubbed her hands together. "They don't call Poseidon the Earth Shaker for nothing. Some are expecting a tidal wave. I think it will be an earthquake, boy. A big one. And when it comes, we take up arms, and then the viper does its grisly work among the Spartans." Maira smiled even as she spoke. Suddenly, her arm thrust out again, and Galen knocked into it. She turned her hand and gripped his chiton, tugging him close to her. Galen was surprised by her strength. Her eyes danced from side to side, frenzied. "We know you're cozy with the prince," she said. "Like I said, we have eyes and ears, Galen. Choose your friends well. And remember this: there isn't a Spartan alive who'd raise his shield to protect you."

"But it all seems sort of vague, doesn't it?" Galen asked, hoping to redirect Maira's aggression a little.

"Where's your trust in the gods, boy?"

"They haven't exactly favored us in the past, Maira. That tattoo on your arm and the one on mine are proof of that."

Maira huffed. She smoothed her rumpled chiton and said, "The Spartans don't control the gods."

Ahead of them, Zoi and Nikolas chattered on. Nikolas had wound his fingers in Zoi's long hair, and he was tugging it playfully. Galen watched as Zoi pushed him away, her profile lit by the setting sun, her mouth open in laughter. "What will the viper look like?" Galen asked Maira.

"Only the gods know. I hope it's something fierce," Maira said, looking up at the sky as if the gods were going to send the viper down from Olympus at that very moment.

"Mind what I said, boy. Not a word to the prince. Or to anyone," Maira said.

Galen nodded. The palace came into view ahead of them. Typically, the palace was guarded by two Spartan soldiers whose red cloaks dangled behind them, while broad shields rested against their bodies. When he'd visited in the past, Galen noted how the soldiers never addressed him, though they nodded their heads at Nikolas, clamping their heels together for the prince. But now, the palace was flanked by several rows of cloaked soldiers. Galen tried to count them, but lost track at forty.

Nikolas and Zoi froze where they stood, and Galen and Maira soon caught up to them. A slew of possibilities offered themselves to Galen, as he thought about the force assembled before them. Perhaps the Persians had launched an attack nearby. Perhaps Nestor had alerted the palace about Zoi, the strange girl who had resisted three helots without effort. Maybe this was Poseidon's sign. Maybe someone had leaked the plans about the rebellion. Galen could tell that Maira was thinking along the same lines. The woman's face was still, her eyes wide, her mouth a little open, as if she'd been caught breaking a law then and there.

"For the last time, Your Highness, I beg of you not to take me to the palace. I'd rather live among the helots, among my uncle's kin," Zoi said, taking a few steps backwards.

"But you will look so beautiful in palace gowns. And the food is excellent. Besides, my mother *is* lonely. She will love you," Nikolas said, tugging Zoi's hand without looking at her. His eyes were taking in the splendor of the soldiers. "Someday," Nikolas said, and this time he did look at Zoi, "I'll stand before them, leading them as their king." Zoi smiled weakly, resigned. "Every Spartan warrior has a helot at his side, to help with the armor and such," Nikolas continud, turning around to look at Galen. "That will be you, Galen. Imagine the two of us in battle," Nikolas said, his eyes glossy.

80

"Dreaming of killing men, are you?" Galen asked. A mean thing to say, he knew, in light of how the Crypteia had worked out, but he felt charged and angry. Perhaps it had been the sight of Nikolas tugging Zoi's hair. Or Nikolas' naïveté, how unknowingly he strolled beside one possibly powerful enough to ruin him. Nikolas sobered at once. "It isn't all about fancy red cloaks, you know," Galen went on. "Spears are for gutting a man. Swords are for slicing throats and limbs. And the soldiers take helots into battle for more than just polishing weapons. Our job is to take the warrior's shield and body back to Sparta. You know that, too." Midway through the speech, a small voice in Galen's head urged him to stop. He ignored it.

"Easy, boy," Maira warned.

"It won't always be that way. When Persia falls..." Nikolas said, trailing off as he turned to look at the rows of soldiers again.

Galen wished he could believe it, wished he would live to see a Sparta at peace. At moments like this, Galen could see the influence of Queen Isaura on Nikolas, how her Ithacan upbringing clashed with Sparta's military nature, how it was said that her gentle spirit had been passed on to her only son.

"What are they all doing here?" Galen asked, gesturing towards the soldiers.

"One way to find out," Nikolas said, and led them towards the palace gates.

Zoi alone did not move. She was left behind, and when Galen turned to look at her, she was doing it again, closing her eyes, concentrating on something within her. For a moment, Galen thought the snake on her thigh was moving, uncoiling. He fell into a stupor looking at it. A clank of shields behind him, held upright by the soldiers now in sight of Nikolas, shook Galen out of his trance. He walked back to Zoi. Speaking low, he said, "Whatever you have planned, spare Queen Isaura and her son. Don't, and I'll come after you, viper or not."

81

Zoi's lip trembled as she took a step forward. Together, the foursome fell into the shadow of the soldiers before passing through the palace doors.

11

Four Doric columns stood at the palace entrance, which gave way to a long hallway. Galen's sandals scraped the stone floors and the sound was like a broom sweeping. Nikolas led the way, and Zoi now walked behind him, in his shadow. Galen rushed to join them, but Maira pulled him back whispering, "Don't forget your place, boy."

"I've been here before," Galen said to her, but the woman ignored him, and kept her slow pace behind the prince. The long hallway opened up to a vast courtyard with a green lawn, several stone benches, and pots filled with lemon balm long past flowering. In the center of the courtyard was a temple, an open-air building surrounded by thirty-six columns. Inside, Galen could just make out a statue of Ares. They moved past the temple and into another hallway. Here, the floor was covered in mosaic tiles depicting monsters. In one corner sat Medusa, the Gorgon, hunched over on the ground. Her arms, set in gray tiles, were wrapped around her knees. Her eyes were two points of red glass. Her head swarmed with tiny snakes, all crafted out of greenstone. At the other end of the hallway was a picture of the Hydra, the poisonous serpent that Hercules slew, the one that sprouted two heads for every one Hercules lopped off. It was said that all Spartans were descendants of Hercules. Galen watched Zoi walk between the two monsters, noting that she did not glance at the mosaics at all.

Finally, the hallway opened to a large, airy room. It, like the rest of the palace, was made of stone, but here, cedar beams were hoisted alongside the walls, and the place felt warmer for it. A fireplace took over the space on one wall, animal skin rugs littered the floor, and here and there lay cozy cushions on the floor. At the far end of the space lounged Queen Isaura of the Eurypontids, her Ithacan gown draped lushly around her body. She was reading intently something written on a wax board. Even from where he stood, Galen could see the intricate lettering.

"Mother," Nikolas called out and the queen lifted her head. At once, Maira dragged Galen to the fireplace, and knelt in the ashes, still warm from the overnight fire. Galen imitated her reluctantly. He'd never once followed that particular slave tradition.

"My Nikolas," Isaura said, laying the tablet down. She rose and clapped her hands, then opened her arms wide. Nikolas hugged his mother warmly, then he turned to Galen and gestured him forward.

Galen gave Maira a gloating look before leaving her there on the hearth. He made sure to dust his knees off before approaching the queen.

"Your Majesty," Galen said, bowing low once Isaura released him.

"Welcome," she said, smiling, but her eyes did not follow suit. Isaura had seen Zoi, and her brow furrowed at the sight of the bedraggled girl.

84

Nikolas reached behind him and pulled Zoi forward. She fell to her knees before the queen, and whispered, "Your Majesty."

"The Eurypontids owe this girl a great debt, mother," Nikolas said, and his voice echoed through the hall. Galen wondered at this gift, Nikolas' ability to modulate his speech, to sound like a regular boy one minute, and a natural leader the next. "I have asked her to keep you company in my absence."

"Rise, dear," Isaura said. Zoi stood slowly, keeping her eyes on her feet. Galen watched the proceedings with a knot in his stomach. If he had to, he thought he could take Zoi down, pin her so that she couldn't move, and so Galen stood at the ready.

"Look at me," Isaura whispered. "Such pretty eyes. Tell me your name, girl."

"Zoi, niece of Brygus, son of Bazil of Mycenae," she said.

"And your uncle approves of your stay here?"

"My uncle was killed in the Crypteia last night, Your Majesty."

The wax tablet that Isaura had been holding clattered to the ground. "The Crypteia? Last night?" Her lips trembled, and her hands rose in the air, seeking Nikolas, who she grabbed and held to her chest. "My boy," she whispered.

"I'm fine, Mother," he said. "You've no cause to worry."

"No cause? No cause?" Isaura asked, shaking her head, as to clear her mind and mouth from what she was about to say. She took Nikolas' hands in hers and turned them over, examining the palms and the knuckles. She glanced at Galen a long moment, then resumed her examination of Nikolas. Her lip was trembling. "Well then," Isaura whispered. She released Nikolas' hands, and bent over to pick up the tablet. "Can you read, Zoi?" she asked, changing the subject.

Zoi opened her mouth to answer, but just then, a clank of shields announced the entrance of King Morfeo to the hall. The space was so large, and so open, that Morfeo seemed small in the distance. Galen had only seen Morfeo once, long ago, when Acayo first joined the agoge. It was clear then that Acayo took after his mother, Queen Cyteria. In life, Cyteria had been fair, blue-eyed, and sharp featured, her face, like Acayo's, eagle-like in its severity. It was said that the Queen's great-grandmother was a daughter of Zeus himself, who'd come down to earth in the form of an eagle one clear night and mated with a woman from eastern Sparta, from whom would descend the Agiad line. The blood of eagles was said to course in Acayo's blood.

Galen didn't believe a word of it.

In reality, King Morfeo was a tall, slender man that moved with tremendous grace. His long fingers twitched as he walked and spoke, and his dark eyes were narrow and set close together. His nose was a large, sharp thing, and his chin receded into his neck, so that he, too, seemed like a bird of prey of some sort. But Morfeo lacked the regal good looks of his wife and son. What he had, instead, was a piercing gaze, and a snarling upper lip, and the height of a Persian, so that everyone in Sparta had to look up to him to see his face.

"You've come on an interesting day," Isaura whispered rapidly to them as Morfeo approached. "I was just reading King Morfeo's report from the front at Salamis," she said, indicating the tablet. Spartans were taught to read only as much as necessary—names, the designation of numbers, and other, practical matters. It was said the Ithacans read for pleasure.

"As you can see, King Morfeo of the Agiads has returned from Salamis alive and well. He's brought a mass of Persian captives with him," Isaura said. "The assembled force is here to keep them subdued. They're being kept in the yard for now."

"Why aren't they at the Agiad palace?" Galen asked.

"Not as big," Nikolas said, and waggled his eyebrows.

Yet another reason for Acayo to hate Nikolas, thought Galen.

"There's something else. A girl among the captives. She's...different," Isaura said, her brow crinkling in concentration. It seemed she would say more, but Morfeo had reached them at last.

"Good afternoon, Isaura," Morfeo said. He spoke very slowly, and pronounced each word precisely, like the singers did when relating a particularly dramatic moment in the tale of a hero.

"Morfeo," Isaura said. She pressed the tablet she'd been reading close to her chest. "How fare the captives? Have they been fed?" she asked.

Morfeo's eyes raked the length of Isaura's body—from the top of her head to the hem of her gown. "Sometimes," he said, "your Ithacan nature is so troubling." Morfeo hid a little yawn behind his long fingers, then said, "Only an Ithacan would care about *captives*." He swallowed thickly, as if he'd tasted something awful. "The captives are not a concern. They'll be parceled out as slaves. Or killed."

Galen's heart pounded in his ears. His toes were curled, his shoulders hunched, his mouth set. Everything about Galen tensed, as if he were getting ready to pounce. Captives. Parceled out as slaves. *More helots to join the miserable ranks in Sparta, Persian or not,* he thought. Again, Galen felt the urgent need to strike out, to let loose a volley of punches and wrestling holds he'd learned in the agoge, but this time, on King Morfeo. Then, he felt Zoi's chilled fingers wrapping around his wrist, and his body felt loose again. Only his heart beat faster.

When Galen looked at Zoi, he was shocked to see how she shuddered, how she kept her eyes locked on the floor. She gripped him still, and Galen realized she'd been steadying herself, not helping him calm down after all. Galen wiggled out of her clasp, sliding his hand into hers. Zoi might be the viper the helots were hoping for, but she was also just a girl, one that had crept into Galen's daydreams. She squeezed his hand, and Galen tried very hard to keep from smiling.

Queen Isaura gathered her gown and took a few steps away from Morfeo. "It is curious to me, Morfeo, that we Greeks, who call ourselves the most civilized people on earth, seek to enslave others." The Queen let her eyes rest on Galen for a moment, and her eyes filled with tears. "We reduce ourselves, our humanity, by doing so," she whispered, shaking her head and regaining her composure. Isaura cleared her throat, and continued: "You've not greeted our son, Nikolas, nor his friends, Morfeo."

"Ah, Isaura. You've acquired a Spartan woman's tongue, that's certain. Forgive me," Morfeo said, and bowed a little. "The trials of war make one forgetful." He turned and shook Nikolas' hand.

"You may remember my friend from the agoge, Galenos," Nikolas said. Galen nodded tersely at the king. "And this is Maira." Maira, who was still in the back of the room, kneeling in the ashes, did not move a jot.

Morfeo said nothing, but looked at Galen a long time, his hands clasped, his fingers in motion, as if kneading his own knuckles. "Befriending helots, are we now? Is this what Sparta has come to?" Morfeo wondered aloud.

Galen stared at his feet. He could hear his heart beating loudly in his ears. He was aware of Zoi standing next to him, hearing Morfeo's scorn, and Galen was filled with shame and anger.

"I have the right to choose my own company," Nikolas said. "Galen has many talents. He has a soldier's heart."

"My son has told me of your friendship," Morfeo said. He arched an eyebrow as he spoke. "Acayo says young Galenos is a fine wrestler, and good with a spear. Is this so, helot?"

Galen looked directly at Morfeo, knowing that it was wrong, knowing well that his eyes should have remained fixed on his own feet. Yet he couldn't help himself. He was still replaying what Nikolas had said, "He has a soldier's heart," and it had given him courage. "The prince speaks too highly of me, Your Majesty," Galen said. "But I have been taught well at the agoge, and the spear feels at home in my hand."

"Pity," Morfeo said. "A boy like you should have his freedom."

Galen's heart leapt at the idea. But when he looked at Morfeo, he saw that the king had a terrible smile plastered on his face, as if what he'd just said ran contrary to what was actually in his mind.

Nikolas cleared his throat, and went on with the introductions. "This is Zoi, niece of Brygus, son of Bazil of Mycenae, who has come to live with Mother." Morfeo looked directly at Zoi for the first time that afternoon, and his breath caught visibly. Zoi, holding Galen's hand, could not still her trembling, would not look up to meet Morfeo's eyes. Galen wanted nothing more than to scoop her up and run away with her, away from Morfeo's terrible gaze.

"Zoi? A lovely name for a lovely creature," Morfeo said. His eyes had grown wide, but soon, he smiled, as if he'd just had a wonderful thought. "Would the three youngsters like to see the captives? Real live Persian wretches, brought low. I might even let Nikolas kill one if he's up for the sport. I heard about his success last night," Morfeo said, grinning.

Nikolas glanced at Galen and Zoi. His eyes trailed down to their hands and lingered there a moment.

"Young prince?" Morfeo asked.

"I don't think that would be---" Isaura began.

"We'd be honored," Nikolas interrupted, and now it was Galen's turn to squeeze Zoi's hand. They followed a few paces behind Nikolas and Morfeo, who chatted together about the front at Salamis, about Acayo's progress at the agoge, and the ripening pomegranates in the courtyard.

"What's he playing at?" Galen said low.

"Nikolas or Morfeo?" Zoi asked.

"Nikolas. He hates the Agiad king."

"Shh."

"They can't hear us. Listen to them prattle," Galen said, a little louder, testing his theory. They walked a bit more, through another courtyard, this one with an enormous well in the center, and three ladies-in-waiting working to pull up the giant, heavy bucket. Zoi craned her neck to watch the girls work, and Galen could sense longing in her, the desire to be that carefree, that concerned with simple things. He wished for that kind of peace too, every day.

"Are you well?" Galen asked her. He'd whispered in her ear, and caught her sweet scent. It made him feel dizzy.

"What do you care? You've decided I'm an enemy," she said, but she did not release his hand.

"I asked, are you well?" Galen persisted.

"No," she answered, and fell silent before the iron gates at the back of the palace grounds.

12

They heard the grunting and shouting of at least a hundred Persian captives before they saw them. When the prisoners finally came into view, Galen gasped. Though twilight had descended, the captives were still easy to make out. The Persians were bound together at the wrists. Their ankles, too, were tied with rope, so that they shuffled as one to walk, resembling a grotesque centipede. Everywhere Galen looked he saw injuries, gaping wounds, and broken men.

"Here we are," Morfeo said, shouting proudly over the din.

Fifty red-cloaked Spartans guarded the Persian prisoners of war.

"So many," Zoi said.

Morfeo turned to her. He put a long finger under her chin and raised her face. Galen could feel a rumbling in Zoi's body, vibrating through her and into his hand. At his feet, the earth rose in little plumes and swirled around Zoi's ankles. Her hand went frigid, so icy, that Galen's fingers began to go numb.

Morfeo looked down at the ground. He stamped the rising cloud of dust. "We have many enemies," he said to Zoi, and released her chin. "You'd do well to note it."

Nikolas, who had begun walking up and down the line of prisoners, called out to them from the end of the line. "What's wrong with this one?" he shouted.

Morfeo, Galen and Zoi approached the place in the line where Nikolas stood, pointing. There, chained between two bald, tattooed Persians, was a blond-haired girl, slumped on the ground. She was small, and frail, and wore a torn, dirty shift. The men on either side of her held up her arms, the chain digging into the skin at her wrists. It looked as though her shoulders were about to pop out of their sockets.

"This is no soldier," Nikolas growled, and pivoted to face Morfeo. "Release the girl."

Morfeo laughed, and the sound was so unpleasant, that even the fierce Persians took a few steps away from him. "This isn't just a girl, young prince," Morfeo said. He crouched in front of the girl, grabbed a fistful of her knotted, lanky hair, and lifted her head. She grunted and spat at Morfeo. "This," Morfeo said, wiping her spittle off his cheek with his chiton, "is our new sibyl."

Galen crouched too, taking Zoi with him, so that they might both peer into the girl's face. The girl looked up. She had round, bloodshot eyes, a small, upturned nose, a small mouth, and a broad, high forehead. She blinked once, twice, and then fainted.

Beside him, Zoi gasped, and tried to wrench her hand away from Galen. But he held her tight.

"Let me go!" Zoi shouted, again and again. The Persians moved forward a little, drawn by the commotion.

"What is it?" Galen demanded. "Who is that? Zoi!"

92

"Let me go!" she yelled. That was when Galen felt it, a painful pulse in his hands, a sharp shock, and he released Zoi at once. In every spot their skin had touched, Galen had a raw, burning blister.

Zoi ran straight down the line of prisoners, headed to the gate. Her chiton fluttered as she ran, and the tattoo flashed momentarily. Both Nikolas and Morfeo ran after her, and Galen was shocked to see that Morfeo reached her first, trapping her at the entry. Zoi was clinging to the gate, desperately trying to fit through them, forcing her left leg and shoulder between the iron bars. Nikolas had stopped running halfway, and Galen had not moved at all. They stood and watched as Morfeo whispered something to Zoi, saw how she softened, how she released the bars one finger at a time, and allowed her self to be led away by the Agiad king.

Nikolas turned, shouting at the assembled forces, "Get the girl prisoner out of the line!" and ran after Zoi and Morfeo.

That's when Galen heard it, low and stuttering at first, those words from his fearful dream. "Please. Galen, please," the girl was saying. She looked up at him, and their eyes met. "Don't let them take me to the ephors, or the viper will destroy us all," she said, her voice only a thread, so hard to hear. "You are Sparta's best hope, Galenos. Please, Galen, pl---" Her mouth went slack, and her head fell back.

13

With shaking hands, Galen felt her slender neck. The pulse beat strong. He stood, and called out, "Guards! Guards!" Galen watched as a Spartan soldier undid the rope around the new sibyl's ankles, as another released the chains at her wrist. She fell to the ground with a thump, moaning lightly.

"Where do we take it?" one of the soldiers asked the other.

"You should take *her* to the palace healer," Galen said.

The soldier turned swiftly to face Galen. "You would do well to keep your crusty mouth shut, helot scum," he growled. Then, the soldier lifted the sibyl roughly and disappeared into the palace. Galen watched them go, his limbs trembling in anger. Of course, there was nothing he could do, no changing what he was, and so he tamped the feeling down as best he could.

The wind had picked up, cold and sharp. By now, a smudge of stars overhead twinkled. The milky galaxy seemed close that night. It was said that Hera, the mother goddess, had

94

spilled her milk when trying to feed the great Hercules, and that the milk had become the stars above Galen now. Most nights, that bright splotch in the sky was the last thing Galen saw before falling into dreams of the red cloak. But Galen had not dreamed of this girl's voice in days, not since the eve of the Crypteia. He'd become so accustomed to hearing it, her pleas in his sleep, that he'd stopped taking note of it, wondering what it might mean. He'd thought the voice had belonged to Zoi. There was something familiar about the tone of it, after all. But here was the unmistakable voice at last, coming from the mouth of this drab, skinny girl. Even worse, she knew about the viper. She'd begged for his help. But how could Galen keep the girl away from the ephors and the Rock of the Sibyl? It was the sibyl's rightful place, and the gods knew, Sparta needed guidance.

Galen's eyes lingered on the soldiers' spears, all held at the same angle, so that the sharp points lined up perfectly. *Such training*, he thought. Whoever went against King Morfeo's wishes could expect those spears pointed in his direction. Galen felt as if he were already on the edge of one of them, teetering to and fro. What were his options? If he voiced his suspicions about Zoi, the viper and the helot rebellion, it would mean Zoi's death, surely. Should he join Zoi and take up arms against Nikolas and the queen, both of whom he loved? Then there was the young sibyl, the voice in his dreams…

Galen didn't know what to do, but his legs tingled, and he thought that if he didn't do *something*, he might burst. If he were at the agoge, he might pick a fight, just to feel his fists colliding with someone. But he could not fight in the palace. So he ran. Through courtyard after courtyard, his sandals slapped the mosaic floors. A singer, playing his lyre in the corner of one room, plucked delicately on the strings of his instrument, and the music followed Galen into each room, at odds with the din in his head. He stopped, at last, in Queen Isaura's chamber, where they'd last left her.

Maira was no longer in the ashes, nor was she anywhere about. The fire had been kindled again, and it crackled and warmed the room. The queen was seated on a pillow, a stylus in her hand as she scratched letters into clay. A candle burned beside her. She was biting her lower lip in concentration. Her ankles were crossed, revealing a pair of golden anklets that reflected flickering candlelight. Galen watched her a long time, catching his breath. *If I could write*, he thought, *I'd put it all down in an anonymous message to the queen. I'd tell her to run away, back to Ithaca, and to take Nikolas with her...*

"Galenos," Isaura said softly, interrupting his thoughts.

"Your Highness."

"Come," she said, and pulled a nearby pillow close to her. "Sit. Nikolas is tending to Zoi, who, I'm told, has fallen ill." Isaura patted the puffy seat and the scent of anise filled the air, the pillows having been stuffed with wool sprinkled with the spice.

Galen sat down. He felt as if he should be doing something else—planning, fighting, and keeping an eye on Zoi himself—rather than sitting on a pillow.

"So, my son is smitten," Isaura said, smiling. "Zoi is very beautiful."

Galen didn't say anything, but he could feel his ears growing hot and, most likely, turning red.

The queen brushed some lint from her gown. "I'd hate for my son to get hurt," she said, absently. But when Galen looked at her, he saw her eyes were glossy. *Always in tears*, he thought, and his heart ached for the beautiful Isaura who seemed to carry such sadness in her all the time.

"I won't let any harm come to Nikolas," Galen said, and the queen nodded.

"I know it, Galenos." She arranged her long gown for a moment, cleared her throat, and said, "Spartans are loyal, and a Spartan's word means a great deal. Leandros, our king, was quite faithful to his friends." She paused a moment, gathering

96

herself. Though her face contorted a little at the memory of Leandros, she did not weep. "I appreciate your devotion to my son. Very Spartan of you," she said after a moment, sitting taller on her pillow.

"I'm no Spartan, Your Majesty," Galen said, and at once regretted it. *Now I've insulted her*, he thought.

"Even so," Queen Isaura said. Galen heard a hard edge in her voice then and his heart sank. The Queen had not spoken to him as if he were a real person, not just a helot, since Nikolas first joined the agoge. And now Galen had ruined it.

"Even so," she said again, "The love you have for Nikolas is a strong one, but you cannot protect him from every mistake," Isaura said. "Even mistakes that come wrapped in beautiful packages."

"Zoi," Galen whispered, and the queen nodded.

"Don't let her come between you," Isaura said.

"No, Your Highness," Galen said, coming to his feet.

"Nikolas is in his chamber. He's waiting for you."

"Yes, Your Highness. I take my leave," Galen said with a little bow. He started towards Nikolas' chamber in the north wing of the palace, when he thought to turn around. "Helots are not allowed swords," he said to Isaura, "but what little strength I have is yours, if you need it."

Isaura nodded, unable to speak, and Galen left her company.

14

Galen stood before the broad doors of Nikolas' chamber, his hand resting on the iron door pull, when he heard the shuffling of feet in the adjacent hallway, and a soft grunting sound, as if someone was struggling with a heavy object. Galen waited for whoever or whatever was making the noise to move further away before peering around the wall.

There, in the dim light, was Morfeo, dragging Zoi behind him. Her eyes were closed, and Morfeo held her by the armpits, her long legs dangling and scraping against the stone floor. The skin on her heels was torn, and her blood streaked the stones. Morfeo was struggling with the work of pulling her, and Galen remembered how Zoi had made herself heavy back at the agoge, how hard it had been for three helots to budge her. *Her power still courses through her*, Galen thought. *Thank the gods she's alive.*

Galen looked frantically around him for some kind of weapon, anything that he might use. In the corner was a tremendous two-handled amphora, painted with the black figure of the great Achilles, holding aloft his spear. Lifting it, Galen measured the vase's heft. *It's no weapon*, he thought, *but it will do.* Quietly, he stepped into the hallway, and found it empty. At the end of the corridor was another door, leading to the banquet hall. Morfeo had left it open.

Zoi's blood left a trail into the hall that Galen followed with his eyes. It turned abruptly left, into an alcove in the room that Galen could not see unless he entered the space and revealed himself. *So much for the element of surprise*, he thought. He'd planned on creeping up behind Morfeo and bringing the amphora down hard on the king's head. With any luck, he wouldn't see Galen at all. But now, the vast banquet hall was too open a space for such a move. The tall ceilings echoed sound as well as any peak in Mount Taygetos.

Galen ground his teeth in frustration. What in Hades was Morfeo doing to Zoi? She'd been afraid of him back in the queen's chamber. Terrified. Galen could still feel her hand in his, how she'd gripped him hard, and his heart banged in his chest. *I'll go get Nikolas*, he thought, but just as he turned to go, he heard Morfeo speaking. The banquet hall's acoustics delivered the sound to Galen's ears.

"Zoi. Sweet one. How you've grown," Morfeo was saying, and Galen's imagination ran wild. In his mind, he saw the king's dreadful, slender hands on Zoi's face, on her neck, on her…He hefted the amphora on his shoulder, and took a step into the room. Then he heard Zoi stirring.

"What happened?" she said.

"You fainted. The girl was a shock to you. For me, too, I admit," Morfeo said, and laughed a little. Galen found himself cringing at the sound.

"My feet hurt," Zoi said, whimpering a little.

"My apologies. You were impossible to lift. What *has* your mother been feeding you?"

"Stop it," Zoi said, and her voice sounded fierce.

"But she has taught you a thing or two," Morfeo said. "I can't say I'm not filled with pride." Morfeo laughed again, and the sound bounced around the cavernous hall so that even the amphora in Galen's hand vibrated with it.

"I'm not a pet that's learned a new trick," Zoi growled.

"No! My pet snake? I'd never suggest such a thing," Morfeo said. "The truth is, you're the son I never had!" he said, with a confiding air.

"Can I go now?" Zoi said.

"I waited for you last night."

"I helped you, as you asked. It's not my fault Acayo wrecked everything. I'm done, Morfeo."

"You've spurned my proposals before, and I've been a patient man. But all that is over now. Sheer luck has brought you to the palace," Morfeo said, and though he whispered, the words were amplified.

"Not luck," Zoi said. "I didn't want to come. Nikolas brought me against my will."

"Will? What is that?" Morfeo said, laughing. "We'll have to await the sign, of course. There are reports of the earth rumbling near the mountain. It will make a good diversion for you to step in and do..." Morfeo laughed again, "what you do."

"I don't think--"

"What you don't have, my dear, is a choice. The rebellion is at hand, whether you want it or not. And the queen will be so easy to dispatch."

There was silence for what felt like a very long time. Galen still held the amphora, and it shook dangerously in his hands. Then he heard Zoi at last, asking, "What about the girl?"

Morfeo laughed, satisfied. "The ephors are so eager for a new sibyl, they'll do anything to get their hands on one."

"I'll do what it takes, Morfeo," Zoi said. "Then I'm going to leave. Forever."

Galen put the amphora down gently. He felt bitter surprise. The cold spot under his ribs throbbed, and Galen wished he could cut it out. But Zoi's touch lingered. With a savage kick, Galen sent the amphora sailing through the air. It shattered against the wall. He stood there staring at the pieces, drawing long breaths.

Footsteps sounded in the banquet hall, and soon, Morfeo and Zoi appeared. Morfeo's face was still, like stone. Zoi's dark eyes were soft, pleading with Galen silently.

"Explain yourself, boy," Morfeo demanded.

"I was on my way to Nikolas' chamber and kicked over this amphora. My apologies, Your Majesty," Galen said, and bowed his head a little. *I will not get on my knees before a traitor*, Galen thought, though his legs trembled a little.

"Are you hurt?" Zoi said, laying a hand on Galen's shoulder.

He wanted to answer yes. Yes, deeply hurt, but he shook his head, and jerked away from Zoi as if her touch burned. As always, the place where her hand grazed his shoulder was cool.

Zoi blinked wetly, but did not speak. Morfeo placed his hand on the back of her neck as if guiding an animal. "The queen expects you, now that you're well, Zoi," he said with one last look at Galen. "Do you think that because the prince calls you a friend that you are better than the rest of your lot?"

Galen ground his teeth. He did not look away.

"You're a bold one, I'll give you that," Morfeo said. "Clean up this mess, boy. I will make your master aware of the damages incurred here." Finished speaking, Morfeo steered Zoi down the hall. Then he stopped, as if struck by a sudden idea. He turned, addressing Galen, "What I said earlier about your freedom? One must be prepared to strike when the opportunity arises." Morfeo said no more, and stalked down the hall with his hand clamped on Zoi's shoulder.

If Morfeo was pulling the strings of this "rebellion," then there would be no freedom for the helots, after all.

15

Galen found Nikolas pacing in his chamber. The room was spare, with only a small bed on the floor, and toys from Nikolas' childhood piled into one corner. There was, among these, a wooden sword, covered in nicks and splinters, and a miniature Spartan shield, carved from ash. Galen's throat ached with wanting at the sight of these things he'd never had.

"Nikolas," Galen began, but Nikolas did not stop walking. He swung his long arms forcefully, and the muscles in his face were tight. "I just heard Zoi speaking with Morfeo in the banquet hall."

Nikolas waved Galen away. "You're mistaken. We settled her in her new chamber, with one of mother's ladies-in-waiting. She's fast asleep."

"Listen to me, Nikolas. Zoi's not what---"

"I don't want to go back," Nikolas said suddenly, and Galen knew he meant the agoge. He could also guess why.

"Because she's here?"

"Exactly," Nikolas said, and kicked the little toy shield hard, so that it snapped in two. Galen thought of the amphora outside, and the beating at the hands of Feodoras that would come of the news of its destruction.

"If you don't go back, what would people think? What would your father say?"

"I don't care. He's dead, isn't he? What does it matter what the great and noble Leandros would think?" Nikolas asked. His voice had taken on an ugly tone, one Galen wasn't used to hearing.

"You don't mean that," Galen said, watching Nikolas as he paced the room. "I know you don't want to hear it," Galen said, "but Zoi is not what she seems. She's dangerous. And a liar."

Nikolas halted and looked at Galen. He narrowed his eyes. "You can't have her," Nikolas said, taking a step forward.

"I. Don't. Want. Her," Galen said. Perhaps once he did, when he'd first seen Zoi, walking alongside Brygus in the market, her hand wrapped around a fraying rope, leading a small goat up and down the dusty roads. But that didn't matter anymore. Galen remembered his vow to the queen—"What little strength I have is yours,"—and he remembered how Isaura had praised Galen's loyalty to Nikolas. Even if it meant wringing Zoi's treacherous neck himself, Galen would keep his promise to Isaura.

"I saw how you held her hand, Galen. It was pathetic, really. It was---"

"She means your mother harm. All of us. All of Sparta," Galen interrupted.

"You have no love for Sparta," Nikolas said.

"Listen," Galen said, softening his tone in the hopes that Nikolas would pay attention. "I just overheard Zoi talking with---"

"I'm tired of your disapproval of her. Your condemnation," Nikolas said, waving his hand in the air as if he were swatting a fly. "She saved your life. Have you any shame?" Nikolas asked, standing very close to Galen now.

Galen faltered. Here he was, on the edge of a blade again. He'd been harboring hope for a rebellion, even when his reason told him that such a thing might spell doom for the Eurypontids, for the people he loved. Now all he wanted was for Nikolas to see the truth, to shake off this haze Zoi had enveloped him in.

"Hear me out," Galen said after a moment, deciding on his tack. "Maybe it's vengeance she seeks. For what happened to Brygus."

"That wasn't our fault, Galenos!"

"I tell you she's dishonest. She's a traitor!"

"Say it again," Nikolas challenged, and his voice came out low and gravelly.

"She's a double-crossing bitch!" Galen yelled, and, for the first time in his life, Nikolas laid Galen out on his back with a violent jab to his left temple.

"Stupid helot," Galen heard Nikolas say, before everything went dark.

When he regained consciousness, Galen found himself in the healer's chamber, lying on a wooden pallet. His head throbbed, and he tasted iron in his mouth. His bottom lip was ragged, and there was a nasty cut on his face, from where he'd hit the floor. Worse than that, he was so angry he couldn't think. *He hit me,* Galen thought, amazed. He prodded the tender spot on his temple. *By the gods, he could have killed me.*

Galen's eyes adjusted to the dim room. The healer had put a foul smelling ointment on his cut. There was more on his hand, the one Zoi had blistered with a touch in the yard. The healer had left a small jar of the stuff next to him, as well as a cup of water. Galen sat up, sipped some of the tepid water, and looked around.

Against the furthest wall was another pallet, and coiled on it, the young sibyl. She was shivering, though she'd pulled her thin shift over her knees and had tucked in her arms close to her body, folding herself so that she took up very little space.

She spoke suddenly, startling Galen. "I see how you see me," she whispered. "I am a pitiful sight." She sniffed a little. Her speech, Galen noted, had a Persian lilt to it.

"No, of course I don't see you that way," Galen lied, sitting up. He grabbed a horsehair blanket from a hook on the wall, and laid it over the girl.

"Thank you," she said, without turning her head, which she'd covered with her arms, as if in shame.

Galen wished she'd turn around. He'd thought there was something familiar about her face when he saw her tethered to the line of prisoners. Besides, he'd always been fascinated by the stories of the sibyls. When he was a child, Feodoras would threaten to take him to the Rock of the Sibyl, the entrance to the cave where Meroe, the Spartan Sibyl, once lived. It was said that Meroe devoured children. In his childish fantasies, Galen had imagined testing himself against this monster of the Rock. Now, he wondered if the new sibyl hungered for blood, too.

"That's a myth," she said, interrupting his thoughts. "At least, in the case of seers."

Galen jumped backwards. "How did you---"

"I see what you see. Even now, the veiled world, the one you inhabit, remains in my mind, though we are here together." She moaned softly. "By gods, it makes my head hurt."

"I don't understand," Galen said. He took another step backwards.

"You are Galenos. Your master is a wicked man named Feodoras. Do not worry about the amphora you broke in the hall, for Feodoras is ill and cannot be concerned with it. His body is weak, though he knows it not. Hades prepares a place

106

for him in the underworld as I speak." The girl's voice trailed off. She curled into an even tighter ball, her arms squeezing around her head, and grunted in pain.

After a moment, she spoke again. "You dream of wearing the Spartan cloak, and I tell you that this will come true at a great price. You will lose the one you love, and save the one you hate."

"These are riddles. I'm not sure what you mean," Galen said. "The ones I love and hate? Who are these people?"

"My sight isn't always clear," the sybil said. "The only thing that is cloudless in my mind is you, Galenos. Always you." The girl kicked the horsehair blanket away, and Galen could see that her limbs were suddenly covered in sweat. She turned her head, and her blond hair spilled out over the edges of the cot. She looked at Galen with teary eyes, and her breath rushed out at once.

Then, with the force of a wave, Galen realized who this girl reminded him of. She had Zoi's eyes, and there was something about her small, pointed chin, and the length of her fingers, that was like Zoi, too. But she had a smattering of freckles over her nose and cheeks that were different from Zoi's even, brown skin. Reflexively, his stomach flipped a little at the thought of her.

The girl doubled up again. "Gods, please," she hissed, and then, uttered something in Persian that was at once beautiful and tortured.

"Sibyl," Galen called, and approached her once again.

She didn't answer at once, but stayed very still. "My name is Korinna," she said after a long while. "You are wondering why I hurt. I hear you now, and I hear your thoughts in my head, and it's like someone is twisting a knife in my brain. Honestly, Galen, it would be better if you slept and did nothing but dream."

Galen wondered if he was dreaming now.

"No, you are awake," Korinna croaked. Then she cried out and gripped her hair.

"What can I do?" Galen asked, feeling frantic. The sibyl was breathing hard. Galen had a thousand questions for her— about the viper, the ephors, the dream of the red cloak—but the more questions arose in his mind, the more the girl writhed in pain.

"The ephors," she said, struggling to speak. "Don't let them take me to the Rock. The ephors do not serve Sparta," Korinna said. "They guard a monster. You are Sparta's best hope, Galenos, but I am yours."

"I'll try. I—I—I'll do what I can," Galen said, promising the impossible to this stranger, even as he backed out of the healer's chambers.

16

Galen's head was still humming with all that Korinna had said. Three times he opened his mouth to speak, to say something to Nikolas, who strode angrily a few feet ahead of him. But then, the bruise on the side of Galen's head would thrum with pain, reminding him of Nikolas' last words to him—*stupid helot*—and he would have to keep himself from tackling the prince right then and there.

Besides, Galen had other things to worry about. He'd made a promise to Korinna, to keep her away from the Rock of the Sybil. *Why in Hades had I promised such a thing?* he asked himself. Certainly, the girl had answers, though these were conundrums in themselves. Perhaps it was pity that had moved Galen. Or how much she resembled Zoi…

Galen rubbed his face, willing himself to focus. The Rock of the Sybil was a few hours walk along the Hyakinthine Way, east of Limnai and the army barracks. Officially, the Rock was called the Sanctuary of Artemis Orthia, a sacred place to honor the goddess Artemis, but only the priests used that

109

name. The face of the sanctuary seemed like any other temple, made of wood and stone.   However, it was built into the mountain, so that wood floors gave way to granite far into the structure. The cooler depths of the cave could be felt at the Rock of the Sybil's entrance, coming to visitors in puffs of unpleasantly cold air. Some said the Rock was actually a series of deep tunnels that led straight to the shores of the Underworld.

Ahead of him, Nikolas kicked at stones fiercely, sending them skidding off in all directions. They'd been sent away from the palace by an angry Isaura. She'd taken one look at the swelling and discoloration on the side of Galen's head, and pointed her finger towards the door.

Nikolas had paled, but said, "Father is no longer here, which makes me the man of this house. You cannot force me from my home, woman." He'd used the voice that gained him respect in the agoge, that slow speech and rich timber used by senators. It was the very tone Morfeo employed.

"A man does not strike others in childish anger. Even helots. When you know the meaning of the word 'man,' then will you have my obedience." Her word final, Queen Isaura turned away from them, her back straight as a spear. A line of soldiers clicked their heels as she passed them, then turned as one to escort Nikolas and Galen out of the palace.

What could Nikolas do? To stay put, to undercut his mother publically, would be to make her vulnerable in the palace, an especially dangerous thing to do while his role as future king still hung in the balance. It was bad enough that senators loyal to the Agiads were questioning the decisions the Queen made in her husband's stead. And while the Eurypontid throne remained empty awaiting Nikolas' eighteenth birthday, Morfeo's influence grew at home. So Nikolas left the palace, and Galen followed him. He thought of Zoi as he approached the palace gates, flanked by so many Spartan soldiers. He wondered where the soldiers' loyalty lay—with Morfeo or with Nikolas. Galen prayed that it was the latter, and that the men in the red cloaks would know what to do with one such as Zoi, should she and Morfeo launch any kind of attack.

It was very late when they neared the agoge at last. A fog had rolled in off the Eurotas River, and so the figures that moved slowly in the distance were only vague shapes. A fire glowed and crackled outside. Galen and Nikolas slowed their pace, and Nikolas stumbled over a cartwheel, left in the middle of the road. Galen grasped Nikolas' elbow to help steady him, but Nikolas shrugged him off. Closer now, they heard the plucking of a lyre, and they knew that the students were gathered around the fire, to listen to the singer.

They reached the edge of the circle of students. The firelight burned off the mist, so that Galen felt as if a veil had been lifted from his eyes. Nikolas sought Timios, his sparring partner, and sat with him. Galen found a tree stump on the outskirts of the circle, and sat. He could hear the clanging of iron pots coming from the kitchens, and he knew he should join the work now that he was back. But he thought of Korinna's prediction concerning Feodoras' illness, and he looked around and saw that his master (who never missed the singer's visit) was nowhere to be seen.

Galen wanted to listen, but his eyes were drawn to Nikolas and the scowl on his friend's face. Life in the agoge would be unbearable without his friendship, but Galen did not know how to make amends. Nikolas would not listen to reason. He'd been blinded by Zoi, or bewitched. Even worse, he'd treated Galen like a slave back at the palace. Nikolas had never done that before. Galen searched his heart for forgiveness, and found none.

Beside Nikolas, Timios sat with his knees drawn up, his forehead resting on them. How pale Timios looked. Every so often, the small boy shivered. Timios was the son of a Spartan senator. He had no love for the Agiads, and had once helped Nikolas and Galen put a garden snake into Acayo's food bowl.

Out of all the agoge students, Nikolas and Galen liked Timios best, and counted him as a friend.

Perhaps it was the words of the singer's song that was bothering Timios. Galen stretched out his legs, and listened as the singer unfolded the story of the Spartan Sibyl. Galen was not surprised. Singers often tuned their story selections to the news of the moment. Certainly, half of Sparta had heard about the mysterious girl from Persia, and Galen guessed there had been a collective sigh of relief at the thought that Sparta had a sibyl of its own once again.

"Our sibyl, Meroe, daughter of Lena and Taras, came to us as a child, on a ship with black sails, cradling her infant sister, Lamia, in her arms. The ship sailed the broad back of the sea all the way from Karkinos, the island of Spartan exiles," the singer said. He played the clear-tuned lyre expertly, his fingers dancing on the strings though he could not see. When the singer raised his head, the firelight was reflected in the milky white of his eyes.

Galen slid off the stump and sat on the ground to listen. He leaned against the old stump and his eyes grew heavy. But then he remembered stories of men who'd hit their heads in battle, or in play, and had fallen asleep too soon after the injury and not woken again. So, Galen rubbed his eyes, determined to stay awake for at least as long as the singer played.

The music slowed, and the singer went on: "For Taras had heard a prophecy—that he would pay a steep price for leaving Sparta and having taken with him so many sons and daughters of the land. So cruel Taras sent his gifted daughters away, on a ship laden with goods, with slaves who knew nothing of navigation at the oars, as an offering to the gods. Only long-suffering Lena, daughter of the mighty sea-god Poseidon and the nymph, Pitana, for whom one of our villages is named, had a plan. Secretly, Lena commanded a master sailor to take the ship's helm and steer it towards Sparta. So the girls, gifted each with Poseidon's powers, arrived safely on our shores."

The boys shifted excitedly around the fire. Spartans believed they descended from heroes and gods. In the north, near the village of Pitana, was the Menalaion, said to be the former home of that great Spartan beauty, Helen, for whom all of Troy once burned. Galen had not yet met a Spartan boy who did not claim that his family's ancestry began with Hercules. *Of course, Meroe, the Spartan Sibyl, had to be Poseidon's granddaughter. And I'm Ares' great nephew,* Galen thought, cynically.

"Upon landing, the young Meroe, who was only twelve, gently laid her baby sister at her feet, raised her hands, and said, 'Father Zeus, if you gods have returned me to my homeland out of exile for a purpose, then let me be of use for all of Sparta.' Then, she predicted the death of our King Leonidas at Thermopylae, how he and his three hundred men would fend off thousands of Persian soldiers for days, and how the Persians would behead our beloved king in the end.

"Meroe and the babe, Lamia, were put in the care of the ephors in the Rock of the Sibyl, and the blood sacrifice was made to the gods so that Meroe would be pleasing to Artemis and the gods in her role." The singer strummed a few more notes, then his fingers lay very still on the lyre.

Nestor rose from his place close to the Singer. He clapped his hands loudly, and the students lifted their heads. Some of the sleepy ones startled awake. "Bloody wonderful, as ever," Nestor said, clapping some more. "And now that you've heard the story, you can guess that the new sibyl will require a blood sacrifice, too. She will begin her duties to Sparta on the eve of the full moon, which leaves us little time. So, I've talked it over with the ephors, and we've decided that our own Timios will provide the blood offering."

Galen stood at once, and watched in horror as Timios cradled his head in his hands.

"We won't kill you, boy," Nestor chastised. "Stand proud, Timios! Your failure at the Crypteia will provide the new sibyl with a powerful blood sacrifice. The lash against your back won't be for naught," Nestor said. "What blood you shed will please the gods. May they grant you a long life," the head of the agoge said, smiling. By the light of the fire, his grin seemed ghastly.

Why would you admit to your failure at the hunt, Timios? Galen thought, his heart beating with pity. The singer, too, looked as if he might start weeping. Every so often, one of his fingers twitched, and the lyre sung out a single, sad note.

Suddenly, Nikolas stood, too. Galen shook with excitement. *Nikolas will speak out against this,* Galen thought, and he bounced on his feet. Clearing his throat, Nikolas made his way towards Nestor.

"Hear me, teachers and students of the agoge, so I may say what the gods command of the house of the Eurypontids. Let me wield the lash first, and draw the first sacrifice to the goddess, Artemis," Nikolas said, while Nestor beamed with pride.

Then there was chaos among them. Acayo was on his feet, begging to brandish the whip, too. There were shouts of "No!" including Galen's, and cheers, as well. Timios sat, horror struck, his mouth open and his eyes brimming with tears.

Nestor shouted, "Silence!" and the students simmered down and sat again, except for Galen, who remained on his feet.

"It is good and worthy of the prince to handle the whip. Those of you with stomachs strong enough for it may also take a turn. Know that you will be drawing blood from a friend, from a brother, and know that your hearts will ache forever. It is good of you to know this, so that when the time comes, and a Persian has your brother in the sights of his cowardly arrow, you will fight to the death to protect the man beside you that is even more than kin, lest you hear his cries of agony." Nestor looked at all the students in turn, and they dropped their eyes to the ground under his stare.

"To your dormitories!" Nestor said. On their feet as one, they shuffled off, including Timios, who seemed bolstered in spirit somehow. Only Galen remained, and he stared hard at Nikolas, who stood by Nestor.

"To bed, helot," Nestor said to Galen. Nikolas broke the stare first, and Galen saw that the prince's arms trembled.

17

The eve of the next full moon was three days away.
That gave Galen some time to think about how he might keep
his promise to Korinna. Her words haunted him—that he
would lose the one he loved and save the one he hated. He
caught himself repeating the prophecy aloud as he worked,
trying to make sense of it.   To make matters worse, all night
long he dreamt of wearing the red cloak. The scene would end
in his mind and start back up again, an endless ring of dreams,
and Galen would wake up exhausted.

In the agoge, the days leading up to Timios' punishment
were tense ones. The boys of the agoge avoided Timios' eyes,
would not sit with him in the mess hall, or choose him as a
sparring partner. Only Nikolas spent time with Timios, and the
smaller boy seemed to appreciate it, cracking a smile now and
then at something Nikolas had said. Galen watched them from
a distance during meals, but didn't approach. Whenever

Nikolas' eyes caught his, Galen still saw anger plainly on the prince's face.

On the morning of the whipping, Nestor gathered the boys for wrestling practice. A square, sandy arena called a skamma awaited them. It was marked off with rope laid on the ground. Paired up, the boys took turns in the pit, grappling with one another. Nestor served as referee, and he carried a short whip with which to strike at any boy who performed an illegal move. The whip rarely whizzed through the air. But when it did, those gathered around the skamma winced at the sound, then cheered when the offending player got his just reward. The rules were simple. To win, a wrestler needed to earn three points. Points were gained if an opponent stepped outside of the skamma, if his back touched the ground, or if he conceded defeat. As for illegal moves, a wrestler would feel the sting of Nestor's whip if he bit, punched, kicked his opponent or tried to gouge his eyes.

It was clear that Nestor was trying to get everyone's minds off Timios' whipping later that afternoon. He bounced around the skamma, making grand, heroic gestures as the boys fought. He laughed hard and long with each win, and was so enthusiastic, that the boys soon caught on, following suit. Galen couldn't join in the spirit of enjoyment. His gaze kept falling on Timios, standing far from the skamma, his slender arms wrapped around himself. Nikolas, too, did not seem to be enjoying the morning's matches, and stood close to Timios.

Galen was so lost in thought he didn't hear Nestor call his name. "Galen! Boy!" the man called out, and when that didn't get his attention, he lobbed a small stone at Galen, that struck him square in the chest.

"Hey!" Galen yelled, turning, then stopped short when he saw Nestor glaring at him.

"Get yourself on the skamma, boy," Nestor said, pointing to where Acayo waited, cracking his knuckles.

117

Galen disrobed slowly. Wrestlers fought without clothing. That way, there would be no cloth to hold onto, no advantage to wearing a thicker chiton, or one with bronze buckles. He cursed the dreams that had ruined his sleep. His reaction time would be slow for sure. Everyone knew Acayo was a dirty wrestler. He thought nothing of pulling back fingers until an opponent tapped out, or of grinding his knee into a boy's genitals. Once, Acayo had gotten the whip when he dug his thumb into Nikolas' eye during a match, causing a blood vessel to burst and his left eye to be red for three weeks.

Nestor signaled for the match to begin, and Galen made the first move. He rushed the prince and wrapped his arms around Acayo's waist, carrying him over the rope that marked off the skamma. Galen dropped the Agiad prince onto his back.

"The first point goes to the helot!" Nestor shouted. But the move had winded Galen, and he stood, bent over, in the center of the ring. Acayo had gotten the air knocked out of him, too, and he walked slowly towards Galen.

"Hope you enjoyed that," Acayo whispered. "It'll be the last point you score."

Galen said nothing. Out of the corner of his eye he saw that Nikolas had approached the skamma. He was watching the match with his arms folded, his jaw tight. Timios stood right behind him.

At Nestor's signal, Acayo and Galen began circling each another. Acayo feigned a grab, and Galen fell for the trick, grasping at Acayo who stepped out of the way quickly. Before he knew it, Acayo had clambered up on Galen's back, his arms wound tight around his neck. He could feel his airway tightening, the pressure in his head beginning to build. Galen fell to his knees and Acayo held on.

"The viper's coming, boy," Acayo whispered into Galen's ear. Shocked, Galen's legs buckled, and Acayo flipped him on his back easily.

"A point for Prince Acayo!" Nestor yelled, and the crowd cheered. Only Nikolas and Timios held their applause. Galen and Acayo rose to their feet, standing only inches away from each another.

"What do you know about it?" Galen whispered, then coughed, his neck and throat on fire.

"Zoi, that loathsome little reptile Nikolas is so fond of, can help set you free," Acayo snarled, "that is, if she can stop throwing herself at every man she finds." His mouth curved into a smile. But the muscles in Galen's arm tensed, and before even he knew it, he'd reached back and cuffed Acayo in the jaw.

Instantly, a searing pain burned into Galen's shoulder. Nestor held his whip over his head ready to bring it down on Galen again. "Another infraction and you are disqualified, boy," Nestor shouted over the din of students shocked at what they'd just seen.

Acayo rubbed his jaw. He ran his tongue over his lips, licking at a bead of blood that was forming at the corner of his mouth. Already, his left cheek was swelling.

Galen had walked to the edge of the skamma, straining for self-control. *How many times am I going to get in a fight over her*, he thought to himself. Then he felt a hand on his shoulder. Nikolas' hand.

"Keep it together," Nikolas said in a low voice. Galen met Nikolas' eyes, and saw that the anger had gone from them.

"Any suggestions?" Galen asked. This was like old times. Galen always served as Nikolas' coach during wrestling matches and vice-versa.

Nikolas looked over Galen's shoulder at Acayo, who was busy tying his long hair back. "The Agiad prince has beautiful locks, don't you think?" Nikolas said mischievously. "It's a good thing you don't have any," he said, thumping the top of Galen's head.

119

Nestor called Galen back to the center of the skamma. The two faced off again. This time, when Acayo came close, Galen wrapped the prince's hair around his hand, once, twice, and fell to the ground, dragging Acayo with him. Acayo's head bounced hard on the sandy surface, and Galen laid his leg over Acayo's chest, pinning him.

"A point for the helot!' Nestor roared. The crowd cheered, save for Brutus and Linus, who stood too close to the skamma for Galen's comfort.

They faced each other again. One more point and Galen would be declared winner. He longed for the match to be over, so that he could talk to Nikolas again, this time, he hoped, without fighting over Zoi. But the last point proved hard to earn. Acayo kept slipping out of Galen's grasp, until at last Galen had him with a chin lock. He wrenched Acayo's chin hard to the left. "Yield," Galen growled, but Acayo had somehow managed to get a hand on Galen's stomach, and he curled his fingers into a claw, and clutched at the nerves there. It felt as if Acayo would tear out his guts, and, sensing that he was about to pass out from the pain of it, Galen released Acayo's chin, falling on his back and giving the point to the prince.

They both lay on the skamma for a long time. The sun was getting high overhead, and the heat of the day, paired with physical fatigue, was making it difficult to maneuver. Galen's stomach cramped and he breathed deeply, easing his muscles. *One more point, either way, and it's over*, Galen thought, and got back on his feet.

They began the next round warily. Around them, the boys shouted and clapped. When Galen clasped Acayo around the waist again, trying to toss him out of the ring, he found that his strength failed him, and he couldn't lift the prince more than a few inches off the ground. Acayo took advantage of this misstep, swept Galen's leg out from under him, knocking him down, then, threw his body across Galen's. Galen struggled to keep his back off the ground, the muscles in his stomach tensing and burning. Meanwhile, Acayo worked at Galen's fingers, pulling two of them back towards his wrist.

"That's a gutless move," Galen complained against the pain of it.

"Wrong. It's how I win this match," Acayo said, yanking on Galen's fingers hard. There were two distinct snapping sounds, like the cracking of a small branch underfoot. Galen dropped to his back, clutching his hand, groaning.

Nestor declared Acayo the winner, and the Agiad prince got to his feet, clapping, and kicking sand over Galen's prone form. Brutus and Linus slapped Acayo's back, and chanted, "Hail the House of the Agiads!" to the thunderous cheers. Galen rolled over on his side, clutching his hand. He watched feet stepping around him, over him, as the students dispersed to get ready for the evening's event. Dust rose around him, and Galen coughed on it, thinking dark thoughts.

18

"He's a cheat," Timios said to Galen, his voice small. Nikolas took hold of Galen's good hand, and pulled him into a seated position. Galen moaned on the way up. He moaned again when Nestor examined his crushed hand. Nestor, Nikolas and Timios had stayed behind with Galen after the students left, and now they watched him with concerned looks.

"It was a fair match," Nestor said, though he frowned. Clutches and finger bends weren't against the rules, officially, but most wrestlers avoided those particular moves. They were judged as cowardly, akin to the use of arrows. Spartan soldiers eschewed the bow and arrow altogether in war, believing that shooting at a target from far away was for the weak hearted. "Let's hope it's a sprain," Nestor muttered, drew a bit of cloth from a pocket in his chiton, and expertly wrapped Galen's fingers together so that they could no longer move. "I'll have a word with Feodoras about your duties for the next few weeks," Nestor said.

Galen had not yet found the words to speak. The pain in his hand blinded him, as did the rage he felt towards Acayo. His eyes filled with tears, but that would not do. Blinking them away, Galen got to his feet, and he found that his hand throbbed even more as he moved.

Nikolas and Timios walked him back to his quarters. "Stay in tonight. Rest," Nikolas said, eyeing the deep bruising that was beginning to form on Galen's stomach, and the welt on his shoulder from Nestor's lash.

Galen ignored him. Turning to Timios, he put his good hand on the smaller boy's shoulder. "You'll be fine," he said. "Nikolas will be at the lash. It was good of him to volunteer," Galen said, understanding Nikolas' motives suddenly.

Timios nodded vigorously, as if trying to convince himself of it.

"It's not so bad," Galen said, indicating his shoulder where Nestor's whip had struck him, though his tone wasn't convincing. "I'll be there," Galen said. "Cede when you've had enough." Timios nodded his understanding. Only once, in all the time Galen had been in the agoge, had a student not yielded at the whip. The boy, an eighteen-year old named Orestes had allowed himself to be lashed over one hundred times. His back and calves resembled a butchered creature, and he died at the post, his body collapsing before the horrified eyes of the entire agoge. Pride had sent Orestes to Hades too soon, and yet the Spartan senate honored such stubbornness by naming a squadron after Orestes. Galen had overheard Nestor say this was a poor move on the part of the senate, lest they wanted all the boys in the agoge to get themselves killed in order to save face. Honor was one thing, but arrogance in the guise of honor was another.

Galen watched as Timios and Nikolas walked off towards their barracks. He lay down on his cot, and tried not to think about his fingers. Closing his eyes, Galen thought of Zoi at once, and two sensations went to war in his chest at the thought of her. She angered him, this mysterious, powerful girl. And yet, if he tried, he could still feel her cool hand in his. How well it matched the shape of his palm…How tantalizing her shoulder brushing his…

For a little while, at least, he forgot about his hand. But the appearance of a middle-aged woman at the foot of his cot startled him, and his fingers flared with pain again.

"Who are you?" Galen asked.

The woman carried a satchel. The corners of her eyes and mouth were lined, though these curved upwards so that she appeared to be smiling. "Prince Acayo sends me to you," she said, and began unloading her satchel. Ointments, bandages, and bottles filled with white powders were laid out on the small table next to Galen's cot.

"What? To finish the job?" Galen said, tense. He'd hidden his hurt hand behind him.

"I am a healer," she said. "My name is Candra. Now, let's see the hand." Candra was stronger than Galen suspected. She twisted his forearm around expertly, until his hand was lying in her palm. Undoing Nestor's wrapping, Candra revealed a sorry sight—Galen's fingers were as fat as sausages, and a deep, purple tinge had overtaken the skin.

"Mm. Broken," she said. Candra grasped the two fingers gently, palpating them. Galen winced, and she murmured, "Shh, shh." Still holding his hand, Candra said, "Look to the horizon, young man. What do you see?"

Galen began to answer, "In the distance is the Eurypontid palace. And behind that, Mount--"

But he could not finish the sentence. Candra had pulled on both fingers pitilessly, setting the bones in place. Galen screamed, then bit his tongue and tasted blood. He lay on his cot breathing hard. "Witch!" he yelled at her between gasps.

"You want to use those fingers again?" Candra asked calmly, and Galen nodded. Taking care to be gentle now, she rubbed a greasy ointment on his fingers, and bound his hand more tightly than Nestor had done. Then, she lifted a spoonful of white powder towards Galen's mouth. "Open," she said.

This is it, he thought. *This is how Acayo will kill me. With poison.*

"Open," Candra said again, more forcefully this time. "It's for the pain." Still, Galen would not open his mouth.

"I didn't know you came from cowardly Athenian stock" came Acayo's voice from a few feet away. "Take your damn medicine," he said.

"Trust me. I took an oath not to hurt my patients without just cause," Candra said softly, and this time, Galen did open his mouth. The powder was bitter, and it stuck to his palate and throat until Candra gave him some water to drink.

She packed her things, and bowed before the prince. "Your Highness," she said, and Acayo dismissed her.

Acayo sauntered over to Galen's bedside. In his hands was a bundle wrapped in linen. "Where's my thank you?" he asked.

"Go to Hades," Galen said. He wouldn't admit it, but his hand felt better.

"A typical, ungrateful response. And here I was, ready to make you an offer regarding your...status," Acayo said, and made as if to leave. But Galen didn't take the bait. He watched Acayo's back grimly, his lips clenched.

Acayo laughed. He turned around again. "Ah, pride. I know it well," he said. He pulled a short stool towards him and sat on it. He rubbed his still swollen jaw. "Judging from your reaction at the skamma, I'd guess you've already heard about the viper and the helot rebellion," Acayo said.

"I don't know what you're talking about," Galen muttered.

125

"Sure, you don't. I wonder what Zoi did for you that's made you so loyal," Acayo said, raising his eyebrows. Galen stirred, and Acayo winced, expecting another blow. When it didn't come, the prince relaxed. "Father says that with her help, the helots will gain their freedom."

Galen swallowed loudly. It was a trap of some sort. It had to be. Acayo was just waiting for Galen to say something about the rebellion, to have him executed for treason. *But why did he send his healer?* Galen wondered, thinking again how his hand felt much relieved.

"I think you helots could make good citizens, as does my father," Acayo went on. "In fact, who do you think riled up the helots? Put the idea in their heads?"

Galen looked away. Kings and princes did not start *slave rebellions*. What they started were *revolutions*. "I don't believe you," Galen muttered at last, half-heartedly.

"You've been backing the wrong house, helot," Acayo said, picking some dirt out from under his thumbnail. "You trust the Eurypontids? They'd sooner burn the whole city down than release their slaves."

"That isn't true--" Galen began, wanting to argue that Queen Isaura had a different view altogether, but he stopped himself. It was best to let Acayo talk himself out. He might let something slip.

"Believe it or not," Acayo said, waving his hand dismissively. "I come bearing an offer. Your freedom for your assistance." Acayo weighed the bundle in his hands dramatically, then, began to unwrap the linen slowly. The bright, red color emerged like a wound, growing, until it was clear that what Acayo held was a Spartan cloak. "Just your size," Acayo said, running his hand over the cloth. "You help me, and no one will call you a helot again. You can join the army, grow out your hair, marry a Spartan woman who will bear you Spartan sons."

126

Galen longed to touch the cloth. Here it was, the most important element of his dream coming true. But if Morfeo and Acayo were at the heart of it, was his dream really a nightmare?

"What would you have me do?" Galen asked, his eyes still on the cloak.

"Help me rid Sparta of Nikolas, once and for all," Acayo whispered.

Galen could not control the look of shock on his face. His first thought was to leap off his cot and tackle Acayo. But he caught sight of something gleaming in Acayo's left hand. A weapon, for sure.

"Why me?" Galen asked, stalling.

Acayo seemed annoyed by the question. "You think all of Sparta doesn't know why you're friends with Nikolas?" Acayo asked, his voice dripping with disgust.

Galen shook his head. "I don't know what you're--"

"Drop the ruse. You're hoping the Eurypontids will set you free. Everyone can see how badly you want it, Galen. Running around the agoge as if you were a real student, as if you and Nikolas were brothers," Acayo said, shaking his head. "But I'll concede that you can handle a spear better than anyone here. So, you're useful. I'm going to kill Nikolas. You are going to help me." He brought his face so close to Galen's that he could smell Acayo's strong, stale breath. "You don't really have a choice here. You say a word to Nikolas, or to anyone, you're as dead as those scrawny goats you butcher in the kitchen."

"Why don't you get Brutus or Linus to help you?" Galen asked, hoping to wring more information out of Acayo.

"A nice stew that would put me in," Acayo said with a laugh. "Those two aren't trustworthy."

"Neither am I," Galen said.

"Your freedom rests in my hand. I think I can trust you. Picture it. You can grow out your hair. Marry a beautiful girl. Have a few helot girls on the side. Vote in the assembly. Kill

Feodoras. Whatever makes you happy," Acayo said in a low voice. "And you won't say a word about what we've done to anyone, or you'll lose it all."

Sparta will have one king, Galen thought, *and it will be the wrong one.* The plot was coming together. With Nikolas out of the way, the Eurypontid line would be destroyed, and the Agiads could make a case for themselves as singular rulers. But why was this in the hands of Acayo, so incompetent and weak? Still, he was right about one thing. Galen couldn't say no.

"Fine," Galen said. Then asked, "When?"

A smile erupted on Acayo's face. "Not tonight. That weakling Timios gets the whip tonight and I want to enjoy it. Gods, I hope it kills him," Acayo said. "Father says I'm supposed to wait for a sign before I kill Nikolas," Acayo said, rolling his eyes. "It'll give us time for your hand to mend, anyway. Stick close to Nikolas. I'll be ready. And when it's done," Acayo said, lifting the cloak so that it unfurled, "you'll have what you've always dreamed of."

"Does your father know I'm helping you?"

"Gods, no," Acayo said with a wave of his hand. Acayo mimicked Morfeo's gestures exactly as he spoke. Even his face contorted to look like his father's.

"How do I know you'll keep your promise?" Galen asked.

Acayo folded the cloak carefully, and laid it on the cot. "Keep it. As a measure of faith."

"The dagger, too," Galen said, and Acayo's face registered surprise. He drew the silver, slender thing from a small, leather scabbard along the inside of his wrist. He twisted the elegant weapon in the air as if to examine it. "Well," he said, "I have others," and dropped the dagger atop the scarlet bundle. "It's funny," Acayo said, considering Galen as if for the first time.

"What is?"

"Father always said the helots are more beast than man. It's not your fault, of course. Father says that the beatings at the hands of their masters drive the helots' souls out of their bodies for good. Look at you. Ready to betray your so-called friend so easily." Acayo tilted his head in thought. "Remember, not a word," he said after a moment, and left Galen to his turbulent thoughts.

19

A bright, waxing moon rose over the agoge. The boys stood in the glow of it, in silence around the whipping post, their eyes averted from the wooden stake that Timios would soon grip, exposing his back. Galen's stomach was a knot, and he wasn't alone. He'd overheard the sound of someone vomiting behind the barracks, and wondered if it was Timios, or Nikolas, or one of the other agoge students, overcome by what they were about to witness. Life in the agoge made them into hard-edged men, but that didn't happen right away. They still had all the fears of being children to overcome. It was little wonder that many Spartan men did not remember their agoge years. Their time at school misted over as soon as they left it. Mnemosyne, the goddess of memory, showed them a great mercy.

Soon, Nestor appeared at the door of the barracks, with Timios behind him. The boy walked confidently, his back straight, and Galen wondered what kind of talk Nestor had given him to bolster him so. Timios would be the youngest boy to go to the post in a generation, and Nestor's face was tight with the knowledge of it. Behind Timios was a row of cloaked men, their dark hoods over their heads and eyes. All five of them shuffled as they walked, and two leaned on polished canes. The last of the hooded men was accompanied by a smaller figure, also hooded. Nestor led the line straight to the post. Timios blanched at the sight of it, but did not drop his shoulders. His eyes met Galen's, and Galen nodded tersely at him.

The students began to murmur. "The ephors," they were saying, and Galen studied the hooded figures. How small they seemed. He knew they were older men, chosen for the position because of their many years of experience. Once, perhaps, these men had been as large as Nestor, and as strong. Now all they had left was whatever wisdom they'd gained…and power. Tremendous power. The ephors advised the kings. Nothing happened in Sparta that did not get cleared by these five first. The ephors drew their hoods, and revealed their wizened, wrinkled faces. One of the ephors had a thick red beard, and the lines around his eyes and mouth weren't as deep as those of the others. He was the youngest ephor, but he wasn't young. Few Spartan men reached such an age. War was ongoing, and most expected never to return home. Few Spartan men knew their grandchildren. But these men had *survived.* Galen could feel it, how the students grew quiet again, how their bodies hunched, submissively, in the face of such strength.

Then there was the smaller figure, the one whose arm was clutched by the tallest of the ephors. There was visible trembling, and every so often, the figure would start slipping to the floor, only to be held up by the ephor again.

Nestor cleared his throat. "Timios, son of Tymos, may Father Zeus love and respect you as much as I do. May he grant you always success at battle and a long life. May the blood you sacrifice today please the gods, that our sibyl's tongue speak true forever."

131

At that, the ephor holding up the hooded figure tugged on the coverings, and the hood fell back, releasing Korinna's fine, golden hair, and revealing her small face to the students. There was a gasp, and a few of the bolder students in the back whooped at the sight of her. Their reaction wasn't surprising. Sibyl-lore was full of scandal. It was said that the old sibyl was mistress to the ephors, and that she was kept at the Rock with only a gosammer veil for clothing. Galen felt sick at the sight of Korinna, dangling so hopelessly from the ephor's arm. Her face was scrunched up in pain. He tried to clear his mind, aware that his thoughts were her thoughts, that he somehow caused her pain. He thought of a blank slate, of a clear sky, of an empty bowl, each in succession, and he noticed how Korinna's face relaxed, as if her ache was subsiding.

The smallest of the ephors spoke next: "Blessed boys of the agoge, blessed Timios, the gods are grateful for your sacrifice tonight, and you shall all be rewarded, if not in this life, in Elysium." His voice, though croaky, carried easily in the air.

Then, as if on cue, Timios turned his back on the students. He gripped the wooden post high, his fingers curling around the stake so firmly that his knuckles gleamed white. Every muscle in his back quivered. The students grouped closer to one another, and almost to a boy, their arms were crossed tightly.

Nikolas approached Nestor slowly. Putting the coiled lash in his hand first, Nestor whispered something in Nikolas' ear, then, stepped far away. Galen expected something, a signal from Nestor, a prayer from the ephors, something, anything, to come first. But before he knew it was happening, Nikolas had taken a step forward and released the whip, the leather slicing through the air and cracking against Timios' skin, opening up a gash a foot long that bled like a fountain. Timios screamed in agony. Korinna screamed, too, and the ephor holding her by the arm shook her vigorously. Timios' hands slipped a few notches down the pole, but he righted himself, and held on again.

Nikolas, trying to control his quivering, let the whip fall to the ground. Before he could step away from his place, Acayo was already there, bounding towards the whip, ready for his turn. He picked it up with a flourish, swung the lash twice around his head as if he were playing with it, the plaited hide of the whip blurring in the air. When he threw it at last, the crack sounded for miles, and Timios collapsed under the force of it, his head striking the pole as he fell, rendering him unconscious.

The two welts on Timios' back bled profusely, soaking the ground beneath him. Nestor gently lifted the boy to a seated position. The ephors gathered around Timios, and one of them drew a lambskin from a pouch at his side, which he used to dab Timios' wounds until it was wet through. Then, the tallest ephor dragged Korinna towards Timios. He passed the blood-soaked lambskin across her forehead; the red streak gleamed on her pale skin. The students drew close, eager to see what she would do.

The ephor released her arm, and Korinna fell to her knees in front of Timios. His eyes fluttered open, and a small moan escaped his lips. "Sweet boy," she said, and rested his chin on the palm of her hand. From his vantage point, Galen could see her face, bathed in moonlight. Freckles dotted her nose and cheeks. Her eyes were quite large and brown. Her blond hair had not been combed, and hung in long, knotty strands. Still, she was very beautiful, far prettier than most of the girls who lived around the agoge, though Spartan women were known for their beauty. *So much like Zoi*, he thought, and watched Korinna wince out of pain, then shake it off. He remembered what she'd said back at the palace, that his thoughts caused her pain of some sort. Galen tried clearing his mind, but found he could not. So instead, he thought of empty bowls, and a long bolt of black cloth, a cloudless sky, and the dark depths of a deep cave.

Korinna closed her eyes, her mouth parted a little, her head twitching slightly. Then, clutching Timios' chin, she said, "Timios, son of Tymos, you shall drink from a cup of champions, your grandchildren will know your name, and you shall know theirs." A smile came to her face, though her eyes were still closed, "And you shall be a happy man," she said, and when she opened her eyes, she released Timios and sat back on her heels, hanging her head low and catching her breath.

The students whooped and shouted. Acayo, who'd been standing with the whip still in his hand, threw it down with great force, then, kicked it for good measure, sending the lash skittering away from him like a frightened snake.

Timios stood unsteadily, and Nestor offered his arm. The red-bearded ephor stepped out into a clear space. He raised his arms and said, "Behold the god-given power of the Sibyl of the Rock. We await the favors of the full moon, when Artemis is most pleased, to bring the sibyl to her home." Korinna searched the crowd for Galen, and finding him, she opened her mouth as if to speak.

No, Galen said to himself. *Not here. We have two more nights until then. I'll get you out,* he thought, as clearly and deliberately as he could. Korinna brought her hands to her forehead, but when the moment passed, she looked at Galen and nodded, mouthing the words "Thank you," twice.

The students dispersed, and Galen made his way towards Nikolas. "How are you?" Galen asked Nikolas, who had turned a sickly shade of yellow the moment he touched the whip and was still that color.

Nikolas shook his head, unable to speak. They watched as the ephors led Korinna away, drawing the hoods over their heads again as they went, and they saw Nestor speaking kindly to Timios as he guided him towards the healer.

"Only two lashes," Galen said. "It might have been worse."

Nikolas shuffled his feet, making patterns in the sand.

Galen waited until the last boy disappeared into the barracks. He scanned the area and saw no one. "There's something you need to hear," he said to Nikolas. "Meet me in Ares' temple. You take the short route," he said, running off around the barracks, going the long way. He needed to tell Nikolas about Acayo's plot, and about Zoi and Korinna. Galen felt burdened with too much secrecy, drowning in it. Ever since the Crypteia, life at the agoge had become more difficult. More and more, he felt on the precipice of something, as if the world was balanced on a pin, and it could be tipped in any direction, changing everything. The helot rebellion, the war with Persia, the new sibyl, Zoi—there were too many forces at work for Galen to manage alone.

He needed his best friend now, more than ever. Pain in his temple flared suddenly, reminding Galen of his fight with Nikolas. *That won't happen again*, he told himself. Pushing the memory aside, Galen stepped into the temple.

20

The temple was dark as pitch as he entered, but light flared suddenly as Nikolas, who'd gotten there first, lit a small torch. He set it in a small, wooden holder secured to the wall, then kneeled before the altar. Galen waited for him to finish, suppressed his appetite as Nikolas dropped a bit of cured meat to the ground, and gathered his thoughts.

"Morfeo is plotting to undo the Eurypontids," Galen began.

"What else is new?"

"It's not funny, Nikolas. He has it in his mind that Acayo and I should murder you. Acayo offered me freedom, Nikolas. Freedom in exchange for your death," Galen said, and watched, horrified, as Nikolas' arms went taut. "You must know that I'd never---" he started to say.

"I know," Nikolas said, guiltily. "I used to beg father to release you from bondage, do you know that? And each time he'd grow angry, murmur about the will of the gods, and send me out of the room. Mother's only a little better. When I mention your freedom to her, she starts to weep. To think that Morfeo---"

"This isn't about me!" Galen shouted. "To Hades with my freedom," he said, and felt a twinge in his throat as he did so. "Zoi is in league with Morfeo."

"Impossible," Nikolas said, that edge of anger in his voice again.

"It's what I've been trying to tell you. And I swear to the gods if you hit me again, Nikolas, I will lay you out cold."

Nikolas shook his head. "Go on," he said.

"I overheard her talking to him in the palace. He wants her to do…something. Something to help rid Sparta of the Eurypontids. You know she's capable of great power, Nikolas," Galen said. His conscience stung. He'd left out mention of the helot rebellion again.

"My mother," Nikolas said. "She's alone in the palace with her. With Zoi."

"I know. What do we do?"

"I'll send word with a messenger tonight. She is to be guarded at all times, on my orders," Nikolas said, thinking aloud.

"And if Morfeo intercedes?" asked Galen.

"It will buy us time, at least," Nikolas said.

"There's something else," Galen said,

"More?"

"I know. It's been some week. The new sibyl---"

"Is beautiful," Nikolas interrupted.

"Let's not start that again," Galen warned. "She needs our help. She says the fate of Sparta depends on her not being placed in the Rock."

"And you believe her?" Nikolas asked, surprised. Galen was always the skeptic between them.

"She knows…things," Galen said vaguely.

137

Nikolas, unsatisfied, began to say something, when they both heard someone approaching the temple.

"Hide," Galen urged, and Nikolas got to his feet and crawled into a shallow, cramped hole in the wall to the left of the altar. He struggled to draw his long, skinny legs all the way in, and managed it with a painful grunt, just as Acayo, Linus and Brutus entered the temple.

"You aren't alone," Acayo said.

Galen made a show of looking around. He feigned shock, raising his eyebrows and opening his mouth.

"We heard voices," Linus spoke now, taking a step closer to Galen.

"A man can't pray in peace?" Galen asked.

Acayo circled the small space. He tapped the figure of Ares with a long finger until it toppled over. "What offerings does someone like you have to give?" he asked, and Galen motioned to the strip of meat covered in sawdust.

Brutus bent over and picked it up. He dusted it off on his chiton, and took a mighty bite. "Thanks," he said.

Galen couldn't help but wonder about the nature of the gods. Shouldn't lightning come down at this very moment and strike Brutus? Shouldn't Ares himself appear and impale the boy right then and there? All was still, and the little figure of Ares lay face down in the sawdust, powerless.

Acayo's eyes lingered on the space into which Nikolas had crawled. When he turned to Galen, he was smiling. "Remember what we talked about, helot," he said, crouching to pick up the remnant of scarlet cloth that once belonged to King Leonidas. "You like this color?" he asked, dangling the scrap in front of Galen's face.

Galen tried very hard to keep still. Acayo stood so close to him, that all he had to do was reach out and grab Acayo's ankles to topple him. But Brutus and Linus were close, too. And if he started a fight, Nikolas would be sure to reveal himself to come to Galen's defense.

"You do, don't you?" Acayo taunted. "I like it, too, especially when it bleeds out of people I hate. Timios yielded too quickly for my tastes."

Without warning, Brutus kicked Galen in the mouth. He tasted the iron before he saw the blood splattered on the ground. *Please stay hidden,* Galen thought, desperately when he saw Nikolas' sandal emerge from the hole.

"Well done, Brutus. I feel much better," Acayo said, clapping slowly. Then, to Galen, said, "I don't trust you, helot. Wait for the signal. You'll want to help our friend Brutus here, not go up against him." Acayo dropped the scrap of cloak on Galen's lap, then turned and left the temple.

When they were out of earshot, Galen muttered, "Stay where you are Nikolas. They'll wait outside for a good while longer."

"I'll kill them," Nikolas said, sounding, suddenly, exactly the way Galen remembered King Leandros' voice.

"Not yet," Galen said, running the back of his hand across his mouth. *Not so bad,* he thought, realizing his teeth were still in place. It was the third time that day he'd thought an injury could have been worse. *What am I turning into?* he wondered, and left the temple, his whole body aching.

As he reached his cot, an answer came to him suddenly, like a torch being lit: *A Spartan. This is what it means to be a Spartan. To shrug off injuries as if they were spider bites.* And he wondered if the same were true in reverse. Did becoming a Spartan mean inflicting injury without remorse? He fell asleep to that disturbing thought, and slept fitfully all night, plagued by dreams awash in red.

21

After breakfast the next morning, Feodoras mustered the agoge helots and gave orders in a quiet voice. He threatened no one. Insulted no one. The man's skin was pallid, and blue veins were visible on his face. Even his breathing was shallow, though he was seated.

Korinna was right, Galen thought. *He's ill.*

"You, boy," Feodoras said to Galen. "The cook wants to make a pork stew tonight. A piglet will do," he said, and tossed two drachmas at Galen, which he caught with his good hand.

Galen stood for a moment, jostling the heavy coins in his palm and eyeing Feodoras. The man coughed, his eyes grew watery. "What are you gaping at?" he growled, but Galen, savoring the moment, waited a beat before looking away.

As they were dismissed, the helots began whispering intensely, wondering about what they'd just seen. Already the rumors zinged through the air—perhaps one of the helots had poisoned Feodoras, or maybe Aphrodite, the goddess of love, had punished Feodoras for forcing helot girls into his bed.

Knowing the cause of Feodoras' ill health, Galen did not stop to chat. He'd planned on returning to the palace, hoping he might check on Korinna, maybe even find a way to spirit her away from there. What he'd do with her next, he had only a rough idea.

Earlier, he'd had a chance to talk with Nikolas. "I've sent the messenger to the palace," Nikolas said. "Zoi is to be under heavy guard."

"It's a start," Galen said thickly. His jaw was aching from Brutus' savage kick. His shoulder smarted from Nestor's whip, and his broken fingers throbbed. *I'm a mess*, he thought pitifully. "How's Timios?" Galen asked.

"Hurting. The healer said he was feverish all night." Galen frowned, but Nikolas clasped him on the uninjured shoulder. "Don't worry. Didn't your sibyl predict a long life for our Timios?" Nikolas said, smiling.

"I'm going to go get her. Today," Galen said, and Nikolas' smile faded.

"Not without me."

"Without you," Galen said. "You're too conspicuous, *Your Highness*."

"I can order the ephors to--"

"The ephors only heed the word of the king. And you aren't a king yet."

Nikolas stared up at the vault of the sky for a moment before adding, "You can't get into the palace on your own."

"Not going through the front doors," Galen said.

Nikolas pursed his lips as if he were thinking about the wisdom of letting Galen go alone. Then, Nestor decided for him.

"Nikolas!" Nestor roared. "You're to lead the morning's hike!"

Nikolas muttered, "Of course," and gave Galen a pointed look. "If there's any trouble, blame me," he said, taking a hammered bronze cuff off his arm and giving it to Galen. "Tell them I sent you. Trade the cuff if you need to," he said, and was off towards Nestor.

Using a spare bit of cloth he kept tied to his belt, Galen secured the cuff, which bore the crest of the House of the Eurypontids, inside his chiton. Tied in another place, near his left hip and inside his chiton, was Acayo's dagger. Galen watched as Nikolas lined up the students he would lead into the mountains. Nikolas walked before them, his hands clasped at his back. The boys stood attention, chins held high, as respectful of Nikolas as they were of Nestor. Galen thought, not for the first time, that he was seeing a king of Sparta in action.

Galen took the road to the market, and when he was out of sight of the agoge, turned towards the palace. All along the way, his mind churned with what he was about to do. He rubbed his shorn head as he walked. It would be a shame to cut off Korinna's hair. Blond locks were so rare in Greece. Some people even tried bleaching their hair, with strange results. Once, even Feodoras had appeared at the agoge with hair tinged a funny green color. The helots had spent the day averting their eyes, afraid that they'd burst into laughter if they looked upon him. In secret, they began calling him "Seaweed."

Galen hoped to get to Korinna first, to rid her of that hair, and try to pass her off as a helot. It wasn't a very good plan, he knew. Perhaps the girl, with her sight, could offer a better one. With that thought in mind, Galen made his way through Sparta's city center, on his way to the Eurypontid palace.

He'd stopped at a fountain to drink when he first felt it—a rumbling under his feet that lasted only a few moments.

142

The water in the fountain sloshed and spilled a little. A small, brown hare darted out of its burrow at the edge of the road. Across the road, three girls who'd been practicing a dance caught sight of the creature and chased after it, laughing.

Galen had felt small earthquakes, but never experienced a big one. In the old stories, Poseidon was the earth-shaker, and when angry, he'd cause the sea to rise and crash into the earth as easily as if the earth's ocean was a bowl of milk the sea god had upended. Easing his feet out of his sandals, Galen felt for more movement in the ground. But all was still, and he began to wonder if he'd imagined the earthquake in the first place.

Further up the road, Galen saw a small house whose north wall had caved in. Outside of it, an old helot poked at the rubble with a walking stick.

"Is anyone hurt?" Galen asked, but the man shook his head. Oddly, he was smiling. It was a toothless smile. "Are you well?" Galen asked again, taking a step closer. Perhaps the man had been hit on the head by falling debris.

"Better now that the viper's on her way," he whispered, and he looked up into the skies, still smiling.

"What do you mean?" Galen asked, feeling as if he was losing his balance.

"The sea god sends a sign, boy, and you don't know enough to heed it," he said, shaking his head.

"So the earthquake? That's the sign?" Galen asked, a tightening in his belly.

The old man gripped Galen's upper arm hard, and dug his long, jagged nails into the flesh. "Captive no more, boy," he mumbled. Galen tore away from him, and when he looked at his arm, he saw that the man had drawn blood, right over his helot tattoo, so that the script was now unreadable.

Galen ran the rest of the way to the palace, his head flooded with images of Queen Isaura maimed or killed, of Zoi calling forth a veritable forest of enemies to destroy the palace and all of Sparta. He ran, though part of him had been excited

143

by the old helot's eagerness. The imagery of his dream came to him again, of himself wearing a red cloak, but he pushed the idea away. He'd made promises to the queen, and to Korinna, in that order, and he meant to keep them.

Guards stood at attention at the palace gates, their eyes darting from side to side, sensing that something was off. There was a distinct buzz in the air. The helots on the street spoke only in whispers, and they kept their eyes on the skies and on the distant mountain ranges, as if this viper they were waiting for would slither down Mount Taygetos, or swoop down from the sky. Galen knew the truth. The viper was a head shorter than he was, had the kind of eyes that broke a man's resolve, and was more powerful than even Galen could guess.

It's no use going through the front gate, not without Nikolas, thought Galen. Luckily, he and Nikolas had used another entrance as young boys, one only the ephors used. The Bronze House, the temple to Athena, was just south of the palace, up on a modest hill. The statue of the goddess was made of bronze, and etched outside the building were depictions of Hercules' labors. These too, had bronze details, and the whole temple glittered in the sunlight.

Few Spartans visited The Bronze House these days, as they thought the place was haunted. A Spartan general, named Pausanias, had, a few years past, tried to betray the city to the Persians. He sought Athena's sanctuary, but the clever ephors walled him up in the temple, starving him to death. Some said Pausanias' traitorous spirit had been barred from even Hades, and that he haunted the temple. Even so, the ephors and the kings and queens of Sparta kept a passageway open behind the statue of Athena, a winding tunnel that led into the palaces.

Nikolas had once taken Galen through the tunnel. They'd been caught carving a message onto the walls of the girls' school when they were thirteen. The idea had been Galen's, and he suggested they write: "Girls of Sparta, N and G bear swords for you, but not for killing." Because Galen did not know how to write, Nikolas began the carving. Pleased with themselves, they didn't notice that behind them stood the mistress of the school, a giant of a woman with a coil of braided hair piled so high it was a wonder she could hold her head up. She planted two heavy hands on either of their shoulders, and lifted them up by their chitons.

"Run!" Nikolas had shouted, and they both kicked free, ducking into The Bronze House. When the woman entered, she saw nothing but an empty space, the mild, golden face of Athena looking down on her. Meanwhile, Nikolas and Galen were hiding in the space behind the statue, and so they followed the dark tunnel, feeling their way in the blackness with their hands and feet, until they saw a chink of light ahead. The light poured down from above, in between the cracks of a wooden door on an iron hinge.

"Don't be locked, don't be locked…" Nikolas had whispered, and when he pushed, the door gave way, opening up to a hall in the back of the palace.

Now, Galen made his way through the tunnel alone. He stubbed his toes on small, jagged rocks every few feet, and cursed aloud each time. The darkness in the tunnel was so total, that his eyes ached from the strain of looking for any glint of light. The going was slow, and when another earthquake rippled underfoot, Galen prayed that the tunnel would not collapse. He walked for a long time, and stopped when a terrifying thought came to him. What if he'd passed the entrance to the palace? He'd been searching for light, yet how easy would it be to cover the door with a rug and better hide it from view? In moments of terror, time slows, and Galen felt as if his every drawn breath took minutes to get to his lungs. He slowed his pace even further, and decided on taking fifty more paces. After that, he'd turn around, back to the Bronze House, and retrace his steps from the beginning, this time running his fingers along the low ceiling.

145

A plan in place, Galen's breathing eased. Ten paces. Twenty. And suddenly, Galen tripped over a low, soft mound.

The mound yelped, and Galen heard a furious scrabbling in the narrow tunnel.

"Who is it?" Galen yelled, groping the air in the hopes of catching whoever it was. "Answer me!" he roared, swinging his arms wildly.

The earth rolled again, a minor quake this time, and Galen heard a small, familiar voice cry out.

"Zoi?" Galen called, and dropped to his hands and knees, reaching out until he touched her cool skin. He felt a set of fingers on his face, feeling his chin, his nose and lips.

"Thank the gods it's you," she sighed, but Galen pulled away.

"What are you doing here?" he said.

"I could ask you the same."

"No more games, Zoi. The earth is shaking, and the helotry is gearing up for a rebellion. What will Morfeo have you do? Out with it," Galen said, all in a rush.

"You think you're so smart, Galen," Zoi said, a note of anguish in her voice. "You overhear a conversation or two, and have it all figured out. What you don't know could fill up Taygetos."

"Perhaps you can rid me of my ignorance," Galen said.

Zoi was quiet a long time, so long, that Galen wondered if she'd somehow crawled away. "Zoi?" he asked. "What are you thinking?"

When she spoke, her voice cracked a little, so Galen knew she'd been crying. "I'm thinking of where to begin," she said. She waited a moment longer, sniffed, then said, "The Spartan sibyl, Meroe, made a prediction sixteen years ago. She foresaw one Spartan prince betraying the other. There's more. Meroe foresaw Poseidon's great fury at the prince's betrayal. That the sea-god would shake the earth. The helots have taken it as a sign that they should rise up and demand freedom." Zoi

146

spoke in whispers, and she paused here and there as she told the story, measuring her words.

"Acayo," Galen said, the prophecy aligning itself with recent events. The sibyl had foreseen Acayo's betrayal of Nikolas, and Morfeo was doing all he could to ensure it would come to pass.

"Or Nikolas," Zoi corrected.

Galen tensed. He'd overheard Zoi talking with Morfeo. She was in on the plot. "I know more than you think I do," Galen warned. "Be careful what you say."

"A sibyl's predictions are never clear-cut. Who is to say that Acayo will be the one to betray Nikolas, and not the other way around?"

"I'll say it again, in case I wasn't clear the first time. Be careful what you say." Galen sought the dagger inside his chiton and wrapped his fingers around it.

Zoi went on, ignoring Galen. "Meroe was killed soon after the second prophecy was made. Her daughter, a witness to Meroe's murder, was sold to a Persian. Her name is Korinna. I believe you've met."

"The new sibyl?" Galen asked.

"The same," Zoi said.

"What does she have to do with this?" Galen asked, his throat dry.

"I've no idea," Zoi whispered.

"You're lying," Galen said.

"I swear it! I have no idea--"

"Shut up. Here's what I know. Morfeo is an ambitious man. He understands the prophecy only one way—the destruction of Sparta will lead to the reorganization of government. One Sparta, one King. That's what he wants. He doesn't seem the type to care about freeing slaves, so why is he inciting a helot rebellion?"

Zoi stirred, but did not speak. Around them, the earth rumbled.

147

Galen felt real fear stirring in his chest. He wished he knew the full extent of Zoi's powers. Still, now was not the time for caution. He had her trapped. "Answer me!" he yelled. A shower of earth fell from the ceiling, and Galen could feel it coating his face and lips.

Zoi's voice was small when she spoke. "Morfeo has promised several of the helot rebel leaders that he will grant the helotry full citizenship if they lead the insurrection and help him carry out his plans."

Galen thought about Acayo's offer of the red cloak. He twisted the dagger in his hand.

"I don't think he will, in the end," Zoi continued. "But he'll use the rebels to do away with certain obstacles."

"The Eurypontids," Galen said, the plot coming together in his mind. "The queen," he amended, thinking of her palace full of helots, of Maira, and the eagerness he saw in her eyes, and the old man in the street, celebrating his coming freedom among the ruins of his house. "If she dies in the rebellion, Morfeo can't be blamed."

"Exactly. He'll use the moment to gain Spartan support. He will be grief-stricken, but strong. And he will squash the rebellion because he designed it. With the House of the Eurypontids completely destroyed, the House of the Agiads stands to rule Sparta alone."

"The night of the Crypteia," Galen began slowly, finding the need to ask but fearing the answer, "you were helping Acayo trap Nikolas, weren't you?"

Zoi was silent.

"But then Linus went too far in making you seem the victim, didn't he?" Galen asked, remembering the tree limb Zoi had dropped on his head.

"Morfeo holds the fine thread of my life in his hands," Zoi said after a while. "Please understand, Galen."

"I can't understand what I don't know fully," Galen said, his voice calm, though he felt a growing ire in his chest. "What about Brygus?" he asked.

"He was a good man," she said. "He took me in when I was small. He knew nothing of what I could do." Zoi shifted in the dark. "Focus, Galen. The Eurypontids are all in mortal danger," she pleaded.

Galen felt his stomach turn. "Is Queen Isaura alive?" he asked, his voice shaky.

"She is fine, for now."

"I swear, if you hurt her---"

"I don't want to!" Zoi said. "But I'm all caught up in it, like an insect in a web!"

"I don't understand," Galen said, frustration growing.

"Morfeo owns me. He owns me as surely as Feodoras owns you. If I don't do what he says...." she said, trailing off.

"Then run away with me. To Messenia. I'll pretend to be a helot in your service, and with your gifts, we can easily---"

"Galen," she said, stopping him. "I don't know how to get out of this. I can repair wounds, I can stir the earth, I can make myself heavy as a stone, but I can't stop this—this malice," Zoi said, sniffing loudly.

"Of course you can. You just slip away from it, from Morfeo."

"I mean the malice that's in me," she cried. "I'm not a good person. I've done terrible things. I've been doing them since I can remember."

"I don't believe that," Galen said softly.

Zoi was quiet a long time. When the ground shook, she sat closer to Galen, her arm pressed up against his. "I was five when I first realized what I could do," she whispered.

"Your powers are amazing," Galen said.

"Are they?" she asked, gripping Galen's wrist. He felt a strange sensation in his stomach then, something close to nausea, and then a deep, overriding need to sleep. His eyes closed. Then, Zoi let go.

Galen's eyes flew open, though there was nothing to see but darkness. "What did you do?" he asked, his strength coming back to him.

"Slowed the flow of your blood," she said. "I did it for the first time when I was five. To the sibyl. I didn't find out she'd died until later."

"You w-were under orders?" Galen asked, and felt Zoi nodding. "How is it that you can--"

Zoi laughed a little. "It runs in the family. Curses, some call them. Here's mine—if it's alive, I can manipulate its properties. Make it move. Make it light or heavy. Heal a wound. That's my curse."

"Sounds like a gift," Galen said.

"I can crush lungs. I can paralyze a bird's wings mid-flight. I can choke a man with his own tongue," she said. "Fun gifts."

"You haven't done those things," Galen said, though he wasn't sure.

"But I can. And it's what Morfeo wants me to do, Galen," Zoi said. She reached over his lap and gathered his injured hand into her own. In the dark, she undid the wrappings as gently as she could though Galen clenched his teeth in pain. When her hand covered his fingers, he felt a sting that subsided, and then, that familiar, deep cold spread through his skin, so that it felt as if his hand had gone terribly numb for a moment. When it was over, he was able to flex his fingers with ease.

"Thank you," he whispered.

Maybe it was the darkness that made it all feel like a dream. Both of them blinded by it, Galen cupped Zoi's face with both hands and ran the pads of his thumbs across her eyebrows. She turned her head so that her mouth pressed against his left palm. Galen had several thoughts at once. This moment, right now, had been a wish of Galen's from the first time he'd seen Zoi. She turned her head again, and now their foreheads were pressed together. She lifted her hands and touched the stubbly hair on his head. Galen could smell honey on her breath, and he almost forgot that Zoi represented a threat to the queen and to Nikolas, whom Galen loved as a mother and brother. He thought of the fatal wound Acayo had given him, and how Zoi had saved his life. And there was Korinna's prediction and Galen's dream of becoming a Spartan and wearing the scarlet cloak of the citizen.

The kiss surprised him. He'd never kissed anyone before, though he'd bragged to Nikolas about sleeping with a helot girl earlier that spring, unwilling to fall behind the prince in experience. At first, he yielded to it—to Zoi's cool lips pressing softly against his, then, her mouth opening, trying to deepen the kiss. But something wasn't right. Unsure suddenly of where he was, Galen dropped his hands to the ground and patted the earth. When Zoi moaned a little in his mouth, Galen pulled back, his head slamming against the tunnel wall.

They were quiet again. *I don't even know myself anymore,* Galen thought, frustrated. *Why had that felt so wrong?* Zoi was a beautiful girl and Galen had been fantasizing about her for ages.

"You've good instincts," Zoi said quietly.

There it was, Galen thought. *Instincts.* He'd always been perceptive, certainly more so than Nikolas. Even as a child, Galen had had a keen sense of whom to trust, whom to come to for help. So it was that he gave his heart and loyalty away so easily to the queen and her son. But Zoi had always made him uneasy, a feeling he ascribed to his pining for her. With Zoi, there was always a bit of intrigue, yes, but also, apprehension.

Galen again felt for the dagger in his chiton. "Are you the viper the helots are hoping will come?" he asked.

"No," Zoi answered quickly.

"I don't believe you," Galen said.

Zoi didn't speak. But he heard her choking back a sob. Then, he felt the tips of her fingers on his hand, releasing his own, one by one, until the dagger was loosened from his grip. "I don't want to be anyone's symbol," she sighed. She slipped her hand into his.

Galen wished he could see her now. Would she appear trustworthy like this, lost in a vulnerable moment? He'd closed his eyes when she'd kissed him, and had kept them closed. Now, opening them again, he saw, in the distance, a thin line of light on the ceiling. The entrance to the palace was very close.

"What about you?" she asked. "What are you doing here?"

"I promised the sibyl, Korinna, that I'd get her out of the palace before the ephors could install her in the Rock," Galen said.

"And were you going to do that before, or after, we ran away to Messenia together?"

Galen chuckled, in spite of his lingering doubts about Zoi. "Before. I keep my promises," he said.

Then, the ground shook again, and more clumps of earth began to rain down on them. A cracking sound came from overhead, like wood splintering. "We need to move!" Galen shouted, got on his feet, and tugged on Zoi's arm, dragging her towards the palace.

"You're going the wrong way!" she yelled, and pulled in the other direction.

"I made a promise to the sibyl. To keep her from the ephors."

Clods of dirt fell now. "It's starting, Galen," Zoi said. "Go!"

"No!" Galen shouted. "You don't have to follow orders. Help me stop this."

"I'm not the viper, Galen," Zoi said. "I'm just the preview. For Morfeo, I'm the distraction that Acayo needs to

make sure he's the only surviving prince in Sparta. Look to
your friend, Nikolas," she said.

Above, the tunnel was giving way, and spears of light
were piercing the darkness. Now, Galen saw that Zoi was her
old self. She stood tall, her feet spread wide apart. Her long,
dark hair was braided to resemble a fish's spine, long and
straight down her back. And there, flashing in the shafts of
light, was the serpent's scale marking on her leg.

"Take a good look, Galenos," she said, noticing his
gaze. She lifted the hem of her chiton with one hand and pulled
a part of it off her shoulder with the other to reveal that the
marking he took for a tattoo was actually her flesh, mottled and
green as her eyes, and that the scales spread over her torso.

"Monster," Galen hissed.

Zoi's eyes filled with tears. "No Galen. I'm not the
monster. I'm bound to the real monster." She tied up her
chiton again, her fingers trembling. "Save Nikolas, and I'll take
care of Korinna," she said, without meeting his eyes.

"How can I trust you?"

"You can't," she said. "But you don't have a choice.
Who will it be? The prince or the sibyl?"

"Do not touch a single hair on the head of Queen
Isaura," Galen growled.

"I'm trying to be on your side," Zoi said.

Galen studied her now, how her mouth was set in a grim
line, her hands balled into fists. Around them, the world
rumbled, and Galen felt the subterranean shaking deep in his
chest.

"Try hard," he said, then he ran back from where he
came, towards the entrance to the Bronze House.

153

22

The statue of Athena blocked the opening of the tunnel into the Bronze House. It had fallen over in the earthquake, and now, the goddess' massive body covered most of the entrance. Only a gap about a foot wide remained through which Galen could see that the Bronze House was filled with helots, dancing, celebrating, and singing hymns to Poseidon, the earth-shaker. Galen had never seen a helot celebration and it filled him with joy. In the corner of the temple stood two young helot men, about Galen's age, taking turns carving their tattoos out with a knife. The blood trickled down their arms. The two grunted through the pain, and let out sharp, loud laughs every so often. A woman who stood so close to the tunnel opening Galen could have reached up and touched her sandal hoisted her small daughter on her shoulder. "Free men and women!" she shouted, bouncing the little girl up and down, while the helots in the temple cheered.

Galen longed to join them, forgetting all about Nikolas and Korinna and Zoi for a happy moment. He had never wanted anything so badly in all his life. He pulled at the wooden floorboards around the opening, grunting with the exertion it took to yank them free. One board came loose. The others would not budge. Then, he heard it, a man's voice coming from within the crush of bodies, shouting, "Down with the Spartans! We outnumber them, brothers and sisters! May their blood flow to the Eurotas and color it red!" There were cheers again, louder this time. Galen stilled his hands. He watched as more helots came into the temple. They brought with them weapons, some of which were already crimson. With each new set of arms, the helots cheered.

They're turning the temple into a fortress, thought Galen. He wondered where the Spartan soldiers were. Had Morfeo commanded them to do nothing? To stand by as their city was overtaken? Another look into the temple confirmed his worst fear—there were at least ten children among the rebels, standing close to their parents, small hands clinging to chitons, their eyes wide with terror.

The woman nearest him had put her daughter down. The child, five or six years old, tapped her bare foot on the floor to some rhythm in her head. Galen didn't like seeing the children there among the adults, so small and helpless. He remembered when he was small, how Feodoras had never shown him a kindness. For a moment, he considered warning the little girl, showing her the tunnel and the way out. Galen reached out a hand. His fingers nearly touched her slender ankle. Then, he stopped. What if she squealed, or pointed him out to the adults? They might think he was a spy, or they might yank him into the temple and hand him a sword. Galen's heart pounded at that last idea. He could nearly feel it in his hands, a long sword with which to gain his freedom...

"Down with King Morfeo!" one of the helots shouted.

155

"Down with the Queen!" another answered, and the helots took on the chanting, back and forth, calling disaster on the royal houses of Sparta.

Back to the palace, Galen thought, terrified, and angry with himself for wasting time. He ran, stumbling over debris and fallen rock, hoping Nikolas was not yet in danger. Lost in thought, the passageway seemed far shorter this time. Galen found the door easily and pushed it open. He poked his head into the corridor, and looked around, confused, realizing that in spite of the dust in the air, and the overturned amphorae, and the shouting he heard, that this was, in fact, the Eurypontid palace. Except it was in chaos.

The queen, he thought, and pulled himself up and out of the passageway. A steady rain of dust fell from the ceiling, and Galen saw the beginning of a long, jagged crack there. He heard the pounding of feet on the floor, and the intermittent shouts of women. Turning in the direction of the shouts, Galen paused only to make sure that Nikolas' bronze cuff was still secure in his chiton, and to pick up a shield that had fallen to the floor.

The corridor spilled out into a courtyard, the one with the small temple to Ares, and Galen saw in horror how it had collapsed. The head of the god having rolled out of the temple, lay still and broken in the grass. The queen's chambers were in the eastern wing of the palace, so that she might rise with the sun, Nikolas had explained once. Galen stopped for a moment, got his bearings, then took off again, past the large hall where he'd overheard Morfeo and Zoi conspiring, then, turning left into another corridor. What he found there stopped him cold. The floor was littered with fallen men and women, all of them with shorn heads. Galen scanned them for wounds, but found none. Even more curiously, he noted that their chests rose and fell softly, regardless of the awkward positions in which they'd fallen. *They're sleeping*, Galen thought at first, then remembered Zoi's demonstration of her powers in the tunnel.

156

How sleepy Galen had become with a single touch. He stepped over the men, trying hard not to crush fingers and noses as he went, until he reached the door of the queen's chamber.

Galen pushed at the timber door gently, afraid of what he would find inside. There were female voices shouting within. *If she's hurt the queen*, Galen thought apprehensively. The door cracked open a bit, and before Galen could pull it further, a cold hand grasped his wrist hard. Instantly, Galen fell asleep.

23

Galen woke inside a lush chamber. The stone walls were painted in rosy tones, the color of a sunrise. There were enormous pots of herbs, including the largest, greenest oregano he'd ever seen. In the center of the room was a bed covered in lambskin. The posts of the bed were made of cedar, and they touched the ceiling. And sitting on the bed was Zoi, her arms wrapped around her legs, her right foot tapping nervously. She was sitting in a patch of winter sunlight, and all the fine hairs on her arms and legs trapped the light and appeared to glow. Galen followed the light to an opening in the ceiling, through which could be seen a patch of blue sky. When he looked at Zoi again, she'd caught his eyes. Her mouth parted, but she did not come to him. Galen tried to lift his head.

"He stirs," an unfamiliar voice said. Galen found he was having trouble focusing his eyes at close range, as if he'd become suddenly far-sighted. Before him stood two large girls, their upper arms the size of Galen's thighs. Then, the girls merged into one, fuzzily, slowly, until his vision cleared at last. The girl was holding a long sword like an expert.

"Thank you, Diantha," Galen heard another voice say. This one he recognized and he felt as if he could take a deep breath again, for the first time in hours.

"Queen Isaura," he said, sitting up. The world spun for a moment.

"Slowly, Galenos," the queen said as she approached. She kneeled by him and put a small cup to his lips. Galen drank the mint-flavored water.

"What's happened here?" he asked.

"The helotry is in rebellion," Isaura said darkly. She gripped Galen's face, and he held his breath, shocked at her touch. "Swear to me you have no hand in this, Galenos. Swear it!" she whispered fiercely.

"None, Your Majesty. I swear," he said.

Queen Isaura looked into Galen's eyes, as if searching for a sign, then released his face.

"He speaks the truth," another voice, this one behind Galen, said. He turned and saw Korinna, wearing an orange, Ithacan-style dress. The hem was embroidered in silver thread, some of which hung in a fringe that brushed her ankles. Her long, blond hair had been combed and braided, and held back with a band of cloth, dyed to match the dress.

She's beautiful, Galen thought, unable to stop himself. Korinna cringed for a moment, then smiled.

He stood, felt a little woozy, and leaned on Diantha, who was a head taller than he. Zoi chuckled, and Korinna glared at her. There was another girl standing by the herbs. She was small, with a short, thick waist, and she gripped a short sword with all her might. "Your Majesty," the girl said, "we must get you to a safer place.

159

"I am not leaving my home, Helena," the queen said, spinning around to face the frightened girl, who fumbled with her sword and had to bend to retrieve it.

"Where are the soldiers?" Galen asked.

"Morfeo has led them to the Bronze House, where the rebels have gathered," Isaura said.

Galen thought of the children he'd seen inside. "All of the soldiers?" he asked.

"He left a small guard here," the queen said, throwing her arms up and sitting beside Zoi on the bed. "But they were overcome by a—a—what did you call it?" she asked, turning to one of her ladies-in-waiting.

"A woman, my queen," Diantha said. "It was so fast, and I was hiding behind a low wall, but I swear she had scales, and a long, forking tongue. She wrapped her mouth around the neck of a soldier, but then I shut my eyes. The screaming was bad enough."

"A drakaina, Your Majesty," Korinna said, tucking her hands into the long sleeves of the dress, clutching the material from the inside.

Korinna looked at Zoi, who'd risen from the bed. The sibyl's eyes widened as Zoi approached quickly, and clasped Korinna's wrist. Galen got to his feet.

"I've saved your life twice, sibyl. Watch what you say," Zoi said. Though her voice sounded dangerous, Galen saw tears in her eyes.

"Zoi," Korinna said. "Have you no love for me?" she pleaded.

"Girls!" the queen shouted. A helot man, broad-shouldered, carrying a makeshift spear and shield, had broken through the door. Isaura signaled Diantha and Helena, who raised their weapons. Before Galen saw any more, Zoi thrust her hand into the nearby potted herbs, threw her head back and closed her eyes. The plants grew thick tendrils, flowers that blossomed and died on the vine, and fat, woody roots in what

160

seemed to Galen the time it took to blink twice. He found himself surrounded by the sweet-smelling plants, walled away from the queen, her ladies and their attacker. The plants shifted, creating a crackling sound that drowned out noises from outside the living enclosure. Galen found himself in a small clearing in the middle of it, along with Zoi and Korinna.

"What did you do?" Galen shouted, tearing at the plant. "Get rid of it! The queen, Zoi!" But Zoi did not move an inch, so steadily was she staring at Korinna.

Korinna looked terrified. "You're so much stronger than you were," she said.

"We have wonderful gifts, Korinna," Zoi said.

"Curses, too."

"Shut up."

"Take it down!" Galen yelled at Zoi, who took no notice of him.

The two girls stared hard at each another, though they wore pained expressions. *Whatever this is*, thought Galen, *they don't hate each other.* He was reminded of his battles with Nikolas—sometimes violent, but always short-lived affairs. The way brothers fought, Galen imagined. Like family. And now, seeing them together, Galen saw how much alike the girls were. Small chins, large eyes, slender wrists but strong hands, almost mannish. Only their hair was differently colored. *They're related*, he realized, wondering why it had taken him so long. *Sisters maybe, or cousins*, he thought. There was no mistaking it, and Galen wondered if their powers came from the same source.

Now, the voice of the queen and her ladies could be heard. The plants that surrounded them shook, as if someone were trying to cut through. Galen could hear his name being screamed as if from a great distance, and it made him panicky.

"They can't know about the drakaina," Zoi was saying.

"Half of Sparta saw her!" Korinna shouted.

161

Galen began clawing at the plants, tearing at leaves and branches. But each time he ripped at the plant, more of it grew in place. The queen, shouting his name, sounded very far away now.

"It must have been a mistake," Zoi said, gripping Korinna's shoulders now. Her terror seemed to weigh her whole body down, so that she crouched a little and had to look up into Korinna's face. "Morfeo," she said. "Morfeo wouldn't put her in danger like that. He wouldn't."

"Morfeo?" Korinna spat. Her face turned ugly at the name. "How long, cousin? How long before you learn that those you trust hold no love for you? That those you are so keen on hurting are all you have?"

Galen stopped pulling vines. *Cousins then,* he thought, his suspicions confirmed.

"The drakaina listens to Morfeo," Zoi insisted. Her voice was laced with anguish.

"It is vengeance she seeks! It always has been!" Korinna said, throwing her arms around Zoi's neck. "Listen to reason," she cried, her face hidden in Zoi's hair.

A muffled scream filled their ears. "The queen!" Galen yelled, and the girls looked at him at last. "I don't know what is happening," he said, "but we can't let her be captured by the helots. Or killed. Remove this wall, Zoi," he pleaded. "Please."

For a moment, Zoi's eyes softened. "Do you hate me, Galen?" she asked. "I don't think I can bear it if you do," she said softly.

Galen's heart pounded. He wasn't sure how he felt, actually. He feared Zoi--that was certain. "People are dying because of you," Galen said, trying to keep his voice flat.

"They die in war all the time!"

"Soldiers *choose* that fate, Zoi. Helots don't. We don't get to choose anything!" Galen said. "Remove this wall! Use your gifts for something other than devastation!"

162

At that, Korinna groaned. She fell to the floor, her head in her arms.

"Oh, no," Zoi said, trying to catch the girl as she slid. They landed on the floor together, Korinna crying in pain.

Empty bowl. Flattened field. The surface of the river, Galen thought, anxious to clear his mind and alleviate Korinna's hurt.

Zoi flattened a palm against the girl's sweaty brow. "There, there," she whispered, until Korinna fell limp, though her eyes were open.

"How did you---" Korinna muttered. The look of pain in her eyes was gone.

"I've learned a few new tricks," Zoi said. "It is not all about devastation," she said, looking at Galen pointedly. She watched him a moment, then said, "Come with me, Galen. We can run away together, to Messenia, as you said."

"We can't leave now, Zoi. We can't leave everyone in this mess."

"It's because of what I am, isn't it?"

Galen stared at the living wall. He didn't know what to say. Could he be with a creature like Zoi? Instead of answering her, Galen touched the wall and whispered, "Take it down. Please."

Zoi's mouth settled into a grim line. Her eyes darkened, as if something burned behind them. "You're making a choice now, aren't you?"

She ran her fingers along the hedge-like wall, and immediately, it began to wither. "Tell the queen I've joined the fight against the rebels. As for the drakaina--"

Korinna shook her head. "Morfeo is only using her. And you. You must know that. Stay here. Help us."

Zoi's heart was clearly torn. She looked up to the skylight, then back down at Korinna. "I'm going to Morfeo. I've spent enough time here, and if he finds out I helped keep the queen alive..." Zoi's face crumpled before she could finish speaking, as if she were trying to keep tears back. She faced the barricade she'd created, planted a foot in a Y bend in the roots, and heaved herself up, one foot following the other, towards the skylight.

"You're helping us then?" Galen shouted up at her. "You're on our side?"

Zoi's small form was hard to see in the brightness. Galen thought he saw her nodding, or maybe she was shaking her head. "Zoi!" he shouted, but she was gone into the glare. It was hard to tell the moment she disappeared from view.

Galen started to follow her; his impulses, as ever, were hard to rein in. "Stop," Korinna said, taking hold of his chiton. She gestured towards the plants, which were dry and brittle now. Leaves fell rapidly, and through the branches, Galen saw that the room was empty.

24

Galen rushed out into the hallway, stumbling over the sleeping helots. "Zoi did this," he said, turning to Korinna. "Put them all to sleep."

Korinna nodded. "She could have killed them. But she chose another path," she said.

Galen scanned the hallway. The palace was quiet. He stepped gingerly over the bodies that were beginning to turn in their sleep, moaning and stretching. "They're waking up," he whispered, holding out his hand to Korinna. She took it, and followed his lead down the corridor.

Galen's mind turned from one option to the next quickly. Zoi had left them to join Morfeo, the queen and her ladies were taken hostage, and Nikolas was still in danger. He found he could not focus on any one possibility for long before his brain hopped to another. Down the corridor they went, hand in hand, until they were clear of the sleeping helots. Galen stopped then, and faced Korinna.

"Your head. It's not hurting anymore," he whispered.

"Only a little. Zoi eased the hurt some," she said.

Without thinking, Galen's hand went to the cool, silvery skin on his side. "Can you still…do you still…?"

"See what you see? Hear what you hear?" Korinna supplied for him. She nodded. "Your perceptions are like a veil over my own."

Galen said nothing. He didn't like having her in his head, and he hoped that she didn't hear *everything* he thought. Half of his musings were panicked, full of self-doubt. The other half involved Zoi. The way her chiton clung to her form…

Korinna cleared her throat, and Galen stopped short. "Listen," he began to say. "I know I promised to help you. And I will, but I don't like the way you--"

"No," she whispered fiercely. "Look." She pointed to an open courtyard in the distance. The five ephors were picking their way through the ruins of Ares' temple. One held a bouquet of herbs tied together, which burned at one end, releasing a stream of heady scented smoke. "They mustn't find me," Korinna said.

Galen gripped her arm and pulled her down another hallway. This one led to the kitchen, the floor underfoot no longer tiled, but paved with smooth stones. He tugged her through a doorway and into an open-air patio. In the center was an oven. The fire underneath had gone out, but tendrils of smoke still rose slowly. To the left of the oven was a medicinal garden, and herbs were planted to the right. A door in one of the exterior walls stood ajar. Galen headed for it.

"How do you know where you're going?" Korinna demanded.

"Grew up in a kitchen," he said. "They're all the same." He opened the door and led Korinna in. It was a pantry, stocked with clay pots, casks, cooking utensils, dried herbs and salted meats. Galen drew the door closed, leaving it slightly ajar so that they'd have some light. He indicated a barrel to Korinna, and she took a seat. Then he drew the dagger from his chiton.

Korinna threw up her hands at first, then, lowered them, understanding what Galen was going to do. "I've never cut it," she said, fingering the ends of her hair.

"I've never grown mine out," Galen said. Korinna laughed quietly. "We don't have much time," he said. "I cut your hair. You talk. Tell me everything I need to know to save the Eurypontids."

She waited a beat, ascertained his thoughts, and nodded, lowering her head so that Galen could better reach the hair that hung down her back. She waited until she felt the first tug, the first rasping sound of the blade against her hair. Swallowing thickly to keep herself from crying, Korinna began:

"My mother was Meroe, the Spartan sibyl, daughter of Lena and Taras, Spartan exiles," she said,

"I've heard about her, from a singer at the agoge," Galen interrupted, gripping another hank of hair and running the dagger through it. The locks fell to the ground and covered his feet. "Meroe and her sister arrived in Sparta in a ship with black sails. Poseidon is said to be their grandfather," Galen said, surprised that he'd remembered so much.

"It's true," Korinna said. "One day, my great-grandmother was bathing in a lagoon near the sea. The god looked up from his watery depths and saw her, the water on her skin sparkling in the sunlight. He rose to greet her, in the form of a young man, and seduced her," Korinna said. Color rose to her cheeks.

"Go on," Galen said, his voice creaky.

"Nine months later, my grandmother, Lena was born. She had no godly gifts to speak of. She married Taras, and bore my mother, Meroe, and then another daughter, Lamia. Then it became clear that Poseidon's powers had skipped a generation. By her fifth birthday, Meroe could foresee the weather. By her sixth, she knew when an animal would grow sick and die. At her seventh birthday, she foretold the death of a schoolmate. And by her tenth, she was having visions of nations at war, the fate of thousands of men clear in her mind."

Galen's hands went still. *Was Korinna this powerful, too?* he wondered. Her hair was at her chin now, and he went on working, shortening the locks further.

"Not nearly as strong," Korinna said, answering Galen's silent question before proceeding. "As for Lamia, her gifts were closer to Poseidon's. While the sea-god can move the earth and the waters, Lamia found she could move living things with ease, experimenting at first with a pet canary of Meroe's. Lamia would force the creature to fly so high that it would become just a yellow dab in the sky, then paralyze its wings so that it dropped like a stone, forcing it back into flight just before it hit the ground. What Lamia could not do was give the bird life again after she'd killed it playing."

Galen opened his mouth to speak, realization striking home. "Lamia was Zoi's mother. And your aunt."

"*Is* her mother," Korinna corrected. "Lamia lives."

"But Zoi claimed her mother--"

"Zoi speaks half-truths. She loves her mother, in spite of everything," Korinna said. "I loved my mother, too, and I'd go on loving her even if she were a monster. We can't help it."

"I wouldn't know about that," he said. When she looked up at him, he shrugged. "No parents, remember?"

Korinna gave him a sympathetic smile and carried on. "While Meroe inherited her mother's kindness, Lamia took after Taras' cruelty and selfishness. After she'd been installed in the Rock of the Sybil, Meroe begged the ephors to let Lamia stay with her, and they, in a rare moment of compassion, acquiesced. So, the two girls grew into womanhood in the caves at the foot of Mount Parnon. They were both quite beautiful, my mother in particular, which made it difficult for the ephors to resist her." Korinna grew quiet, then said: "My mother could not tell which one fathered me."

168

She drew the back of her hands across her eyes. Galen worked in silence, pity thick in his throat. So much hair littered the floor that he had to kick it away, lest he slip on the glossy tresses. The sun had shifted in the sky, and the slash of light coming through the partly opened door had moved across Korinna's face.

"Pardon me," Galen said, bent low, and pulled the barrel upon which Korinna sat so that the sun was out of her eyes. She was jostled, and leaned on his shoulder for a moment before righting herself. "That's better," he said, and got back to work.

Korinna sat up a little straighter, reached up to feel the length of her hair, and said, "I'll make an ugly bald girl."

"All the helot girls are bald," Galen said, trying hard to keep his tone light. "And some of them are quite good looking." Korinna laughed and Galen relaxed a little at the sound. "Can you go on?" he asked her after a moment.

"Of course," she said. "As for Lamia, she fell in love with a frequent visitor to the Rock. King Morfeo."

The dagger clattered to the floor. "Sorry," Galen said, flustered.

"I don't blame you," Korinna said. "He'd already married Cyteria, so Morfeo's affair with Lamia was particularly scandalous. Soon after his visits began, Lamia delivered her firstborn, a son named Thanos. He was taken from her immediately after his birth. In a jealous rage, Cyteria had ordered that the baby be thrown off Mount Taygetos." Korinna's voice dropped even lower, and she twisted her hands in her lap as she spoke. "But Lamia was carrying twins. The second baby, Zoi, was born an hour after her brother, and my mother helped hide her.

"Lamia went mad, Galen. She vowed revenge on Sparta. If she couldn't have her son, no Spartan woman could."

Korinna stopped. The knife blade hummed through her hair. She could feel it cold against her scalp. "Don't move,"

169

Galen warned, remembering the times the barber had cut him accidentally.

"Have you heard the stories? Of the children dying at the mouth of the Rock?"

"Everyone's heard those," Galen said, running the dagger slowly around her ears. "Feodoras used to threaten he'd take me there."

"They aren't stories," Korinna said. She could feel Galen's hand trembling against her head, but she went on anyway. "Meroe didn't notice what was happening for a long time. The Persian war had begun, and the ephors demanded a prophecy of her before each squadron moved out. She was busy caring for me, and doing her job. I was five years old, as was Zoi, when I stumbled into Lamia's quarters and witnessed her grisly habit firsthand. I had spent little time with my aunt and cousin. They kept themselves secluded, in the deepest tunnels of the Rock. My mother told me it was Lamia's grief for her son that ruled her heart now, and though she tried to coax her sister out into the world, for Zoi's sake, she'd failed. Anyhow, I'd been trapping small lizards, and one proved difficult to catch. I followed it down, down, deep in the Rock, and came upon a thing I will never forget—Lamia cradling a limp child, a boy of about six or seven, her mouth clamped on his neck, blood pouring in streams to the ground. In the corner, Zoi watched with bored eyes. It took a moment for Zoi to look up at me, but when she did, there was a clear threat in her eyes—*tell no one.*"

Korinna's skin erupted in goosebumps, the fine hairs on her arms standing on end. Galen found his own body reacting to the gruesome story, and he could not suppress a shiver. Without thinking, he rubbed Korinna's arm with his free hand, as if to warm her, then stopped when he realized the liberty he'd just taken.

Korinna said nothing, only crossed her arms and continued the story. "I ran to my mother, praying to the gods that Lamia had not seen me. I felt sick halfway up the tunnel, and paused to gag, but nothing came up. When I reached her, Meroe was sitting before a chasm in the earth from which sometimes emerged a strong smelling fume. She kneeled before it, her eyes closed, inhaling the pungent smoke. For centuries, sibyls have used the sacred vapors to induce visions, and I'd just stumbled upon my mother's work. My unwillingness to interrupt her gave me time to think, to consider the warning in Zoi's gaze. But my mind kept returning to the sight of that boy's body, his brown eyes open and staring at the dark ceiling of the tunnel. I wondered what the last thing he'd seen or heard had been, and I shuddered to think of Lamia's crazed smile being that thing.

"So I told my mother what I'd seen. Realizing the monster her sister had become, and fearing that Zoi and I were in danger, Meroe made a sacrifice to Poseidon, begging that Lamia be punished. That night, an earthquake shook the ground, and heavy mist enveloped all of Sparta. When it lifted, and the earth stopped rolling, Lamia found she could no longer blink, nor close her eyes, even to sleep, and that her lower body was covered in scales. Her legs had withered so that she had to drag herself with her arms. Because she'd partaken of the murdered child's body, Zoi, too, was changed, though not as gruesomely as her mother. Ashamed and enraged, Lamia hid deeper in the Rock to places unknown, taking Zoi with her. She'd become a drakaina. A dragon woman."

Galen leaned back against the pantry shelves, and looked up. *Drakaina*, he thought. *Dragon, not viper.* He felt as if he'd stepped into one of the singer's songs. The age of heroes was supposed to be long past. And yet here she was, a great-granddaughter of mighty Poseidon, head half-shorn, staring up at Galen, hearing his thoughts, with a tale of a monster loosening her lips.

"Please finish," she said, rubbing her head. "I'll look freakish enough when it's even."

171

Girls, Galen thought. *Even in times like this, they worry about their hair.*

Korinna laughed, loudly this time, and the air seemed to lighten. Galen worked quietly, his hand on her head, turning it gently this way and that. He was thankful for the silence, and he tried not to think of anything other than Korinna's hair, how even this short, the blond fuzz shimmered when the light struck it.

Done now, Galen put a finger under Korinna's chin to tilt her head left and right. "Pretty good," he said. She blushed, and he drew his hand back. "You'll need to change your clothes," he said, indicating her Ithacan gown.

Korinna looked down at the pretty dress, frowning. Galen poked his head out of the pantry, checking to see if all was clear, and disappeared. He returned a moment later with a filthy looking chiton. "Found it in the adjacent room." He lifted the cloth to his nose and made a face. "Smells like sheep guts," he said. "Sorry, but it will have to do." He held out the chiton and Korinna took it.

They stared at each other for an awkward moment. Then Galen said, "Oh. Of course. I'll step out while you undress," and rushed out of the pantry. He heard her rustling with the gown. *Empty bowls, empty bowls, empty bowls*, he thought over and over again.

When she called, "All done," he breathed a sigh of relief.

Galen stepped into the pantry and looked at Korinna in the half-light. The chiton was a bit large for her, but she'd cinched it well at the waist with some rope. She'd tucked a small bunch of dried lavender under the rope, giving the otherwise pitiful clothing a feminine touch.

"How do I look?" she asked.

"Like one of us," he said, smiling.

"A helot?"

"Yes. Unmistakable."

172

"Good," she said, smoothing out the rumpled chiton as best she could.

A strange look drifted across Galen's face. He squatted then, and looked up at her. "Sibyl," he began, "can you see the path before me? What do I do now?"

Korinna shook her head. "I can't control the visions. They come and go as they please," she said. Then, she closed her eyes, and Galen held his breath. She opened them again, exasperated. "Nothing."

Galen rose, kicked at the tresses on the floor. "So that's it. You've told me everything?"

"I've told you everything you need to know," she said.

"No!" Galen said angrily. "No tricks. I want to know *everything*, not just what I 'need to know.'"

"I've said all I should," Korinna said, getting to her feet. The barrel tipped over, crashing into a shelf and sending a slew of jars to the ground.

A voice outside called: "There's someone in the kitchen!" Galen pushed Korinna back with his arm, and kicked open the pantry door, gripping a hunk of splintered wood in his hand for a rough weapon.

A pair of helot men entered the kitchen. One had a black eye. The other walked with a limp. "Oi," the first one said. "What are you doing here?" He carried a dull sword.

Galen dropped the wood, and wiped his brow. "Thank the gods," he said. "We've been hiding from Spartan soldiers in here." He stuck his hand in the pantry and yanked Korinna out. She stumbled to his side.

"My, my," one of the men said.

"She's my sister," Galen growled, and the two grew serious again.

"We've found at least thirty helots asleep outside the queen's chamber," the one with the limp said.

"Rotten, lazy bastards," the other muttered.

173

"Where is the queen?" Galen asked, and Korinna tugged hard on his hand. "I mean, is she dead yet?" he added, trying hard to sound enthusiastic about the possibility.

"We don't know," the black-eyed one said. "But the Eurypontid palace is ours. Not a soldier, not a royal, not even a damned lady-in-waiting in sight." He rubbed his hands together and the sound was like the rustling of dead leaves.

"That is good news," Galen said. He pulled Korinna behind him, trying to put quick distance between them and the helots.

They were just outside the kitchen, back in the corridor, when they heard one of the men saying, "Look at all this hair. And a fancy gown, too." Galen and Korinna took off running, hearing only dimly behind them, "After them!"

25

They raced through the halls, over the mosaic floors and past the broken temple again. They burst through the front doors of the palace, which were, for the first time in Galen's memory, unguarded. Then they stopped. Pandemonium had taken over the city. The ground shook every few minutes, and the sound of crumbling walls followed the movement.

Everywhere Galen looked, something pierced his heart. In the distance, a Spartan soldier dragged an injured helot boy by the arm. Three helot men squared off against a single soldier a few paces off. The helots came after him with wooden clubs, which bounced off his shield easily. When the soldier lifted his sword to strike, Galen turned away. Far up the road, a Spartan phalanx had formed. Rows of soldiers stood like shark's teeth, crouched in a fighting stance, shields up, swords out, keeping a mob of helots away from the Agiad palace. Moans and shouts and ear-piercing screams muddled Galen's thinking, so that he stood and looked and could think of nothing else to do.

"Let's go!" Korinna shouted, pulling Galen's hand. But Galen did not budge. He didn't know what to do anymore. Here they were, his people, fighting for their freedom at last. Was he to run from that? Like a coward?

"They will not be free," Korinna yelled over the din. "Not in our lifetimes. Death and destruction are all that awaits the helotry!"

"You've seen it?" Galen asked.

"No," she shouted. "But I don't need to!"

Galen turned to her, his eyes full of furious tears. "Who's to say you're right? Who's to say?" he argued, sounding like a child to himself. Ashamed of crying, Galen rested his forehead against the palace door. Again, he cursed his fate. *I don't want a half-life,* he thought. *I want to choose where I go and whom I marry and whether I die fighting or not.* He knew Korinna could hear it, but he no longer cared.

He felt her hand, soft on his back. It was the lightest kind of touch. Tentative. It drew him out of himself, and he turned around.

"I know how you feel," she shouted.

"Right," Galen said, sighing. She could barely hear him. "Because you see what I--"

"No, because it's the same for me," Korinna said, standing closer to him. "The ephors enslaved my mother. They will do me no better. And if they do, and I misspeak, or a prophecy leads to ruin, or one of the gods uses me as his or her plaything, then the ephors have me killed," she said, speaking fast.

"Like your mother," Galen said.

Korinna shook her head, casting down her eyes.

For a moment, in a brief flash, Galen pictured Meroe as she might have looked, wrapped tightly by a serpent, her face turning purple as the life left her. "Lamia killed her," he said. "And Zoi helped."

"Zoi didn't know what she was doing," Korinna whispered, but before Galen could argue, a company of soldiers, running in formation, rushed past.

Galen heard one of them cry, "To the Bronze House!" He remembered the temple being used as an armory and fortress. And the forty children he'd counted inside.

Korinna's head rose sharply, having heard Galen's thoughts, having seen the children through his eyes. She closed her own then, as if listening to something deep inside herself.

"What is it?" Galen asked, shaking her shoulders. "What do you see?"

She held up a hand, shushing him. "I see a line of children, running into the hills north of here," she said. "They are safe. Their lives extend far into the future," she said, her speech slurred, as if she'd drunk a good bit of wine. "But we have to go to them."

"But the queen. And Nikolas? Zoi said Nikolas is in danger."

"Nikolas is at the Bronze House," Korinna said calmly. Galen's mouth opened, and she squeezed his shoulder. Then, she took off at a sprint in the direction of the temple.

"Wait!" Galen cried, and overtook her lead quickly. He took a sharp left away from the soldiers, cutting through several empty homes, for all the Spartan women had gone to fight the rebelling helots, too, trained not to heed their gender when the city was threatened. Galen and Korinna darted through people's vacant kitchens, bedrooms and gardens, and when they came out again onto the main street, they found they were ahead of the company of soldiers by a good distance.

Despite the earthquakes, the Bronze House still stood in all its glittering glory. Galen saw the helots packed inside, standing at the entrance to the temple. Some bore arms. Others seemed terrified, their wide eyes gazing out at a hundred Spartan soldiers walking in formation towards them. The soldiers' scarlet cloaks snapped and billowed in the wind. A

177

single, tall figure walked between the ranks. Morfeo, his expression hard, held his arms tight against his body. Behind him, walked Acayo in his own cloak. He was shorter than his father by a good head, but he kept his chin up and seemed tall, too.

Galen and Korinna stopped abruptly, a few paces shy of the entrance. "What will we do?" she whispered.

Before he could answer, Morfeo's booming voice cut through the air. "Helots of Sparta, you've pinned your hopes on a sign from Poseidon! But these were the false hopes of damnable slaves!"

"Traitor king!" they heard from inside the temple. "Deceiver!" "Liar!" came the shouts of the helots.

"Behold your ruin!" Morfeo roared, looking to his right. Galen and Korinna saw her at the same time that the soldiers did—Zoi, flanked by two enormous dogs, her hands on their haunches. She walked slowly, calmly, though the dogs snarled and foamed at the mouth beside her. She stopped before Morfeo and turned on her heel. The dogs turned, too.

Zoi scanned the crowd of soldiers. Her eyes were a bright green, and she'd lowered one strap of her chiton so that her left shoulder was bare, revealing the gleaming scales there.

Drakaina, thought Galen. Korinna winced, her hands flying to her temples. Zoi turned her head, as if she'd heard him, too. Their eyes met over the heads of the assembled force.

Galen wished suddenly that Zoi were the one who could hear his thoughts. She needed to understand that there were children inside the Bronze House. That she need not follow her mother's path, or Morfeo's orders. Beside him, Korinna grunted against the intensity of Galen's thoughts. *No,* he thought. *Zoi can't hear me the way Korinna does.*

So, he screamed her name instead.

26

The dogs at Zoi's side threw back their massive heads and howled at the sound of her name. A hundred helmeted Spartans turned at once to look at Galen and Zoi. One broke ranks, and walked towards them. He had a familiar gait, but it wasn't until he'd pulled the helmet off his head that Galen knew who it was.

"Nikolas," Galen said, relieved at the sight of his friend, alive and well. He was awed, too, by the swirl of his cloak as he walked.

Grabbing a handful of Galen's chiton, Nikolas pulled Galen up, his feet coming off the ground a bit. "Trying to get yourself killed?" Nikolas asked. "Go home, Galen."

Galen shoved Nikolas, and the prince let go. Several Spartans took a step towards them, but Nikolas raised his hand to halt them. "These helots are not with the rebellion!" the prince shouted at the men, and they fell back in line.

179

"There are children in there," Galen said.

Nikolas' eyes narrowed. "What? Did she tell you that?" he asked, indicating Korinna.

"I saw them myself."

Nikolas stepped back. "You were among them? The rebels?"

"It isn't like that."

"Do you mean to join them?" Nikolas asked. His voice was laced with hurt.

"No. I—I—," Galen stuttered.

"The men and women barricaded in the temple deserve their freedom," Korinna said suddenly.

"At what price?" Nikolas demanded. "The helots have taken my mother." Then, turning to face Galen, said, "We are at war with Persia, and now this…this…distraction!"

"It is part of Morfeo's plan," Galen urged in a whisper. "Believe me, please."

"I don't trust, Morfeo, if that's what you're getting at," Nikolas said quietly so that the nearby soldiers would not hear. He turned his helmet over in his hands. "You, wearing a cloak, a free man at my side," Nikolas said, "There's nothing I'd like more. But the rebellion has to be stopped before there can be talk of freedom and Morfeo is brought to justice."

"He is the root of all of this!" Galen said through gritted teeth.

"And what am I to do? Run? Stage a revolution now? Leandros is dead and I am not the king yet. First things first, Galen."

Galen looked over Nikolas' shoulder. There was a tense quiet in the air, as the helots and the army faced off, awaiting Morfeo's orders. But Morfeo was observing Galen and Nikolas from a distance.

Suddenly, they heard the grunt of a man in the front line, and watched in horror as a soldier fell to the ground, a spear sticking out of his neck. The Spartans put their shields up. At the entrance to the temple there was a scuffle. A young man, with thick biceps and an equally thick neck, was pushed out. "He's the one that threw the spear," a helot voice from inside called.

The Spartans roared, their line pulsing, eager to get into the temple. The helot darted left, then right, finally facing the phalanx, breathing hard. Then, Morfeo said something to Zoi they could not hear. She shook her head. Galen could see it, fear on her face. Morfeo whispered something in her ear, and she closed her eyes and took a deep breath. Her arms rose slowly. Her closed eyes twitched. From a distance, the sharp howls of dogs sounded.

Sensing what was to come, Korinna yelled, "There are children in there!" and rushed towards the temple. Galen gripped her by the waist, and she kicked his shins with her heels, trying to free herself.

Just then, the dog on Zoi's right leapt into the air with a deep snarl. It landed on the helot who had been pushed out, and they watched as the man dropped to the ground, his limbs flailing under the dog's savage attack. Zoi watched it all with her head cocked to the side, the way one might watch a pair of birds pecking harmlessly at one another. The man screamed one final, sickening note, then fell silent.

"She did that?" Nikolas asked, but didn't wait for an answer. His face became hard, his mouth a severe line. Then, he slid his helmet back onto his head. When he turned, Galen saw in Nikolas a gravity of expression he'd never seen before, even in the darkest days of agoge training, even when Timios had been at the whipping post. It stopped Galen cold, and filled him, too, with something else—confidence that a Sparta led by Nikolas was a country worth saving. "Get the little ones out, Galen. I'll do what I can here," Nikolas said before turning to join the ranks.

"Be careful," Galen called to him, but Nikolas didn't acknowledge it.

"Through the tunnel again," Galen said to Korinna, but before they could leave, they saw them, hundreds of wild dogs, and a few wolves, too, moving in a pack towards the temple. The animals snarled and bit at one another as they went, enraged. The two dogs at Zoi's side snapped at the wind. All the while, Zoi's hands ran over the backs of the animals, her fingers flexing as if she were playing some sort of instrument no one could see. The dogs were at her command, all of them, and they stopped before the temple, pawing the ground and howling.

Galen and Korinna reached the palace easily, went through the front doors, and wound their way to the tunnel entrance. They encountered no one in the halls. It seemed all of Sparta was gathered near and around the Bronze House.

Galen stopped before the passageway. "I'll go first," he said to Korinna, his eyes trained on the dark drop below. "We move fast. I'm not sure the tunnel held during the quakes. If I say run, you run, back to the palace," he said, and began lowering himself into the dark space.

Korinna laid a hand on his head and he paused. "Remember, I saw the children in a vision. Have faith." Galen nodded, and plunged into the cool tunnel. Korinna came down, feet first. He gripped her legs and eased her down. They picked their way in silence, stumbling over mounds of earth. Above them, wooden beams had cracked, and in places, the tunnel's ceiling had caved in, so that they could look up into the road above. The effect was that the tunnel was no longer dark, nor so hard to navigate, nor was it so secret anymore.

"Do you hear that?" Korinna asked as they approached the Bronze House. There was the sound of screaming people, yowling dogs, and underneath that racket, a faint, crackling.

"What is it?" Galen wondered, straining to make out the background noise. They slowed their pace a little, leaving the openings in the ceiling behind them. "Uff!" Galen uttered when he felt something hard ram him in the stomach.

The scent of burned things filled the tunnel. Galen turned and saw Korinna crouched down, her arms around a small figure. "It's all right," she was whispering.

The little girl Galen had seen earlier turned to face him. Her short hair was singed, as were the ends of her chiton. Tears had left streaks on her blackened cheeks. "The others? Did they follow you?" he asked, and watched as the child lifted her arm, pointing. Galen turned to see a line of sad, bedraggled children. The older ones carried the little ones on their hips. Some had been burned, others bitten. "Is this everyone?" Galen asked one of the oldest among them, a boy, around nine, carrying a toddler. Korinna took the child from his slight arms.

"No," the boy said, out of breath. "The viper sent them. The hounds. I've never seen dogs act that way. They didn't back away from spears, from swords, from anything. Dogs are usually smarter than that," the boy said.

Not ones being controlled, Galen thought. "Go on," he said. "Why the burns?"

"One of the men thought the dogs would yield to fire. They took torches off the walls and pointed them at the creatures. But that didn't stop them. Even with their fur burning they bit and tore with their claws," the boy said. He was crying now as he spoke, and he slid down the wall of the tunnel and hid his face in his hands.

"The temple caught fire," Galen said, finishing the story. "The helots are burning alive." *Gods, what has Zoi wrought?* "You," he said, getting down on his knees. "You're the oldest here. Watch the others. We'll be back." The boy nodded tersely, wiped his face, and got back on his feet.

Galen and Korinna ran the rest of the way to the Bronze House. The heat coming from the structure was staggering, but flames had not yet reached the entrance to the tunnel. Korinna approached it cautiously, but Galen pulled at her chiton. "There can't be anyone left," he said.

Korinna closed her eyes for a moment. "No. There's one," she said, and climbed up into the Bronze House. Galen made to follow her, but found that the statue of Athena still blocked the way, and while Korinna was small enough to squeeze past it, Galen could only get one shoulder out. Inside, the walls were ablaze and the smoke was so thick Korinna could no longer be seen. Galen could barely make out the bodies of helot men and women everywhere, as well as a few dogs and wolves. *A massacre*, he thought grimly. He heard screaming still, and more barking, but realized it was coming from outside the Bronze House. Clearly, the battle raged on beyond the burning temple.

He counted to ten, anxious for Korinna to return. "Korinna!" he yelled into the smoke, the crackling flames swallowing his voice. "Korinna!" he yelled again, this time so loudly that his throat felt raw. A burst of flames licked at the entrance, and Galen ducked to avoid it. He coughed into his shoulder then drew his chiton up over his mouth. Concentrating hard, Galen sent her as clear a thought as he could: *I need you alive, Korinna. I need you back here now.*

Galen waited a few beats, then saw her, walking like a crab towards him, a limp baby in her arms. He shouted at the sight of her, and his hands shook as he reached towards her. She handed the child to him while she climbed through the entrance. Galen held it awkwardly with one arm, and helped Korinna down with the other. He'd never held a baby before, and he trembled now, afraid to drop the tiny thing that could not be more than a month old. Its small head lobbed side to side as Galen moved, and its mouth was open. Its chest was very still.

"I don't think it's--"

"He lives!" she yelled, and sat on the floor, rubbing the child's limbs with her hands. She worked furiously, crying as her hands crawled all over the unmoving baby. She peered into its mouth, turned the small thing in her hands and thumped its back, whispering to it.

Galen confused the sound for the creaking of overhead timbers at first. Then, the baby's cries grew louder, and Korinna held it close against her body. "There, little one," she murmured. "Korinna's got you."

Galen was still crouched over, his hands on his knees, his fingernails digging into his skin. Now he straightened up.

"Here, hold him." Korinna thrust the wiggling baby into his arms while she adjusted her too-large chiton, retying the rope at her waist.

The baby quieted and looked up at him, its eyes crossing as it tried to focus. "You're a new thing, aren't you?" Galen asked. He'd never seen anything so small. "Korinna?" he called. "Will this one be free?" Galen looked up at Korinna expectantly, and she could not help but feel a twinge in her throat, tears menacing again at such hope.

She closed her eyes, and the vision came, bright and clear. A smile broke upon her face.

"That's good," Galen said, not waiting for her answer. "Gods, that's good," he said again, this time to the baby.

A high-pitched scream from within the Bronze House drew him out of himself. Galen looked at the nine surviving children, and handed the baby to the oldest boy. "What's your name?" he asked him.

"Cyr. My father was in there. And my mother. I don't-_"

"There's no time," Galen said. He didn't want to be cruel, but he was sure the tunnel would collapse at any moment. "You can grieve later." Galen had a place in mind for them—a helot community north of the village of Pitana. The men and women there worked mainly for Spartan farmers that kept to themselves. Galen hoped their homes were far enough removed from the palace and the Bronze House to have been spared military retribution for the rebellion. "Can you point to the north, Cyr?" Galen asked.

The boy waited a moment, got his bearings, then lifted an arm in the right direction. "Good. You lead them out, up into the farmlands. Find shelter and food."

Cyr nodded, but he hesitated. Galen saw the fear in his eyes. "Do you have a weapon?" he asked Cyr, who shook his head.

Galen cast his eyes around the tunnel. Up ahead, an ash tree had crashed through the ceiling, its pale branches jabbing at the earth. Quickly, Galen assessed the fallen tree, and with two hands, pulled a straight branch free. He peeled the leaves off the branch, and handed it to Cyr. "If you must defend yourself, there's no better wood than ash. And if you make it out of here alive, you can shape this into a fine spear."

The boy looked at Galen tearfully. Galen pushed him down the tunnel. "Go!" he yelled at Cyr, who straightened at once, gripped the ash branch, and herded the other children out.

Korinna closed her eyes again. "They will be safe," she said after a moment.

Galen watched them disappear down the tunnel, the baby's cries growing fainter the further they went. Then, he turned to Korinna. "Now where?" he asked.

"What do you mean?" she asked, puzzled.

"Close your eyes. Do the thing you do," Galen demanded. "Tell me what I have to do next!" He shifted from one foot to the next as he spoke, ready to move in whatever direction Korinna pointed.

Korinna looked away, rubbing dark ashes off her hands. When she spoke, it was in quiet tones. "Have you ever heard the songs of the heroes? Of Hercules or Achilles or Odysseus?" she asked.

"Of course! We're wasting time. The queen may be dead. Nikolas may be dead. Tell me what I--"

186

"That *is* the point, Galen," Korinna said, her voice steely now. "The heroes make decisions on their own."

"I'm no hero," Galen answered.

"Not yet."

His face had gone white. He was no hero, no matter what Korinna thought. But he knew she'd spoken some truth— he'd relied on Korinna's gifts so far, setting aside his own impulses for what seemed the surer route.

"I'm not always right," Korinna said, hearing his thoughts. She drew closer to him. His hand twitched at his side, brushing her hip. "The visions are not perfect."

"If the gods send them, how could they be wrong?" Galen asked.

"Who knows what the gods want? They bicker with each other. We are their playthings," Korinna said angrily. She swallowed hard a few times, looking as if she expected Artemis herself to come down and strike her for her blasphemy.

Galen settled his hand around her shoulder. He could feel her tremble a little. He gave her shoulder a reassuring squeeze before lifting his hand again. He cleared his throat. "The queen," he said. "We seek her out first. Nikolas can handle himself."

Korinna looked up at him, smiling. "A decision at last," she teased.

Galen said nothing, but took hold of her hand and led her back through the tunnel, towards the Eurypontid palace.

27

The late afternoon had brought rain then a frigid wind, and it felt unbearably cold underground. Galen kept from talking. He found the act of speaking made him feel even colder and sluggish. He was starving, too. Every so often, he'd hear a gurgle, his own rumbling insides embarrassing him. But there was no time for food. Galen's mind was at work, trying to guess where the queen might have been taken, and guarding a forlorn hope in his heart that Nikolas was still safe. Behind him, Korinna stumbled, righted herself, and rolled her head from side to side. *Pain again*, thought Galen.

"It's not so bad," she called back, but Galen was flooded with guilt anyway. *Why this link between us?* he wondered. *And why can't I sense her thoughts, too?*

"Not just your thoughts," she said, slowing down to walk beside him, her arms wrapped around her body. "I see what you see, layered over my own sight. Walking like this, both of us staring ahead, makes it easier. The two images fall into place, one a shadow of the other. I don't expect you'd understand," she said.

Thankfully, they came upon the entrance to the Eurypontid palace. Galen pushed debris away from the entrance, hoisted himself up, then lent Korinna a hand. Once they were above ground, Galen headed off in the direction of the queen's chambers.

"Where are we going?" Korinna asked.

"Can't you read my mind?"

"Your mind is all over the place at the moment," she said testily.

As if to prove her point, Galen stopped at once, then turned left. "The dining room," he called out. "There's a sword over the hearth. And some Spartan armor."

"A disguise!" Korinna said, and Galen turned for a moment, flashing her a wide smile.

"Maybe a Spartan can get the answers a helot cannot," he said.

They reached the dining room quickly. Galen listened at the heavy doors, remembering the last time he'd been there, overhearing Zoi and Morfeo plotting within. Now there was silence, but anger at the memory had already bubbled up in Galen's chest so that when he pushed open the doors, he did so forcefully, and the doors slammed against the walls loudly.

Galen cursed silently, and stepped into the empty room. The heavy chairs were turned over. Some were broken. Tapestries had been torn down. But there, above the hearth, was the sword. Beside it, hung a gleaming breastplate. "Must have been too heavy to take," Galen thought, imagining that the helot looters would not have left such treasures behind accidentally.

Nevertheless, Galen dragged a chair towards the hearth, stood on it, and reached up towards the sword. It wouldn't budge. "Can you help?" he asked.

Korinna stood on a chair beside him, but she was shorter, and no help at all. Galen stepped down, and patted his shoulders. "Hop on," he said. Korinna hitched up her chiton and threw one leg over Galen's shoulder. He could feel his cheeks growing hot. She steadied herself with her hand on his head, and Galen thought for an instant how pleasant it felt to have her touching his hair.

"You'll need a helmet, too," Korinna said quietly, having heard his thoughts.

Galen was about to agree with her when he suddenly felt the point of something sharp against his lower back. "Put the girl down," a deep voice said. Korinna spun around at the sound and lost her balance altogether. She fell to the floor with a thud, a whoosh of breath, then a little moan.

Moving fast, Galen turned to face a tall, slender man who appeared to be a helot. But before he could get a better look, the man had gripped Galen's wrist, twisted it hard, pulled Galen's arm behind his back and pressed him forcefully against the hearth.

"Who—?" Galen shouted in a rage.

"I ask the questions. What's your name?" the deep voice boomed behind him. Galen tuned his ears to Korinna's shuffling. It sounded as if she was kicking the man, but this seemed to have no effect. Trapped as he was, Galen found he could move his hand little by little, aiming to get at the dagger in his chiton without being noticed.

"Galenos, a helot," Galen answered. The sharp thing against his skin pulled back a little.

"Who is your master?" the voice growled at him.

"I work at the agoge. Feodoras is my master, may he rot in Tartarus when he dies," Galen added for good measure.

190

"The agoge? Prove it," the man said, and Galen fumbled with his chiton, drawing Nikolas' bronze cuff out.

"It belongs to Nikolas, Prince of the Eurypontids, and student of the agoge," Galen said. "I've stolen it," he added, assuming the helot was part of the rebellion.

"Liar," the voice said, but the weapon fell away from Galen's back, and he turned around at once. There, before him, was a wiry man, his hair kept short in the manner of the helots. Somehow, the man had been allowed a beard, and this grew in thick curls along his jaw and down his neck. The short sword he'd been holding fell, clattering in the hall. The man raised trembling fingers, calloused and rough, towards the bronze cuff, and touched it tenderly.

"Nikolas," he said, his voice breaking.

"What is this abou--?"

"Release me!" Korinna shouted. Galen looked down to see that the man had put his foot on her chest, pinning her down. He lifted his leg, and she scrambled to her feet, promptly kneeing the man in the groin. He fell like a stone.

Galen suppressed a smile. *I'll have to teach her how to use a spear next*, he thought, rushing over towards Korinna. But the man caught Galen by his chiton with quick, strong fingers.

Though doubled over on the ground, the man had managed to stop Galen from moving away. He narrowed his eyes at Galen, though there was no meanness in his gaze. "You must follow me," he said then coughed mightily. "You're needed at once."

"What is this about? And why should we trust you?"

The man's eyes went to the bronze cuff again, and Galen thought he saw longing there. "Because we are guarding Queen Isaura," he said gruffly. Galen tried to speak again, but the man stopped him by holding up his hand. Galen helped him to his feet. "Save your questions for now," he said, then, sadly, "and

191

your strength. I have a feeling you'll need it before this night is through."

28

They followed the helot man for a long while through the cold evening, eventually coming to a path where the forest grew thick on either side. The man kept his eyes on the brush, wary of any movement that might indicate a hungry animal. Though Galen tried asking questions, the man who'd eyed the bronze cuff so voraciously demanded silence.

Silence was not easy to achieve when they reached their destination, an hour's walk from the palace. There, in a wide clearing, stood a house. Its walls were made of sun-bleached coral, and planted all around the place were flowering bushes, so that it seemed that the house arose out of a rainbow-colored hill. From the top of the house rose a steady stream of smoke, and the smell of cooked fish filled the air.

"Where are we?" Galen asked.

"She calls it her 'little bit of Ithaca,'" the man said.

"The queen? This is her home?" Galen asked, relief coming so quickly that he felt all his muscles release their long-held tension at once. *I could fall asleep on the spot!* he thought happily.

Korinna seemed less pleased. When Galen turned towards her, his face alight with joy, he was shocked to see her worried expression.

The queen lives, he thought joyfully, but Korinna's countenance did not change. If anything, she seemed more upset. *What is it? What did you see?* Galen asked, but Korinna shook her head, and busied herself with the ends of her chiton.

"Her Majesty awaits," the helot said, opening the door for Galen and Korinna to pass through. Galen let Korinna take the lead. Before he could enter, he felt the hand of the helot on his shoulder, halting him. "Nikolas lives?" he asked expectantly.

"I saw him last three hours ago," Galen answered. The man seemed reassured, and squeezed Galen's shoulder thankfully.

Confusion and elation battled for control in Galen's mind as they waited in a small room laden with cozy pillows for sitting. When Queen Isaura entered and greeted them, Galen gave in to the comfort of seeing her alive.

"Your Majesty," he said, bowing before her. Galen could feel Korinna brushing his shoulder as she bowed as well. In the corner of the room, Helena and Diantha hugged one another joyfully at the sight of them, alive and well.

"It is a relief to see you, Galenos," the queen said. "And you've rescued our sibyl! I feared for her, once I heard of what happened at the Bronze House."

"It was a bloodbath," Korinna said, and Galen turned to look at her sharply. "What?" she said defensively. "It was a massacre, pure and simple. Her Majesty has the right to the truth."

"Korinna!" Galen warned, but the queen stayed him with a touch on his head.

194

"The sibyl is wise, Galenos," Isaura said. "Morfeo is a cruel man."

"It is only that I hope the sibyl has not made you feel unnecessary guilt for an order that you had no part of," he said, still staring at Korinna. "Morfeo seeks to destroy the Eurypontids."

"So, I've learned." The queen spoke in a low voice to Diantha and Helena, who took their leave with a deep bow.

"You were taken away," Galen said. "How did you come to safety, Your Majesty?

"They sent the wrong helot," the queen said, her eyes resting on the man who had confronted Galen in the village. "Thank you, Nilos," she said softly.

"You've no other guards here?" Korinna inquired.

"They say that the only free women in all of Greece are Spartan women," the queen said. "I've taken advantage of that. I staff my personal estate as I desire."

"I'm sure His Majesty, the king, wouldn't have liked that," Galen said quietly. "Nor Nikolas."

"I'm sure they wouldn't," she said, "if they knew." She winked, motioning to the soft seats around them. "Please sit," Isaura urged them. "The rest of you are dismissed," she said to the helots. "But you, Nilos, please stay. There may be news you want to hear." The tall man found a seat. He folded his big hands in his lap, and kept his gaze on the floor.

"What is this place, Your Majesty?" Galen asked.

Queen Isaura looked around the pleasant, warm room. Tables were draped with colorful silks, expensive things imported from the east. Scattered here and there were rugs and pillows. In the corner of the room, in a golden cage, was a mynah bird, its speckled feathers resembling a starry sky. The queen caught Galen's gaze on the creature.

"This place reminds me of home. That is Astron," she said fondly, stood and walked over to the cage. She opened it, and thrust in her hand. The bird pecked at a garnet ring on her

195

finger once, twice, then hopped onto her wrist, where it began to nudge a bracelet with a large, rough emerald in the center. She drew the aristocratic looking Astron out of his enclosure, and held him close to her breast. "Sweet one," she said to it.

"Sweet one," Astron said, replicating the queen's voice easily.

"My father kept mynahs in our home on Ithaca. We called them starlings there. They used to chatter all day to one another," the queen said, her eyes a bit unfocused, as if she were seeing that craggy island clearly. "It's the sound of home for me. And this place looks very much like my father's home on the coast."

"It is not easy being away from one's place of birth," Korinna said, as if lost in a sad memory herself.

The queen said nothing, only sat down again, and set Astron in her lap, where he picked at the silver embroidery on the queen's dress.

"Now," the queen said, "Nilos reports that you've seen Nikolas, and he is well."

"I saw him at the Bronze House, dressed in Spartan gear," Galen said. "He was sound. Eager to stop the rebellion." Galen stopped there, reluctant to reveal more and frighten the queen.

The queen dropped her shoulders and exhaled. "He's truly safe then," she said, nodding, as if assuring herself of it. Astron echoed her words, "Safe then," and the queen laughed and patted the small, glossy head.

For now, thought Galen. He rubbed his knees back and forth, unaware of how anxious he seemed.

"Tell her," Korinna exhorted him, and Galen's attention snapped to.

"Acayo intends to murder Nikolas, on Morfeo's orders," Galen said, spilling the words out so quickly that he wondered if Korinna had forced him somehow.

196

Nilos, the helot, looked up, startled. *He's quite loyal to the prince, isn't he?* Galen thought purposefully, and waited for Korinna's response. But she offered none, only closed her eyes and winced.

"Acayo told me himself," Galen added, sensing that Korinna was irritated by his partial truths.

Isaura bit her lip. "Why would Acayo tell you this?" she asked slowly.

Galen hesitated. "I don't know, Your Majesty," Galen said. "Acayo wants me to help." Galen was quiet.

What will she think of me? he thought miserably.

"Go on," Korinna whispered.

"He, um, Acayo, I mean, offered me my freedom in exchange for my assistance." Galen could not look the queen in the face. *Will she see it in me? My desire for liberty?*

"Your freedom," the queen said, sighing, "is an impossibility."

Galen felt a surge of anger. He looked over at Nilos, who sat gripping his short sword tightly. The man's beard was long. His manner assertive. *Nilos is a helot in name only*, Galen thought heatedly, then, looked at Korinna, who was shaking her head. *The queen has granted this man certain freedoms*, Galen thought without breaking his gaze.

The corners of Korinna's mouth were turned down, and her eyes were moist. She looked up to the ceiling, then, a note of resignation in her voice, said, "Ask her for it, Galen. Ask for your heart's desire."

It was as if Galen had been waiting for someone to prod him into action. He fell to his knees in supplication, conjuring the formal speeches he'd heard so often in the agoge. "Your Highness, Queen Isaura, wise as Athena, hear my entreaty. I am good with a spear. I have shown my loyalty to the House of the Eurypontids. I--"

"Galenos," the queen said, raising a hand to interrupt him.

"As I said, I can handle a spear. Just last week I sent a rough one through a notch in an ash tree, over fifty feet away. And I'm a fair wrestler."

"Galenos. Child."

"What I mean to say is that I would be useful to you. I once pledged what strength I had to you, and I shall keep that pledge, but grant me some freedom, kind queen, so that my oath is all the more valuable to you," Galen said. He'd placed his palms on the floor, and his forearms shook violently.

The queen covered her face with her hands. "Oh, Galenos," she sobbed through her fingers.

As if prompted, Astron hopped onto a nearby pillow, turned one, bright eye towards Galen, and said, "Oh, Galenos. My son. My son. My son." The bird would have gone on repeating it, staring all the while at Galen, had the queen not risen, cupped the bird in her hands, thrust it back into its cage and covered the cage with a blanket. The sound returned from within that small, dark space. It's squawking seemed a woeful song. "My son. My son. What have we done?"

29

For a few minutes, all movement in the room, all breathing it seemed, stopped.

"Should I remove the creature?" Nilos asked, and at once the bird began its refrain again.

"No," Isaura said. "The will of the gods is at work."

"They often speak through birds, yes," Nilos said, folding his arms and dropping his chin to his chest.

Queen Isaura told the story slowly, pausing now and again to weep, to dry her face with her gown, and continue. She told of the joy she shared with Leandros, when she learned she was having a child. It was during a sacrifice to Ares that her labor pains had begun. The tradition was to offer the life of a dog to Ares in the dead of night, in the hopes that the god would protect the army on the eve of battle. It had been hard for Isaura to watch the ephors holding down the fine, strong animal, pulling back its snout to expose its throat. She'd trained her eyes on the statue of Ares, an enormous, chained figure, symbolizing the god's best qualities—fearlessness, strength, and callousness—fettered to Sparta forever. The statue of Ares seemed to strain against its shackles before her, and she found it hard to stand upright. Her pains had begun, and she fought them as long as she could before whispering her condition into Leandros' ear.

"How quickly you were born, dear boy, as if you were eager to join the world, perhaps even join the ranks with your father." She said all this in a whisper; into a room so silent even the mynah bird had stopped rustling its wings to hear. "Cyteria, the Agiad queen, was one of your first visitors, and she carried with her young Acayo, a thin, colicky baby, and dared say that hers was the more handsome child.

"Then, the horrible prophecy," Isaura said. "'One Spartan prince will betray the other,' the sibyl said. And the rest that came a few days later, after it became clear that both princes still lived: 'The earth shall tremble. A mighty serpent will emerge from darkness. And Sparta will have no king.'"

"I wanted to run. Back to Ithaca with you, away from this damned place with its rules and rituals and horrid sibyl," Isaura said, lifting her head to face Galen for the first time, no longer to speak in mysteries. "But the ephors demanded your death for the sake of Sparta." This last she said derisively, her lips curling around the word "Sparta" as if it were a curse word.

"Me?" Galen asked, confused. "Why me?" It was the first thing he'd said since the queen had begun to tell the story, and it seemed like the only question worth asking. "Why me?" he asked again, his voice rough.

"That's what I asked," she said. "The ephors and the kings held counsel, trying to decide the best course of action. You've heard of what they do on Mount Taygetos, of course, of the practice of destroying infants that are unfit?" Galen nodded without meeting the queen's eyes. "They'd just come to discuss the mountain when a ragged dog came up behind Leandros and

200

nudged him. The ephors took it as a sign from Ares that the Eurypontids had been chosen to make the sacrifice." The queen laughed coldly, bitterly, then. "Do you know what the youngest ephor said to me later that night, after you were taken away? He said, 'If you make the right kinds of offerings, the gods might give you another child.' As if I would forget my Galenos so easily."

Isaura fell on her knees before Galen and Korinna, and they, shocked that the queen would so debase herself before them, could not speak. She took a hand of each of them in hers. Looking at Korinna, she cried, "May you never know the feeling of having a child you've borne torn from your breast. May the gods spare you that!" Then, to Galen, she said, "Forgive us. We did what we could to turn the tide of fate," and she wrapped her arms around Galen's legs, the way supplicants did at court.

"I—I still don't understand. Nikolas is the Eurypontid prince, he's--"

"My son," Nilos said. All heads turned to watch the helot, who'd grown pale. "My wife died in childbirth. I had fields to plow. I couldn't spend my days tending a baby. The king promised that my boy would grow up to be a prince, and I gave him my Nikolas. He's a good boy, I hear," Nilos said.

"Princely, in every way," Galen said, his voice husky. His head was swimming. He'd tried to tamp down his most unstable and violent thoughts. By now, Korinna had begun pressing the bridge of her nose, grimacing through the hurt.

"Leandros informed the ephors that he would not follow orders. What could they do, those old men?" Isaura said. "But your father believed in the prophecies. He didn't want to kill you, but he didn't want you in harm's way either, wrapped up in a fate of betrayal, the fall of Sparta on your small shoulders. So, Leandros and I made a choice. We gave you away, and adopted Nikolas."

"You put Nikolas in harm's way to save me?" Galen whispered. His stomach was aching, and there was a bitter taste in his mouth.

"How can I explain it?" Isaura cried out, rose, and walked back and forth across the room. "Leandros believed in the prophecy with all his heart. But he also believed that the Eurypontid line must not perish. We'd waited years for your birth, Galenos. There was no guarantee the gods would give us another baby," she said, clutching her hands. "We wanted to-- to keep you safe, and at the same time, protect Leandros' line. We--we needed a son to raise as the heir to the Eurypontid throne." Isaura, who always spoke so calmly, so precisely, stumbled over her speech now. She was speaking too quickly, the long-secreted truth rushing out.

"You thrust a helot boy into the jaws of fate," Galen said slowly.

"Nikolas is not the real prince. The prophecy has nothing to do with him," Korinna interrupted. "He would come to no harm."

"Is this situation not dangerous?" Galen said suddenly. "Are we not at war, right here in Sparta? He could be dead for all we know," he said, realizing then that Korinna probably *did* know. Embarrassed, Galen stared at the ground.

Isaura sat down. She wrung her hands, and said, "You don't understand. How can you? For years I had nightmares of what might have been, of your small body falling, head over foot, into the ravines at the bottom of Taygetos, though I knew that this never actually happened. I took comfort in Nikolas, who was not you, but who became dear to me after a time." She was quiet, and a deep, uncomfortable silence filled the room.

After a while, the queen said, "You were seven, the year Nikolas entered the agoge."

"I have few memories before that day," Galen said. "It's as if my life began when I met Nikolas."

202

Isaura swiped her eyes with the heel of her hand before speaking. "You'd been nursed in the village by a helot woman who was granted her freedom in exchange for the effort, then given over to Feodoras' care in the agoge."

"Feodoras was a brute to me," Galen said, and his voice sounded so dull and cold that the queen flinched and Nilos pressed his sword close.

"Leandros defied the ephors by saving you. For all they know, Nikolas is our son and the Eurypontids are a faithless line, a people that ignore the will of the gods. Galenos," she said, reaching out to touch him, "your father wanted you to be strong. In the agoge, at least, you'd learn what it meant to be a Spartan."

"Even though I would never rule anything but a kitchen." Then, after a moment of silence, Galen said: "Nikolas loves you."

"And I adore him. He is my son. Leandros and I never treated him otherwise." The queen stood gradually, coming to her full height before straightening her gown. "We Ithacans do not rely on sibyls," she said, eyeing Korinna for a moment before going on. "As such, we are free to follow our will, and worship the gods as is their due without fear." Isaura tapped her fingers against her dress. "Galen," she said. "Son." Galen met her eyes, trembling. "We've had the earthquakes, and my ladies-in-waiting claim to have seen a monster in the shape of a serpent, a drakaina. The helots have revolted," she said, glancing over at Nilos, who dropped his chin to his chest. "And so it seems that the Spartan Sibyl, raving mouth and all, knew what she was talking about. You must be careful. Do not trust Acayo. Stay away from him."

Korinna drew her arms and legs closer to her body. Nevertheless, she spoke up. "My mother's visions were godsent, Your Majesty. She was not hallucinating when she divined the future."

"Your mother?" Isaura asked, dumbfounded. Her mind seemed to work quickly. "Korinna, daughter of Meroe, I didn't realize it would be a night of reunions," she said softly, before looking meaningfully at Galen.

"You're wondering if I'm going to betray Acayo, as the prophecy said," Galen demanded. "Sparta has *two* princes! TWO. Didn't King Leandros think, even for a minute, that Acayo was the one to worry about?" Galen asked loudly, getting to his feet. He'd never approached the queen with anything but a bowed head and a full heart. Now, he strode to face her, his face hot with tears, his hands flexing at his sides.

The queen blinked slowly. "You're misunderstanding everything. We never believed the traitor would be you, Galenos. We were worried for your safety," she whispered, lowering her gaze.

"And how well you showed faith in me," he said in a whisper.

Galen spun around in frustration, grunting, then, kicking savagely at a pillow. It darted through the air, tassles fluttering, and struck the birdcage, which fell over in a jangling, clattering heap. The mynah bird flew out, resting on a beam near the roof. "My son," it said once, mockingly, then, began to preen its feathers. Galen threw another pillow at it and cursed aloud.

"Who else knows?" he asked.

"No one," the queen answered. "As I said, Leandros kept it from the ephors. For all they know, Leandros ignored their wishes and Nikolas is the prince."

"What about Morfeo?" Galen asked.

Isaura shook her head. "Nilos and I have kept the secret all these years. But I always thought that perhaps Cyteria knew. As I said before, she was one of your earliest visitors. She held you, and commented on the shape of your face, and the thickness of your hair. Later, once Nikolas had come to live with us, Cyteria visited again. I remember how my blood ran cold at the sight of her, staring at Nikolas with furrowed brow."

"If Cyteria worked it out, then Morfeo must know," Galen said, and began pacing the room sorrowfully. The mynah squawked again, without words this time, but loudly. There was a note of mockery in its call. Galen rushed towards the bird in a rage.

"Calm down," Korinna said. Her face was screwed up in pain at the rush of his thoughts.

"I'm sorry, Korinna!" Galen roared at her, turning away from the mynah that had grown quiet. "I just—I just—I can't just go to sleep or shut my mind off!"

"Your anger is justifiable," Korinna muttered, pressing the heels of her hands against her eyes.

"Justifiable? Justifiable? Gods, have I lost my mind? You!" he shouted, pointing at Korinna. "You knew all along! You saw this—this--" Galen scanned the room, as if he could snatch the word he needed from the air. "This act!" he said at last. "My whole life, Korinna. All of it has been a sham and a disgrace. For what? For a prophecy that would come true anyway?"

Galen spun on his heel and faced the queen. Nilos stood, drawing his sword, but Galen did not falter. He faced his mother, and said, "May Sparta become a kingless, lawless place. I wish it with all my heart. It is the kind of mad country you deserve."

Then, Galen left the room, ignoring Isaura's pleas behind him.

"Galen!" Korinna shouted.

The further away I get from you, Korinna, the better, he thought furiously. Behind him, he heard Korinna cry out, from pain or sadness, Galen could not tell.

30

Galen sought hard ground. He wanted to lie on it, his face exposed to the stars. He walked into the woods behind the queen's cottage, far enough that he could no longer hear his name being called, or the infernal squawking of that bird. The queen had not sent a guard, or Nilos, to come after him.

As he walked, he indulged in thoughts of what might have been. He couldn't help himself. Galen thought of Nikolas' chambers in the palace, of the prince's toy swords and shields, of his many nursemaids, tender-handed women who'd doted on the prince, and he wondered what it would have been like to grow up in such a way. Feodoras had scarred him, physical scars across his jaw, his face, on his back, and ones that nobody could see, for Galen carried them within, nurturing them with bile, waiting for a single, revengeful moment. The unfairness of it all angered him, confused him. And beneath all these thoughts—great pity for Nikolas, who'd been a helot for a few weeks only, and who might not survive learning the truth.

There was a little clearing about a half hour's walk from the house. The long grasses there were flattened. *Probably a deer's bed*, he thought. Galen lay down. A beehive nearby hummed with nighttime activity. The sky was bursting with pinpricks of light. Now and again, one of the stars shot across the heavens. The trajectory was never the same. Some seemed to be coming down to earth. Others followed the arc of the sky left to right. He considered Zeus and his vengeful thunderbolts and wished for a star to fall on Sparta, one big enough to put an end to it all—the Eurypontids, the Agiads, the drakaina in her cave, the ephors, Zoi and Korinna.

Korinna, he thought with a pang in his chest. This last thought hurt him most. Up until now, he'd been guarding his thoughts, conscious of the effect his milling brain had on her. He'd cared about her almost immediately, and Galen supposed that it was the dream that had done it. Galen had been hearing Korinna's voice in the dream for a long time. She was instantly familiar to him when he first saw her.

His thoughts skipped to Zoi, somewhere in Sparta now at Morfeo's side. Galen dug his heel into the earth, frustrated with himself. He'd sensed she was dangerous from the start. And yet, somehow, he'd been duped by a pair of pretty eyes and a pitiful story about Morfeo's "hold" on her.

Then he remembered something curious. Zoi had shown great fear at her first sight of Korinna. *Zoi has no reason to fear anyone, not with her strength*, Galen thought. He pondered this for a while, keeping thoughts of Isaura and Leandros at bay.

Sibyl, he thought as he looked up at the starry sky, *I've something to ask you.*

It took Korinna an hour to pick her way through the forest. Galen felt some regret at calling her in such a way when there might be beasts in the woods. But when she appeared, he saw she'd armed herself with a torch in one hand, and a short sword in the other.

"You've been thinking," Korinna said, her nose crunched up.

"Have I hurt you?" Galen asked, his eyes still on the sky.

"Not much. No." She bent down and dug a small, deep hole in the earth, then she shoved the torch into it, so that it stood without falling over, casting a circle of orangey light around them. She held the sword at her side.

"Nilos gave you the weapon?" Galen asked.

"Yes."

"Nikolas takes after him," Galen said.

"The queen told me that you resemble the king." They said nothing to one another. A small creature shuffled to the right of them, drawing Galen's attention. He took the sword from Korinna's hand.

"What was that for?" she asked, gesturing towards the sword.

"I stand a better chance against anything that comes too close," Galen argued. Korinna lunged for the weapon, but Galen was too quick. He smiled brightly while waving at her with the sword.

"You think too much of yourself right now," Korinna said.

"There's no besting an accomplished grappler," Galen said smugly.

"Indeed," Korinna said, before locking one of her ankles behind one of Galen's, and pushing him with both hands so that he fell on his backside. Even so, he did not let go of the sword as he hit the ground.

"Go flirt with some other prince," Galen said, brushing dirt off himself. Astonished, Korinna blinked thickly, then went for the sword again and missed.

"So easily distracted, this sibyl is," Galen taunted.

208

"Fine. Keep it," Korinna said. At first, Galen thought she was truly angry, but after a few tense moments, Korinna laughed. "I'm terrible with a sword, actually."

"I can tell," Galen said.

Just then, a gust of frigid wind blew through the canopy of trees overhead. The two of them watched as the branches swayed and crackled. When seen between the shifting leaves and branches the stars seemed to sputter one moment, shine the next. They watched the sky in silence before the wind strengthened, and a large bough fell to the ground, snapped in two by the wind. The limb and its leaves fell over the torch that Korinna had secured in the ground, snuffed it out, and broke it. A small flame burned among the broken twigs. It was hardly enough to keep the beasts of the night at bay.

Galen and Korinna took turns feeding the fire, but it wouldn't grow. The earth was moist and the flame flickered weakly. The broken torch wouldn't catch light.

"Thank the gods for the moonlight," Korinna said. The woods were washed in a bluish glow.

"We need fuel," Galen said, frustrated. "Stay here," Galen said, feeling for what was left of the smoking torch. Grabbing it at last, he got to his feet.

"Where are you--"

"Ssh," Galen said. "Listen. Do you hear them? The bees?"

Korinna said nothing, but soon, the sound came to Galen's ears again, the humming he'd heard when he'd first found the clearing.

"To the left, I think," Korinna said.

He walked slowly towards the sound, the smoldering torch in his hand. This would have to be a careful operation. To disturb a hive, a full hive, was to invite disaster. But Galen had seen the beekeepers in the city at their work, how they'd used smoke to quell the bees. Galen tiptoed towards the sound until he felt the vibrations of a thousand buzzing bees in the air.

He was sure of where he was when he felt one alight on his ear, and sting him there. Galen fought the urge to clap his hand over his ear. He'd deal with the stinger later. When the hive itself came into view, bathed in the moonlight, it looked like the head of a goddess, round and indifferent. He raised the smoking torch towards the hive and let the smoke envelope it. Galen listened for the dulling of the sound. It came a few minutes later. The buzzing had slowed. The bees, under the influence of the smoke, became slow and apathetic. With a swift strike, Galen knocked the hive down, and it cracked open on the ground. The hive crawled with the slow, smoke-drunk insects, and Galen had no problem at all rolling the tip of the torch in and out of the honeycomb, gathering globs of beeswax as he went. Some bees stuck to the sticky mass, and Galen felt a little sorry for them, beating their tiny wings and unable to take off.

Galen put distance between himself and the hive. Soon enough, the wind would clear the bees' heads, and they'd grow angry. Korinna had tended the small fire with kindling, and now it had grown a bit.

"I'll wager you've never seen this," Galen said, dipped the beeswax-laden torch into the fire, and watched as it burst into a bright, hard-to-look-at flame. Korinna's face came into view, clearly now, lit by the intense fire. Her eyes seemed to burn with a light of their own.

"Impressive," she said, then squinted at his ear. "You've been stung." She plucked the stinger from his earlobe in one deft move. Then, she dabbed a bit of the beeswax on the sting. "That should help with the pain," she said.

"Now you've taught me something," Galen laughed. "We're even."

A single bee crawled along Galen's shoulder. Its path was crooked, having lost its way in the haze of smoke. When Galen noticed it, he raised a hand to knock it off, but Korinna grabbed his wrist, stopping him. "My mother was called 'The Bee,' did you know?"

210

Galen shook his head. The insect crept closer to his neck. Everything in his body tensed. His ear ached from the first sting, and he didn't want another.

"Priestesses of Artemis are often associated with bees," Korinna whispered. She laid a finger along Galen's neck. He braced for the pain of the sting, but none came. The bee had sidled onto Korinna's finger, and she held it up, peering into its tiny face. "They say that bees travel to and from the underworld," she said. "Spartan tombs are hive-shaped for that reason."

"I've seen them," Galen said, remembering the funeral for Acayo's mother, Queen Cyteria, long ago. The tomb had resembled a massive hive. It made sense, really. If the bee could enter Hades at will, then a hive-shaped tomb seemed a good point of entrance to that dark, unknown place. But Galen hadn't known that sibyls were called "bees," too. Did their gifts come from Hades, that master of death?

"Maybe," Korinna said, reading his mind. "Some of us see past death, beyond our lives. Beyond the lives of everyone we know."

"Have you?"

"Only once," Korinna said. She twisted her hand so that the bee could walk right side up. It traveled past her knuckle and doubled back again, towards the tip of her finger. "Once, I thought I saw a place full of palaces. But they were tall, and they seemed to slice the sky, and their smooth surfaces glittered like bronze. And each palace held hundreds of people," she said, narrowing her eyes as if she might see it again. "I think it was a time far from now. I could be wrong. Maybe it was only a dream."

"I'd like to see such a place," Galen said. He didn't take his eyes off the bee. He was sure that it would sting her at any moment. "But only the gods are immortal."

"There is another way to live forever," Korinna said. "In the songs. The stories. The singers will tell of you some day."

Galen said nothing. They were back to this. His princedom. His destiny. "So, is that your new pet?" Galen asked, trying to change the subject.

"Of course not." Talking to the bee, she said, "Tiny one, give my mother a kiss from me." Then, as if it had understood her, the bee beat its wings, alighted on Galen's nose for a moment before disappearing into the dense forest.

"What was that?" Galen said, rubbing his nose.

"I suppose it gave you a kiss first," Korinna said, bursting with laughter. Their hilarity echoed in the darkness, but a wild dog answered it, howling long and low, cutting short their mirth. They sat closer to the torchlight. Korinna laid the sword on her lap again, and Galen did nothing to stop her.

"You called for me," she said, serious now. Her voice cracked a little as she spoke, and Galen sensed nervousness in her that he'd not felt before.

"I was wondering about Zoi," he began. "When she first saw you, back in the palace, her eyes went wild in terror. Later, when I overheard her talking with Morfeo, she seemed anxious about you."

Korinna thought for a minute. "I think it is guilt you sense in her."

Galen cleared his throat. "She'd mentioned what she'd done to your mother," he said roughly. Korinna turned her head and faced the torchlight. Galen was keenly aware of her movements. "After Meroe died," he said cautiously, "you ended up in Persia. How?"

"You want me to speak of my capture. The details are ugly."

"What does it matter now, Korinna?" Galen asked. He ran his hands through the fire before them. "See? If you swipe it, the fire does not burn. So tell the story quickly." Galen wasn't sure it was good advice. All he knew was that he no longer felt Isaura and Leandros' deception as sharply as he had at first. Perhaps it was good that the truth had come out this way, hastily, like a bolt from the blue. Perhaps he'd gone numb. Galen wiggled his toes, testing to see whether he still felt the ground beneath his sandals.

Korinna began. "I was taken from my Spartan homeland, enslaved as a child, torn from my mother, Meroe. It was Lamia's doing. She'd learned that my mother had called down the curse that turned her into a drakaina, and so Lamia convinced Morfeo to order my mother's execution."

"Why would Morfeo heed her?" Galen asked.

"Two reasons I can think of," Korinna said. "One, my mother's curse betrayed the goodness of her heart. Meroe turned against her own sister in order to protect children she didn't even know. A person like that, wielding so much power in Sparta, and full of good intentions, would be an obstacle for Morfeo, always."

"And the second reason?"

"Lamia loves him. Awful as he is. Morfeo feeds off her loyalty, though he doesn't return the feeling." Korinna and Galen were quiet for a moment. Galen didn't think Morfeo could love anyone. Certainly Acayo seemed to suffer from a lack of affection.

The torch leaned a little, and Korinna put out a finger to right it, before going on with her story. "Zoi put my mother to sleep, the only mercy offered her, and I watched as Meroe was burned alive, the skin flaking off her bones. My eyes went dark. I thought I'd gone blind, Galen. But then, I realized I'd been staring into the fire too long. That night, my hands and feet were bound. We travelled for weeks until we reached the Persian border, where I was to be sold to an Ionian farmer for twenty minae.

"I had my first vision in my master's cart on the way into Ionia. I saw the arrow that pierced the horse's left eye, well before it flew in the air. I cried to my captor in Greek, "Your horse is dead," and he climbed into the cart to bind my mouth closed. Then he heard the arrow zipping through the atmosphere, heard the whinnying cries of his horse, and the plunk of a second shaft where he'd been sitting. The would-be thieves, upon inspecting the cart, devoid of any goods except for me, left us alone and horseless in the Persian wilderness.

"I remember how the summer sun burned. The soles of my feet were torn to shreds as we walked to Babylonia. My value rose to one hundred minae once the farmer showed off my fortune-telling skills in the city square. The farmer became rich beyond his imagining at my sale. I was purchased by Darius, a Persian prince, and left at the temple of the Persian Sibyl, the old and wise Sambethe. We ate milk and bread and the occasional bit of lamb. We picked figs off the trees, and kept a pair of goats. Sambethe used to wash my hair in a creek near our home. She was kind, and eventually, I stopped crying through the night. Once I grew stronger, Sambethe trained me as best she could, teaching me the Persian tongue, how to speak a prophecy so that if my words resulted in tragedy, the blame could only be pinned on the interpreter, not the seer.

"Sambethe was like a balm to my hurt. She was powerful. Gifted. If you can imagine it, Galen, she wore her black hair long, having never cut it or combed it properly, and she embedded glass into her braids, so that if any man dared try to subdue her by pulling her hair, he'd be cut. Once, I saw her whip her long braid around and rip up a man's forearms. He'd asked her the price of my virginity." Korinna stopped, adjusted the torch, and cleared her throat.

"Sambethe was killed by a Greek prisoner of war. As she was dying, she offered one final protection, a gift to me. She warned of a plague upon any man who touched me without my consent—his limbs would rot and fall off. She had me carve the prophecy on a rock at the entrance to our temple so that all men who read it felt their wicked desires thin and disappear. And because she'd been so respected and feared in life, I was left alone, mercifully. I mourned Sambethe, my second mother, deeply."

Unconsciously, Galen slid away from Korinna. She laughed a little. "Let's see," she said, lifting his arm by the wrist. "Any bits of dying flesh? No? Then don't worry, Galen."

"I wasn't worried," he said, though he didn't sound convinced.

"Right before she died, Sambethe held my hands. She had one last vision, which brought a toothless smile to her face. Sambethe said something in an ancient language, one she'd not taught me. She gripped me hard, then her spirit left her. I never knew what that vision was." What came next was a whisper. "On the night Sambethe died, the night of my tenth birthday, I began to see another world shimmering before my eyes. When I'd look into the distance, I would see another landscape, my own Sparta, glimmering there out of reach. With some work, I trained myself to live in both places—Persia under my feet, and Sparta in my vision, like a gossamer veil, allowing me to see both into that world, and through it, into the one in which I actually lived.

"Dear gods, the headaches! My vision would cripple me. I had such a hard time of it, concentrating on two places at once! It felt as if my head would cleave in two. The guardians of the temple tied sashes over my mouth to dim my shrieks.

"And then, after the pain, I began to hear you, Galen, speaking to Nikolas, to that wretched Feodoras. I nearly went mad. I began to confuse prophecies. Worse still, I chose to look into your world instead of mine, forgetting to eat, to sleep. Watching you was like taking a powerful drug I could no longer resist."

Galen had been looking at Korinna as she spoke, watching the way her lips parted over her words, the white line of teeth showing now and again, her small chin dipping. She'd been facing the woods before her, her eyes wide and glossy, as if she were seeing these things, these places, again. Not knowing what else to do, Galen pulled one of her hands away from ground where it rested, and held it.

Emboldened, Korinna went on. "Because of me, the Persian army was defeated at Sestus by the Athenians. I hadn't been careful. I'd read the omens poorly. For that I was to be destroyed, as my mother had been—burned at a stake for the entertainment of the army—when Leandros' forces invaded.

"The Spartan soldiers broke into my temple at dawn. One of them slung me over his shoulder like a sack of flour, and yelled to the others, 'Sparta will have a sibyl again!' to which they cheered, and carried me off.

"And so you returned to Sparta, the land of your birth," Galen said.

"Here I am."

"And you've no idea why the visions started?"

"None," Korinna said.

"I know they hurt you. But I'm glad you see what I see, hear what--"

"—you hear," Korinna finished for him.

They looked at each other for a long, charged moment before Galen looked away. "Do you know what I'm thinking now?" he asked.

"You're scared. You feel betrayed."

Galen nodded. All his life, he'd watched the boys in the agoge, he'd trained with them, and had seen them join the military and the assembly. Some died. Many others came back wrapped in red cloaks to chat with Nestor, or to referee a wrestling match. And all the while, Galen cursed his helot blood. He hated the Spartans, too, for their arrogance and prejudices. Always, always, Galen felt that conflict, of wanting to be part of a world that oppressed him, then feeling small and ugly about his lack of pride.

216

It was good not to have to say it aloud, for some of those feelings shamed him.

"Have you seen anything else about our future?" Galen asked. Korinna's head shot up. "My future," he amended. She smiled, having caught a flicker from Galen's subconscious.

"No, nothing," she said.

"Korinna," Galen said, and held her gaze for a moment. He didn't shield his thoughts. They weren't worth shielding any more, and besides, regarding Korinna, his thinking was still muddled and smitten and afraid, all at once.

Korinna closed her eyes against the rush of feelings. The sound of another baying dog, this one closer, brought her back to the moment. "Yes, Galen?"

In the distance, a human scream sounded. More howling now, accompanied by barks and snarls. *We're not far from another helot village*, Galen thought darkly. An image came to him at once, of the red cloak Acayo had left in his sleeping quarters, and suddenly, Galen had had enough of sitting on the ground, stargazing.

"Let's end it," he said. Korinna smiled. She brought his hand up to her lips and kissed it. Galen couldn't help but laugh, but underneath that sudden, joyous feeling was a sense of purpose. "But first, we find Nikolas. We're going to need all the help we can get if we're going to slay a dragon."

Korinna nodded, stifled a yawn, and moved to rise. Noticing her tiredness, Galen suddenly realized that he felt exhaustion deep in his bones, too. He twisted the beeswax torch deeper into the earth, and laid down.

"What are you doing?" she asked.

"Resting," Galen said, closing his eyes.

"But the dogs," she began.

"We'll be safer if we trek through the woods at dawn. And we have my torch."

"And my sword," she added, pride in her voice.

217

"Perfect," Galen said. He felt the tickle of her shorn hair against his shoulder, and the heavy, reassuring weight of her head resting upon him. It took Galen a long time to fall asleep, but when he did, he dreamed of the red cloak again. When he woke, he wondered if Korinna shared his dreams.

31

Queen Isaura was waiting for them when they returned. She'd had the helots lay out a breakfast of figs, and barley bread soaked in wine. Galen and Isaura did not speak, but he let his mother fold him in a long embrace, and he dropped a soft kiss on her cheek, their tender gestures speaking of forgiveness.

Isaura and Korinna watched as Galen ate, and when he was done, they had their own meal. It was the first time in Galen's life that the custom of having men eating before women was done for his benefit, and already, he was uncomfortable with these aspects of his new identity. It had bothered him to eat while Korinna watched, to chew even as he heard her stomach rumble softly. She shook her head when he made an attempt to protest, and Isuara gently chastised him, saying, "Know your place, Galenos."

Later, when the table was cleared, Isaura presented Galen with a gift. In her hands was a luminous spear, its iron head a classic leaf shape, the rear point fatally sharp. But what made it special to Galen's eyes were the leather wrappings

219

along the shaft, dyed in the brightest crimson Galen had ever seen.

"Your father's," Isaura said, presenting Galen with the spear.

"I couldn't," he said, shaking his head.

"Leandros left it behind accidentally. This weapon has seen many battles, but none so important as the one you aim to fight. You look surprised that I know your intentions," she said, smiling softly. "I've been watching you for years. Every day you grow more and more like Leandros. Forgiving. Assertive. Brave. Duty-bound." She listed the characteristics with a measure of pride, as well as sadness, in her voice.

"You're too kind," Galen said. "Soft-hearted. Bullheaded. Reckless. Guilt-ridden. That's more like the truth."

"It's all about perspective, then," Isaura said, laughing softly. "Such qualities carry grave risks. It's best if you are armed well," she said more seriously.

Then, Isaura tilted the spear onto its end, jabbing the rear spike into the floor. She twisted the top half, revealing an ingenious bronze joint in the center of the shaft, and separated the two halves easily.

Galen couldn't contain himself. "I've never seen a spear like this!" he said, and took the two halves in his hands. He swung them like swords, the bronze rear-tip and the iron point flashing, the spear suddenly having become a doubly fatal weapon.

Isaura laughed. "Leandros always complained about the difficulty of traveling with these spears. Three yards of weapon is no easy thing for a soldier to bear on long-distance campaigns. So, he found a solution."

"It's amazing," Galen said, clicking the two halves together again. The seam was invisible.

They were all quiet for a moment. "Be careful," the queen said after a while. "Now that I have you, I can't bear to lose you a second time."

Overcome, Galen found he could not speak. Isaura took him in her arms, weeping over his shoulder. "Forgive us, son," she whispered.

"I will not let Morfeo destroy Sparta," Galen promised, by way of showing just how much he'd already forgiven her.

Isaura cupped Galen's face in her hands, squeezing hard, and when she let him go, her fingers twitched, as if she wished she could hold on to him forever.

They walked towards the city through a rose-colored dawn. Avoiding villages as they went, for they saw spirals of smoke here and there through the trees, Galen and Korinna took longer than they might have. They talked over their plan. First, they'd seek Nikolas, hoping that he'd returned to the agoge for the night. Then, they'd go straight to the Rock of the Sibyl. That's when things became tricky. How *did* one go about destroying a drakaina? And if they were successful, there was still Morfeo to deal with, and Zoi's vengeance when she learned what they'd done to her mother. But at least they'd have removed one weapon from Morfeo's armory.

If, if, if. The 'ifs' plagued them as they walked and talked. Galen found himself babbling after a while, uttering all the ideas that came to him without pausing to consider them first. So, he stopped himself, said, "I'm sorry, Korinna," and fiddled with the spear.

"You know," Galen said, tilting the spear, "this bit here is called a 'lizard-killer.' I'm thinking it's an apt name."

Korinna nodded. "Is it terrible," she asked, "that Lamia is my aunt and I feel such—such--"

"Hatred?" Galen supplied. "No. She had your mother killed. And if Morfeo had his way, he'd have killed mine," he

221

said. Thinking of Isaura this way, as his mother, felt strange, but right.

Korinna said nothing else, and Galen wished he could read more than sadness and frustration in her face. He reached out and touched her shorn head, which felt softer than his own. He felt a guilty pang whenever he thought about her hair.

They didn't speak again until they reached the edge of the woods, and Sparta spread out before them. It was a city in ruins. Buildings had come down in the earthquake, though the damage seemed random. Here and there, some houses stood as if nothing had happened. There were dead in the streets, covered with cloths and winding sheets. In the distance, funeral pyres had been lit, and the stench of burnt flesh filled the air. Galen scanned the area for soldiers, and saw a few stationed along the road. Their shoulders were slumped, and it was clear they'd been up all night.

"Hide the spear," Korinna whispered, and Galen undid the two halves again, tucking them under his chiton as best he could. There was no hiding the weapon entirely, but it would have to do. A helot had no business carrying a weapon such as that.

They stepped out onto the road headed to the agoge, keeping their heads down. "Breathe," Galen urged Korinna, who'd been holding her breath.

"Right," she said. "How could you tell?"

"You inhale loudly," Galen said, and glanced at Korinna, whose cheeks burned. "I like it, actually," Galen said, then, thought, *Gods, that was awkward.*

"So awkward," Korinna said, chuckling. "But also very sweet. I'm glad my breathing pleases you."

"Now you're making fun of me."

"A little."

"As long as you keep breathing," he said, feeling a twinge in his chest, as if the string of a lyre had been plucked in his body.

222

"I can't promise that," she said.

What are we talking about? Galen wondered, confused. The conversation had taken a strange turn. This time, Korinna did not answer his thoughts, and so he turned his attention to the road instead, focusing his mind on the deep ruts the cartwheels had made, and how they'd filled with water overnight.

They were only a few miles down the road when the buzz of a crowd pricked their ears. The building that housed the Spartan senate was hidden by a tangle of people standing outside the house, a hundred Spartans deep. The assembly was composed of twenty-eight Spartan men over the age of sixty. Evidently, a meeting had been called that morning, and the rest of the Spartan citizenry had amassed outside the Assembly House to listen to what was being said.

"We've walked into a hornet's nest," Korinna said, when a good many Spartan men turned to look at them, gripping their weapons. Clearly, the helots were now enemies of the state, and two young, unarmed helots made for easy targets.

Galen gripped Korinna's hand and led her towards the nearest building, where they ducked behind a low wall. "We have to find out what's going on in there," Galen said. The kings led the meetings of the assembly, which meant Morfeo was making a move.

"But how?" Korinna asked.

Galen looked around. They were in the courtyard of a Spartan home. Potted herbs dotted the area, and a line of wash hung in the early sunlight. Three drab chitons and a long, dark cloak dripped water onto the ground. Galen tore the last off the line, and held it up.

"Will it work?" he asked.

She closed her eyes. "Come on," she whispered, as if willing the future to unfold a little for her. Exasperated, she opened her eyes. "All I know is that we're going to try," she said.

"Good enough." Galen wrapped himself in the cloak, covering his head. "Do I look like an old man?"

"You look like a gigantic wet dishrag," Korinna said.

"It will do." He grabbed Korinna roughly by the upper arm, and began dragging her towards the Assembly House. For her part, Korinna played the role of captive well, sliding her feet this way and that, and letting her eyes roll to the back of her head.

Hidden by the cloak, Galen found it hard to see. Nevertheless, he pushed through the crowd. Some complained at first, but then it happened, a Spartan to Galen's right said, "Look. One of the ephors with a helot captive," and the rumor spread like fire, so that the people parted before him easily.

They stopped near the entrance to the assembly, close enough to see and hear Morfeo before the senators. Then, crouching, Galen pulled Korinna behind a pillar set close to the wall. It was a dark, private place, but Galen kept the wet cloak on, just in case.

The Assembly House had been built with long speeches in mind. A person had only to only whisper on the House floor, and his voice echoed loudly. Theaters were designed the same way, and Galen, who'd been to the theater but never the Assembly House, couldn't help but notice how similar the two places seemed.

Morfeo, on the senate floor, was putting on a performance. "Gentlemen of the Gerousia," he began, for that was the name of the assemblymen. "It is my terrible duty to inform you all that Queen Isaura of the Eurypontids was killed in yesterday's rebellion."

The men rustled, whispered to one another. A few shouted, "No!" and Galen remembered that that many members of the Assembly publically backed the Eurypontids. Galen's heart pounded. They'd only left Isaura in her home a few hours ago. How could it be?

Galen felt a fierce grip on his wrist, then, Korinna whispered in his, "It isn't true, Galen. He's trying to find her, but he hasn't yet. Trust me."

"You've seen it?" he asked, daring hope, and she nodded.

"Spartans!" Morfeo shouted, gaining their attention. "We have before us a dilemma. What is left of the Eurypontid line? A weak boy. A half-Ithacan who disobeyed orders at the Bronze House, attempted to keep our army from subduing the helot rebels, while our women, Spartan women, drew swords and spears yesterday against the helot foes, and died for their country. Nikolas is not worthy of the red cloak."

Some of the assemblymen rose to their feet. Those loyal to the Eurypontids cried, "Lies!" and the clank of swords being drawn was heard. Behind Galen, the great crowd of Spartans pushed and clamored, too.

"He'll bring a civil war upon us," Galen whispered to Korinna, who watched the proceedings wide-eyed and tremulous.

"This morning, the helot rebellion has been quashed, thanks to my leadership, and mine alone. Where was Nikolas in this?" Silence descended on the room. Galen could tell, they were all thinking about what they'd lost in the rebellion—their helots, perhaps even members of their family, the Bronze House burnt to the ground, and all this in the midst of the war with Persia, which had begun to demoralize the Spartans. Morfeo had timed it perfectly.

"I propose that we lay aside this partisan bickering. Eurypontid versus Agiad," Morfeo said, his hand waving lazily in the air, as if he were brushing away the two historic lines. "It has kept us back for far too long. City-states all over Greece answer to one king each. Even the Persians lay the crown upon one head. In this, Sparta falls behind."

The assembly exploded in uproar. "No country can match our strength!" one senator shouted, and the others bellowed in agreement.

"Friends," Morfeo drawled. "It is true that we Spartans are superior in everything. Warfare. Education. Our women. But I ask of you, when you throw a spear, do you use one hand or two?"

"One!" shouted an eager senator, and Galen saw the man bore a family resemblance to Morfeo—long nosed and slender.

"Yes, thank you. One," said Morfeo, "because a two-handed grip makes for faulty balance and an aim less true. Think on it, friends. Sparta needs one hand." Then, Morfeo raised a single fist in the air. Half of the senators applauded. The others watched in silence.

Morfeo scanned the crowd. "Years ago, the Spartan sibyl prophesied that Sparta was to have one prince if it was to survive. The god Ares himself chose the Eurypontids to make the sacrifice, but Leandros," here Morfeo paused, scanning the room, his mouth twisted in disgust. "Leandros ignored the advise of the ephors, and the prince Nikolas lived."

The crowd rustled. Their voices rose again. Morfeo hushed them with a loud shout, "Gentlemen! The kings are descended from Hercules! The gods have blessed us with divine leadership. And today, I will prove to you that a Sparta led by one house, one king, has the gods on its side!" he roared.

Morfeo opened a door behind him and stepped inside a dark room. The senators rumbled, some getting to their feet to see what Morfeo was up to. Galen wondered too, then spotted, down in the front, the five ephors in their cloaks. Anxiety gripped him. His disguise now seemed ill planned.

"As long as no one bothers to count them," Korinna said optimistically.

Then, Morfeo appeared, leading a bloody, dazed Zoi onto the scene. The senators gasped as one. Her chiton was torn in places, and the green scales that made up her skin glittered in the morning light, for the Assembly House was open to the air.

"The gods have sent us a weapon to crush our enemies," he said. Zoi stood, swaying side to side, her mouth open, her eyes wild. There was an open gash over her left eyebrow. "Poseidon's heir is on our side," Morfeo said, and gestured for Zoi to move near him. She did, and Morfeo drew a small, green snake from inside his chiton. It had wrapped itself gracefully around his fingers, sniffing the air as it moved.

Understanding dawned on Zoi's face, and she shook her head violently. Morfeo ignored her, grabbed her wrist roughly and put the snake in her hand. It lifted its head and flicked its tongue. "Show them," Morfeo said. Zoi touched the tiny head with the tip of her finger, and at once, the snake went limp, and lay draped over her hand like a bit of rope. Zoi shook her hand with a fierce shudder, and the dead snake fell to the floor.

"One touch, and the Persian king will be dead. One touch, and this war will be over!" Morfeo shouted.

Filled with pity, Galen stood, nearly rushing Morfeo at that moment. Korinna held onto one of his legs, whispering, "Stop," before he quit struggling against her.

Galen sat down hard. The assemblymen began their discussions, and the place filled with the clamor of men competing to be heard. Galen thumped his head against the marble wall a few times, frustrated. "This is killing her," Galen whispered.

"What we plan to do may finish the job," Korinna said.

"What?"

"Why do you think she follows Morfeo's orders?" Korinna asked.

"She said she fears him." Galen remembered Zoi in the tunnel. How she'd wept. How *human* she'd seemed.

"Zoi fears what Morfeo will do to her mother. Lamia is mortal, as is Zoi. Morfeo holds Lamia's life in his hands, for Lamia still loves him."

"It makes no sense for Zoi to be so loyal to Lamia," Galen argued. "The drakaina is a child killer. A beast."

"You can't help who you love," Korinna said softly.

"I can."

"Can you? Look upon Zoi now," she commanded.

Galen did. He could see that she was crying and that her hands shook, even as Morfeo pointed to her scales for the senators to gape at, even as Morfeo regaled them with her incredible powers. Galen's heart pounded with compassion.

"You loved her once," Korinna said. "And a part of you still does."

Galen shook his head. Zoi had had a choice. And she chose the path of conspiracy and murder. "She isn't like you," Galen said. There was more he wanted to say, but the words wouldn't come.

"You just met me," Korinna said, pulling away from him.

"So?"

"So you've lived your entire life in the agoge, without a kind word from anyone save Nikolas. You're confusing gentleness for affection."

"I know what I want," he said, turning to face Korinna.

"You've cleaved your heart in two, Galen," she said. "A heart can't work that way. Not the way it's meant to work. Like your spear. When it's in two pieces, the weapon isn't really a spear anymore, is it?"

"You sound like Morfeo, talking about two hands, two hearts."

"His example was a good one, though his point was flawed. I'm talking about you. You fall in love too quickly, Galen," she said, her eyes downcast.

He wanted to argue, but found he didn't have the words for it. He had often accused Nikolas of the same thing—of being too softhearted.

"I call for a vote," Morfeo's voice rang out then. "Those in favor of a Sparta ruled by one king, by me, raise your weapon." Short swords and spears went up, one at the time, the iron glinting and trembling. Zoi had been the deciding factor. Even as they voted, the senators could not tear their eyes away from Poseidon's great-granddaughter.

"What of the Eurypontid prince?" a lone, dissenting voice asked.

A wicked smile appeared on Morfeo's face. He bent down and picked up the lifeless snake, then gave it to Zoi. She looked at it in horror. Galen saw the gesture for what it was—a threat to Lamia's life. Zoi knew it, too. "We deal with traitors swiftly in Sparta," Morfeo announced. Then, he turned to Zoi, and said, "Go get him."

The corners of her mouth flickered, and suddenly Zoi seemed more awake than before. She rolled back her shoulders, assessed the crowd, and bolted out through a side door.

32

They were nearly trampled at the entrance to the Assembly House. Spartans dashed everywhere. Around them fights broke out right there on the street, some in defense of the Eurypontids, others siding with Morfeo and the Agiad line. Still others were running home, to either take up arms or prepare to flee.

When the crowd at the Assembly House thinned at last, Galen and Korinna wove through empty homes and cut across fields on the outskirts of town, desperate to beat Zoi to the agoge. But when they reached the agoge, they found it quiet. There were no students anywhere, and Galen guessed they'd been recruited to help tamp down the helot rebellion. He led Korinna back towards the helot sleeping areas, and these too, were vacant. Cots sat unmade, and no sounds came from the kitchen. Galen sat on his cot for a moment, gathering his thoughts. *Where would Nikolas be right now?* he wondered.

Korinna did not sit down. Instead, she lifted the red cloak that Acayo had offered Galen. "It's rightfully yours, you know," she said, and held it open, eyeing the cloth, twisting it here and there. Gently, she sat down beside Galen, and laid the cloak on his shoulders. Her fingers worked the bronze buckle easily, and it clicked into place, cool against his neck.

"I don't think--" Galen began to say, but stopped cold at the sight of Feodoras, stumbling into the tent.

"That's a pretty picture," Feodoras slurred, then coughed, spitting out a glob of blood that turned Galen's stomach.

Galen was on his feet at once. "Where is Nikolas?" he asked.

"You're making demands, now?" Feodoras asked, raising his finger at Galen's nose. The man leaned at an angle, lost his footing, and crashed into one of the other cots in the tent.

Without thinking, Galen extended a hand to help Feodoras to his feet. The man took it, and then, with the strength of someone sober and healthy, socked Galen in the eye.

"Blast!" Galen yelled, pulled the spear from within his chiton, and clicked the two halves together.

"Galen!" Korinna said. "He is ill. And drunk."

"You helots ruined everything with your little rebellion," Feodoras slurred. He coughed again, his chest making a hollow, whooping sound. A bit of blood colored the side of his mouth.

Galen tilted the spear so that the point pressed against Feodoras' forehead. The man stilled. "Once more. Where is Nikolas?" Galen asked.

Still, Feodoras was silent. Galen twisted the spear slowly in the palm of his hand, the point pressing hard against

231

Feodoras' brow. "You hold your fate in your hands, Feodoras, despite current appearances. Answer me," Galen said.

"Ares' temple," Feodoras said. "That's where they've put him." Feodoras' eyes crossed and uncrossed as he tried to focus on the end of the spear.

Galen dropped the spear. Feodoras swiped at his forehead and glanced in horror at the small smear of blood he saw on his fingers. "Will he live much longer, sibyl?" Galen asked Korinna aloud. Feodoras' eyes went wide as he took in Korinna's form, realization coming to him at once.

She closed her eyes. When she opened them, they were wet with pity. "No," she said softly. "He is diseased to the core."

Galen and Korinna turned to leave, halting at the entrance to the tent when Feodoras said, "You aren't fit to wear that cloak, boy." Then, he fell into another series of wracking coughs.

Galen gripped the spear tightly. "Forget him," Korinna said, clutching Galen's arm, "as the gods have." Together they sought the temple to the god of war.

Feodoras had been right. Gathered outside of Ares' temple, stood a ring of armored boys, but they weren't there to worship any god. Acayo led the pack, with Brutus and Linus flanking him. In the center of the circle stood Nikolas, shakily, wearing only his chiton. Nikolas' cloak lay on the ground, rumpled and stained.

"Bastards," Galen muttered. He took a few steps towards the tense gathering, then, stopped. "Korinna. Get out of here," he said, without turning around.

"Hardly," she said.

"Promise you won't get involved in whatever happens next. These boys are trained to kill. They won't care that you are a girl."

"You know what I've been through. I saw more in Persia than you can imagine."

"If you get hurt, I'll--"

"You'll do nothing," she said, her eyes wide open. "You will take your rightful place in Sparta. Swear it. Swear you will not endanger your destiny, Galen."

Again, Galen felt as if he'd lost track of the conversation. The voices of the students were growing louder.

"Swear it," Korinna said again.

I hate these one-sided conversations, he thought, then, asked aloud, "What have you seen?"

"Only that you are meant to be--"

"With you," Galen interrupted. She looked away. *I could kiss her*, he thought carelessly, forgetting for a moment that she'd heard it.

"Don't," she said.

"You could use one," Galen answered, and she punched him in the arm, without much force. Galen made a show of rubbing the spot. Then, he said, "Please. Stay back. We're running out of time."

Korinna looked at him for a moment, her eyes darting to and fro, as if she saw something in Galen's eyes that exposed how stubborn he could be. "Go," she said. Wordlessly, Galen pulled Acayo's dagger from his chiton, offering her the handle.

She nearly smiled. She took the weapon and hid behind a large, jagged rock.

Galen walked slowly towards the boys. A small creek separated the temple grounds from the agoge, and this he stepped in carefully, avoiding the slippery, moss-covered rocks. He was aware of the cloak brushing his calves, and the way the spear felt in his hands—light and well balanced. He did a quick count of the boys. There were twenty-three surrounding Nikolas, including Acayo.

So many are with Acayo, Galen thought. How easily
Morfeo had manipulated them. He'd used the Spartan fear of
the helotry against them. In all of Greece, the Spartans were the
only ones who'd let their slaves outnumber them, and an
uprising had always existed in the realm of possibility. But no
one would have guessed that a king of Sparta would stage the
rebellion, then turn around and crush it, sacrificing helots and
citizens alike, in the quest for power.

Now, he could hear them, taunting Nikolas:

"The Persians would have been defeated ages ago if not
for the incompetence of the Eurypontids!"

"Isaura coddled the helots! Her lack of discipline led to
the revolt!"

And then, as Galen approached, one of the boys cried at
him, "Treacherous slave! Wearing the cloak of the Spartan
army!" and another shouted, "There's your helot boyfriend,
Nikolas! Go give him a kiss!" and the others cheered.

But Acayo raised a single finger in the air, and the quiet
multiplied among the boys until all was silent. He stalked
towards Galen, haughty as ever, his own red cloak wrapped
around his body as if the wind were biting.

"It's taken you long enough," he growled. "You haven't
earned that cloak yet." His upper lip curled into a snarl. "These
boys are useless," he said, indicating the group behind him.
Acayo glanced at the spear. "You're armed. Good. There's an
audience, so you'll earn a fine reputation. You gut Nikolas and
all I have to do is prick him with this," he said, gesturing
towards a knife in his hand, the very weapon he'd used against
Galen back in the dining hall. Galen saw that the tip of the
knife was coated with thick, golden oil. "Viper's venom,"
Acayo said.

Galen craned his neck and saw that Nikolas was holding
his arm at an awkward angle, and he thought at once that the
prince's shoulder was dislocated. There was, too, a gash from
just beneath his eye down to his chin. It was not bleeding at the

moment, but Nikolas' chiton was stained with blood, as was his neck and chest. Nikolas looked up and tried to speak to Galen, but one of the boys pounded the hilt of a sword into his back, and Nikolas fell to his knees with a grunt.

"It doesn't look like you need me to do anything," Galen said to Acayo. "You've nearly killed Nikolas already."

Acayo looked past Galen, hesitating for a moment before he spoke. Then he whispered, "I'm going to be king." He lifted a thin, white hand, and wiggled his fingers. "These hands can't be bloodied by betrayal now, can they? There are so many witnesses, after all."

"Your father--" Galen began.

"My father has nothing to do with this! I haven't seen him since that mess at the Bronze House. I am the future of Sparta, and it is time for me to take control of things."

Galen thought of the prophecy again, "One Spartan prince will betray the other," and he wondered whether this was the moment. Acayo had been plotting betrayal all along. Then it hit him. This *was* that moment. A prince was going to betray another, but Nikolas had nothing to do with it.

"Lead the way," Galen said in a cold voice, hoping that Acayo would be fool enough to let an enemy walk behind him.

Acayo smiled, then headed back towards the yelling, charged up boys. Galen waited until they were near enough to the group before striking. He kicked Acayo hard behind his knees and the prince fell to the ground. Then, Galen stepped on Acayo's back and ran towards Nikolas.

Galen clicked open his spear, and faced the boys. Behind him, Acayo was trying to stand. Galen saw his reflection in one of the shields before him. Acayo's nose was bloody from hitting the ground, and he trembled with rage. But Galen couldn't focus on Acayo. Two of Acayo's cronies ran at him, and Galen took them down with ease, his father's spear whistling through the air as he jabbed at the boys. The other students of the agoge lowered their weapons at the sight.

Cautiously, Galen lowered his spear, too. "Traitors!" he yelled. "Let Prince Nikolas pass!" The boys did not move. The sun was going down behind him, and a flash of light reflected off a helmet caught his eye. On the curved, polished dome of the helmet he saw Acayo on his feet, the poisoned knife raised over his head.

"Galen!" Nikolas shouted, and burst through the line of boys with alarming speed, running past Galen and colliding with Acayo, his fist grazing Acayo's left cheek, the knife clattering to the ground.

"Now's not the time to hold back!" Galen yelled, running after Nikolas. Nikolas was infamous for it—going easy on competitors during a fight. And Galen saw it now, how Nikolas had thrown a short, weak punch, and not followed through with his whole body the way he ought to. His other arm hung limply by his side.

The next strike was Acayo's, and he staggered Nikolas with an open-handed wallop to the ear. Galen held his breath. His fingers wrapped tightly around the spear, his body tensed with anticipation. Once, twice, he tried stepping into the fight, but Nikolas and Acayo were like one person with many limbs, so closely where they grappling, and Galen feared injuring his friend. Around them, the boys shouted, carrying now the distinct note of a public fight—that eager peal that called others out to watch.

Some of the servants came out, those who'd not joined in the rebellion, and they crept closer to the fighting boys. Galen scanned the newcomers, and didn't see Maira among them. He wondered what had become of the old woman in yesterday's skirmishes. But Lasus, Maira's ancient companion was there, and he tugged at Galen's scarlet cloak and laughed.

"Playing dress up?" Lasus asked, just as Acayo landed another blow to Nikolas' ear. Nikolas shook his head, the way wet dogs did, then, put up his fists again.

236

"Watch the knife!" Galen yelled when he saw that Acayo had bent down to pick up the weapon.

"Your freedom, Galenos!" Acayo said, but Galen did not budge from Nikolas' side. Acayo lunged left, then right. Nikolas and Galen mirrored his movements. The Agiad prince was laughing as he moved, his feet light on the ground. Galen stepped forward with his father's spear, driving the point forward, but Acayo blocked the move with his shield.

The noise was so loud, that none of them noticed Zoi when she first arrived, her hair unruly about her, her chiton in shreds. Blue-green scales glittered around her waist, clinging there like barnacles. The pattern repeated itself down her thighs and up along her ribs before it disappeared behind the cloth of her chiton. She looked like a madwoman. Her chest heaved. Her fingers were bent like claws. The sight of her sent half of the spectators running.

"Galenos," she said lightly, and the sound of her voice reminded him of bronze being struck with a hammer—metallic and resonant. He turned towards her, and felt a stab of pity. Her hair hung over her face in thick, wet strands. She said his name again, "Galen?" but it was a question this time, as if she was still the girl she'd been, the girl who'd thought of him as more than an adversary.

"Zoi," Galen said, aware of the fight going on behind him, torn by the sight of her, and the sound of Nikolas, cursing foully as he struggled against Acayo.

He was about to say something, ask Zoi to join them, to come back to herself. That's when he felt the sharp sting of Acayo's poisoned blade near his elbow.

237

33

Galen could feel it at once; the heat of the poison worked its way up his arm. His legs crumpled beneath him. Nikolas dropped to Galen's side, vulnerable now to Acayo. Galen looked towards the boulder behind which Korinna hid, and saw her running full tilt towards him, the dagger flashing in her hand.

"The knife was poisoned," Galen managed to say, before he found that he could no longer move his mouth.

"Save him!" Nikolas yelled at Zoi, who stood as if dumbfounded at the sight. The liveliness was gone from her eyes. Though Galen's own vision was growing blurry, he noticed something strange about her expression. The more he watched her the stranger he felt, until he realized it at last. Zoi was no longer blinking. He remembered Korinna's story about Lamia, how she'd been cursed with open eyes, destined to witness the wreckage she caused without even a moment's reprieve. *Zoi's done too much. Gone too far*, Galen thought, then heard himself whimpering against the pain in his arm, spreading now and affecting his throat and neck.

Korinna was at his side next. She cradled his head in her lap, and he watched disinterestedly as she yelled something to Zoi. But he couldn't hear any of it. The world had gone mute. Nikolas was yelling, too, and Zoi's eyes moved from one to the other without closing. Not once. Korinna lowered her face towards him. *Tears*, he thought, but thinking the word took great effort. She didn't wipe them away.

Someone jolted Galen, and he watched as Acayo came forward, his knife high over his head. Nikolas reached for his shield, and covered himself and Galen at the last possible moment. Galen thought he felt the vibrations of the blade against the bronze shield, but he heard no clang.

Korinna's hands gripped Galen's chiton, and her face came close to his, like a giant, white moon. He longed to caress her cheek. His limbs were useless at this point. Was he dying? Is that what this was? *This is easier than I thought it would be*, he thought.

Then, he saw water rising around him. It bubbled and washed over him, covering his face. There were Korinna's hands on his chiton, and Nikolas' too, tugging him out of the rushing water, but it was no use. He thought he heard Korinna saying, "Please, Galen. Please," and he imagined he'd stepped into his old dream again. He watched as their feet slipped out from under them, and they tumbled into the water and disappeared from view.

From beneath the rising creek Galen saw how the water grew and foamed, knocking over Acayo and Linus and Brutus. Tentacles of water wrapped around their necks and threw them against the rock that housed the temple of Ares, knocking them unconscious. *How strange it all looks from down here*, Galen thought, and didn't notice that his lungs were filling with liquid. Above him stood Zoi, her hands conducting the spray.

Soon, the flood receded, and with it, the items inside the temple floated down towards the creek. The red scrap of Leonidas' cloth floated right over Galen's nose. He wanted to grab it, save it, but it drifted by and was soon out of sight. His vision collapsed into a tunnel, that closed slowly until there was no light left but a pinprick, and then, this too, disappeared.

Galen woke with his head in Korinna's soaked lap. Nikolas was sitting a few paces away, rotating his shoulder with ease. Zoi held Galen's arm, and the limb was freezing cold. Galen wondered what it had taken to draw out the poison, and if he'd ever feel warmth in that part of his body again. His chest and lungs ached, too, and when he drew breath, his whole body felt cold on the inside.

"You've saved him," Korinna said to Zoi, who shook her head, as if it had been nothing.

"Whose side are you really on?" Nikolas asked.

"None but my own," Zoi said.

"You will have to answer for your crimes against Sparta," Nikolas said.

"Is it not enough that I've saved both you twice now?" she said, gesturing towards the whipping post. Galen turned to look, and saw that they had tied up Acayo, Linus and Brutus to the pole. Even their mouths were bound.

"Well done," Galen said weakly.

"Exile then," Nikolas said to Zoi. His brows were knitted together.

Zoi looked away, and nodded. "I shall take my mother and go."

"She won't leave Morfeo," Korinna said.

"I'll convince her," Zoi said. Her eyes were filling with tears, and she could not blink them away.

"Cousin," Korinna said, laying a hand on Zoi's shoulder. She only said the one word, but it was so full of tenderness, that Galen looked away, feeling as if he were intruding.

"What if Lamia won't follow you?" Galen asked after a while. He cleared his throat, which ached a little still.

"I won't leave her," Zoi said.

"Sparta is not safe for you. You must go," Galen said.

"Are you volunteering to escort me out? To Messenia, Galen, you and me?" Zoi asked, but there was a touch of sadness in it.

Galen felt Korinna gripping his arm tightly. *I'm not going anywhere,* he thought, but still she did not relax her hold. Her mouth was set in a tight line. She was narrowing her eyes at Zoi, her gaze hard as bronze.

Ignoring Korinna, Zoi lowered her head, so that she spoke right into Galen's ear. "My mother can be good again. I know she can. She is heartbroken, that's all. Give me another chance, Galen. Give us a chance. I can be good again, too."

Galen felt a lump in his throat, as if he'd swallowed an egg whole. Even as she proclaimed her goodness, Zoi had not closed her eyes once. They were dry and reddened and had seen too much evil, much of it her doing.

"Get away from him, monster," Nikolas said, and pulled Zoi back by her chiton. "You murdered children back at the Bronze House. Everywhere there is the smell of bodies set on funeral pyres. You and Morfeo have brought ruin and terror to Sparta."

Zoi tossed back her hair and glared at Nikolas, the angry look all the more frightful because it was so fixed. "You speak of terror as if it isn't part of the Spartan fiber," she said. "Everyday your precious Spartans toss infants off Mount Taygetos if they are born ill-formed or weak. Every day, Nikolas. I did what I did to protect my mother. Morfeo holds her heart. He could crush her with an unkind word, not to mention a sword, or a torch, or poison. I followed Morfeo only to keep Lamia safe. Your kind does what it does to protect what? A reputation. The strongest city-state in all of Greece is also the cruelest. Tell me again, Your Highness, who is the monster?"

"Enough!" Korinna shouted, getting to her feet. She opened her mouth to speak, but was cut off by the sound of applause.

Stepping over the creek, which was back to its meager, trickling form, came Morfeo, and with him, fifty Spartan soldiers in red capes that hung still in the windless afternoon. To his right were the five ephors, their hoods drawn over their heads. Morfeo clapped slowly. "Well said, my darling," he called to Zoi. "It's amazing how well voices carry in these valleys. I heard everything. Again, I say, well said. Now that I know the extent of your loyalty, I can proceed with *eyes wide open*." He said this last slowly, maliciously, and Zoi averted her face.

"It is the sibyl!" one of the ephors called out, and Korinna wrapped her arms around Galen's body, burying her face in his chest.

"Stay away from her!" Galen said, struggling to stand, to drag Korinna with him. One of the Spartan soldiers chuckled. Others watched him with burning eyes, staring at the red cloak around Galen's shoulders as if it were sacrilegious.

"We've a celebration to attend, children," Morfeo said. "The new sibyl must be installed in the Rock. The full moon rises in a few hours." He clapped again, three short bursts of sound. "Shall we?" he said.

"I won't stand for this!" Nikolas yelled.

Morfeo made a show of looking around first left then right. "Has the Eurypontid princeling grown a spine?"

Nikolas dropped his shoulders and rushed Morfeo, who snapped his fingers, releasing one of the soldiers to intercede, ramming Nikolas with a shield and sending him flying backwards. Morfeo snapped his fingers again.

242

At once, the front line of soldiers moved. They took hold of Zoi, Korinna, Galen and Nikolas, dragging them to their feet.

"Acayo!" Morfeo shouted at his son, still lashed to the pole. "Perhaps you can refrain from embarrassing me further?"

A soldier loosened the cloth over Acayo's mouth. "Father," Acayo said gruffly once he was free to speak, "I am at your service."

"Of course you are," Morfeo said, then waved at a soldier, who promptly untied Acayo, leaving Linus and Brutus, who were still unconscious, tied to the pole.

Meanwhile, Galen struggled against the soldier who held him, but the man kicked Galen in the groin, then, tore the cloak from him, the bronze buckle scraping Galen's neck.

Morfeo picked up Galen's spear, the one that had been Leandros'. "Excellent," he said. Turning to the assembled force, Morfeo lifted the spear in the air. "See here. King Leandros' own weapon, in the hands of this treasonous scum. Where would you get such a fine lance?" Morfeo asked Galen, who said nothing. "Either Isaura, the Ithacan, or Nikolas, the traitor prince, armed this slave! What lengths the Eurypontids go to, my friends. If any of you still question the reason for the helot rebellion, look no futher than the Eurypontids!"

Morfeo undid the two halves of the spear expertly, having seen Leandros handle the weapon before, and tucked them behind his breastplate. With that, Morfeo gave the order, and the soldiers fell into line, dragging their captives up along the Hyakinthine Way, towards the Rock of the Sibyl.

34

From where he found himself, Galen could just make out the top of Korinna's head bobbing up and down as she was pulled along. One of the ephors was whispering to her. Galen saw her hand clamped tight over her ear, as if to block the sound.

Closer to him was Zoi. It had taken four soldiers to subdue her. The first three were put to sleep the moment Zoi touched them. The fourth approached warily from behind his shield. Zoi watched him with a lazy look in her eyes, the closest she could come to shutting them now. *It's a ruse*, Galen had thought, knowing that the soldier would think her tamed, and lower his defenses. But Morfeo had intervened, halting a few feet away from Zoi, and tapping the fourth soldier's helmet.

"Your Highness?" the soldier said, his eyes still on Zoi.

"May I see your spear?" Morfeo asked, taking the lance in his hands. Acayo, who had been walking alongside his father, eyed the weapon hungrily. Morfeo examined the length of it, spun the weapon around once, and pointed the butt-end at Zoi. Addressing Acayo now, Morfeo asked, "Tell me. What does one call this end of the spear?"

"That's the lizard-killer, father." Acayo glanced from the weapon to Zoi, back and forth, a few times.

"Very good. I think our friend here had forgotten that," Morfeo said, speaking to Zoi now. "You know, the Rock of the Sibyl is overrun with reptile vermin. Shall we conclude the installation of the new sibyl with an extermination?"

Acayo leered at Zoi. The soldiers looked to one another, confused. Zoi dropped her gaze, and when the soldier, spear in hand again, approached, she allowed him to press the tip of the spear against the small of her back, and guide her down the road that way.

The path was fairly smooth. The only thing marring the Hyakinthine Way were the unending ruts on the ground from the chariots and carts that traveled in and out of Sparta. Every so often, Galen's foot fell into one, making him stumble. When he did, the Spartan who had him by the upper arm jerked him hard, and said, "Keep up." There was no malice in that voice, just the sure tone of someone with a job to do.

Two soldiers behind Galen flanked Nikolas. They'd let go of his arms, but walked closely by the prince. Nikolas' lanky fingers flexed as he walked, and Galen recognized the feeling. His muscles, too, were tense, ready to spring, to fight, to flee. But then, his mind would churn, thinking things through to their logical conclusion. Four sixteen year olds, even with Zoi on their side, could not stand up against a company of Spartans. *Surely some of these men were loyal to the Eurypontids*, Galen thought. But none moved to help Nikolas, and Galen saw in each of the soldier's eyes a look of uncertainty, as if a threat had settled in among them. *They're following Morfeo*, thought Galen, *because they've no other choice at the moment.*

They went over a crest at the end of the road, making no sound at all but that of the crunching of earth under their feet. There was, too, the murmuring of the ephor up ahead, muttering still in Korinna's ear, though she turned away from the sound. Galen wondered if that particular man was her father, and felt a storm brewing in his chest, so strong, that he tried shaking himself free. But the soldier held on, and Galen only managed to tire himself out.

Finally, after a league or so, they reached the end of the road. From atop the hill, the Rock of the Sybil could be seen. This was not fertile ground. Tough, dry plants grew here and there, but mostly, the earth was sandy and rocky. Black moss clung to the underside of the big rocks. An olive tree, its branches bare, held in a fork of its trunk a massive, twiggy nest, long abandoned. There was a gaping hole in the side of the tree, where an immense branch had once grown. Glistening inside the hole was a twisted honeycomb, built so that it resembled an ocean wave. Galen stared at the hive, but saw no movement there. The bees had abandoned this place, too. The tree, the nest, the hive, and the dark mouth of the temple cave before them painted an ominous scene. Even the soldiers slowed their pace a little, and those in the front hung back, hesitant to get any closer.

For a fraught hour they stood there, waiting for the sun to finally sink beneath the horizon. Again and again, Galen thought, *what do I do?* And Korinna would shake her head each time his thoughts reached her. Zoi had stood facing the cave, not moving. When the last flash of orange sunlight was snuffed out, the oldest ephor bent low to the ground, struck a bit of flint he'd been carrying, and started a small fire. The others fed it with twigs and dried leaves. It was not a big flame, but it lit up the night. They mumbled words over the fire, a ceremonial light with which to inaugurate the new sibyl. Then, the ephors turned as one, solemnly, and addressed the assembled force.

246

"Men of Sparta, you have set your eyes on this sacred Sanctuary of Artemis Orthia, the Rock of the Sibyl, and you have delivered the new sibyl to her home. Go forth now, for the rituals of the goddess are not for soldiers' eyes," said one of the ephors.

The soldiers rustled their shields, looked to one another, and finally turned to their commander, a man with gray hair that brushed his shoulders. "What of the prince, the witch and the helot?" the commander asked. Zoi turned sharply at the word "witch," but the soldier holding the spear to her back pressed forward. She arched her spine but made no other move.

"They are to stay," Morfeo said, and the ephors dipped their heads in agreement.

The commanding officer asked, "They will run, Your Majesty. Even the animals flee from this place."

"The prince and the helot won't leave their precious sibyl," Morfeo said with a sneer. Korinna was in the hands of the ephors, held too tightly for her to get away. "And the other girl, the 'witch' as you aptly called her, has other…obligations tying her to this place, wouldn't you agree, Zoi?"

Zoi looked at Morfeo with blazing eyes. A sharp wind came to life among them, rattling the dry branches. It died away just as quickly.

Reluctantly, the soldiers released them all, then headed back up the Hyakinthine Way, the moonlight glimmering on their armor.

Galen ran to Korinna as soon as the soldiers disappeared over the crest. She was still being held by one of the ephors. "Let her go," he said. The ephor laughed, a low sound, then he slid a long finger between the hem of his hood and his cheek. The fabric fell back, and now Galen was face to face with a man. Just a man. The ephor was old, yes, but his eyes were dark, his cheeks pockmarked from the acne of his adolescence, and long hairs grew out of his nose.

"There is no escaping what the gods wish, boy," the ephor said. Another stepped forward, and he, too, pushed back his hood. This man was younger, his beard reddish and streaked with gray, and his eyes were small and dark. He had a smattering of freckles on his nose and cheeks, and even some on his eyelids. *Like Korinna*, Galen thought, and she turned slowly towards the man who could be her father, as if looking for the resemblance too.

Suddenly, from deep within the cavern, there came a sound like a wind, a low note that stopped up Galen's ears and nose. He wondered if this was the venting of some sacred vapors, the very fumes that Meroe had inhaled long ago.

All eyes turned towards the cave. A dark shadow was moving within. Galen stared into the gloom fixedly. But the dark shadow would not make itself known. One of the ephors, finding courage somewhere in his heart, stepped forward, and with a shaky voice called, "Drakaina, god-cursed, we bring you gifts to satisfy your hunger and soothe the goddess."

There was a rattling sound from within, a series of clicks that sped up, then slowed down. It sounded to Galen like the kind of noises one heard in a forest at night, emerging from unknown throats. Then, a bright object rolled out of the cave, bouncing rapidly until it stopped at the foot of the ephor who had spoken. It was a human skull. A small one. And it gleamed brightly before them, licked clean.

"I guess she's not hungry," Acayo taunted, though he was backing away into the murky night as he spoke.

"That's it. I've had enough of him," Zoi said under her breath, striding towards Acayo purposefully. When she reached him, he looked up at her with fear in his eyes, and she clamped her hand over his face. Acayo's eyes rolled back, and he slumped to the ground, his arm underneath his body bent at a painful looking angle.

"Is he dead?" Nikolas asked, rushing towards the fallen boy.

248

"No. Sleeping," Zoi said, pushed past Nikolas, past the ephors, and into the cave. No one moved to stop her.

"This cannot go on, Morfeo," the red-bearded ephor said when Zoi disappeared into the cave.

The ancient one chimed in, "We've assisted you in this in every possible way."

"We allowed underage boys to join the Crypteia," said another.

"We fed the insurrection with gossip among our helots."

"Sent Leandros on an ill-fated campaign."

"You promised that the drakaina would bend to your will, that she desired to see you installed as Sparta's only king," said the red-bearded ephor. "You claim only you can control the monster in the cave. Do so now."

The oldest one spoke again. "Sparta can have one king, or twenty, it doesn't matter." He paused, coughing. "Our strength comes from the gods, and the gods speak through a sibyl. We have brought many women gifted with the sight to this accursed place. Ten years of it! And the drakhaina has devoured them all." The ephor shuffled over to Korinna and drew a long fingernail across her cheek. She recoiled, swallowing hard. "This one has great strength, Morfeo," he went on. "The drakhaina *must* accept her. Sparta's fate rests in our faith in the gods. Without a sibyl's sight, we cannot defeat Persia." He lifted his cane in the air and pointed it accusingly at Morfeo. "If you succeed, you will have statues cast in your honor. Now you must act."

Just then, they heard the sound of Zoi's voice coming from inside the cave. "Mother," she was pleading. "Mother, please stay with me. They're only using you. Believe me."

Then came Lamia's rattling, crackling voice, like a thing long unused. "Morfeo?" she called. "Are you there? It's been so long, my love."

35

When she emerged, the ephors took a step back as one.
Galen and Nikolas stood their ground. She crawled on her
hands, her breasts and stomach dragging along the hard floor.
Where her legs should have been was a tail, emerging from her
hips with no seeming end. While Zoi's skin was mottled in
green scales, Lamia's scales were a deep red, the color of
pomegranate seeds, struck through with golden spots here and
there. They were on her hands, her back, even her face and lips.
She seemed brittle to the touch, and her rough skin scraped the
ground noisily. Even so, Zoi clung to her mother's hips, her
feet seeking purchase, trying to stop her from leaving the cave.

Morfeo stood before Lamia. She rose up on her tail,
coiling it beneath her to form a massive, glittering base for her
upper body. Towering over Morfeo, the drakaina looked at the
king sleepily, unable to close her eyes. A gust of vapor from
within the cave whipped up Lamia's lanky, dark hair, and it
brushed Morfeo's face. Galen saw him shudder.

"I've brought you a gift," Morfeo said, pointing at Nikolas and Galen.

At once, Galen and Nikolas searched the ground together, looking for more jagged rocks, for sticks, for weapons of any kind. "Be still," one of the ephors hissed at them, and Galen sent a coarse gesture their way, resuming the search for something sharp or blunt with which to defend himself. Then, he stopped, and looked at the ephors again. He remembered the dagger he'd given Korinna. She was looking Galen's way. *You have the dagger still?* Galen asked in his mind, and saw as Korinna nodded. Luckily, the ephor gripping her had loosened his hold. *Then, I'm coming for it,* the thought.

"On three, Nikolas," Galen said, crouching. "One, two…"

"On three what?" Nikolas asked.

"Three," Galen said quietly, and dashed off towards the ephors, who were concentrating on Lamia and Morfeo. Galen threw an elbow at the nearest ephor's chin, knocking the man backwards. Another ephor raised his knife, aiming for the back of Galen's head, but Nikolas blocked him with a savage kick to the man's arm. The knife clattered to the ground, and Nikolas picked it up. As Korinna ran past Galen, she handed the dagger she'd been hiding to him. But it was all for naught. Galen and Nikolas were quickly surrounded by the ephors, their four knives pointed at them.

"Drop the weapons," the red-bearded ephor said. "Kick them here," the man added, and Galen and Nikolas complied. He strode over towards Galen, took hold of his chin and pushed it back, exposing Galen's neck. The knifepoint rose, and the metal caught the moonlight. But in pulling his arm back, the ephor struck the olive tree forcefully, and suddenly, a great thrumming sound filled their ears.

The man screamed, and Galen saw the beginnings of a swarm. The hive was not dead. The bees had only been asleep, deep inside the tree. They clamped onto the ephor's face, alighted on his eyelids and crawled into his mouth. He ran, and the other ephors followed after him, the red-bearded man's screams resounding in the night. Behind them, a cloud of buzzing, stinging bees shadowed them.

Though they ran away wildly, the ephors had taken their weapons. Morfeo had been watching it all without moving to help. Lamia swayed at his side. When the ephors were gone from sight, Morfeo's shoulders seemed to relax, as if an unpleasant element of the evening had been done away with easily. He'd grown paler, and his skin reflected the moonlight.

"It's no easy task nourishing a prophecy," he said indifferently. "Up and down Greece, oracles and seers and sibyls sniff the poisons that rise from the earth and see visions," he sneered. "It is nonsense, all of it." He looked at the boys then, his eyes fell on Korinna. "Sibyls? More like swindlers. Addicts to the fumes that feed their sight."

"Explain Lamia's curse, then!" Korinna yelled at him.

Lamia hissed, drew up to her full height, then sunk down lazily again, as if the effort was too much for her.

"Hold your tongue," Morfeo said at once. "Is Lamia cursed? That is for the gods to know." As he spoke, he stroked one of Lamia's arms, and she, sleepy-eyed seemed to relish his touch. "It is the prophecies that I take advantage of. The sibyl plants a seed, and that seed grows in the minds of those who hear the prophecy, gaining strength until there is no way to undo the people's conviction. Kings have been exiled, princesses have been murdered, and we have gone to war because of these idiotic divinations.

"But the sibyls of the world are tricksters, and they keep their predictions vague and hazy. This is where an ambitious man steps in. We make of them what we will. So, Meroe inhales the smoke of the earth, and says that one Spartan prince will betray the other, and that the world will rock with the force of an earthquake, and that a viper will rise." Morfeo looked at Lamia. He laughed bitterly, sounding slightly mad. "The earth

252

shakes under Sparta every few years, where's the wonder in that? It was just a matter of time before an earthquake struck again. As for the viper, Lamia and Zoi were under our noses all this time. Then, there's the matter of the Spartan prince," Morfeo said, and glared directly at Galen.

"Stop!" Galen yelled, frantic. He'd planned on telling Nikolas about his parentage in a different way. A gentle way. Not like this.

"Does His Highness know who he really is?" Morfeo asked, smiling with pleasure.

"What is he talking about?" Nikolas asked.

Morfeo laughed again, throwing his head back and enjoying the moment. Then, just as quickly, he grew stone-faced again, and addressed Galen. "I knew you would want to help Nikolas the night of the Crypteia. Of course, you would." Morfeo glanced at Acayo, still asleep on the ground. "Acayo was to do away with you first, and then Nikolas. He failed on both counts. The Eurypontids have been difficult to kill," Morfeo said, clenching his teeth as if he suddenly realized something. He looked anxiously at Lamia, who tilted her head towards him, a sickening smile on her face. It seemed to embolden Morfeo. He released a deep breath, saying, "But now that we're here, the drakhaina will do the job nicely."

At this, both Nikolas and Galen yelled, "Traitor!" and bent down to pick up stones, bent on hurling them at Morfeo and Lamia. With a whisper, Lamia slithered away from Morfeo, quickly, moving faster than a lightning strike, and took hold of Korinna. She gasped, struggled against the strong arm that held her, her cries filling Galen's ears.

"No!" Galen said, and he released the stones in his hands at once.

Morfeo assembled Leandros' spear slowly. "Move an inch, and the girl's head will join this one," he said, kicking hard at the skull so that it skittered far away from them. Galen jerked towards Morfeo, then stopped at the sound of Korinna's whimper. Lamia's scales had sliced the skin on her legs, wounds deep enough to hurt but not kill. Galen stood motionless again, breathing hard.

"I made a promise to the ephors that I intend to keep. History will remember those who sided with the Agiads. Sparta is on the cusp of conquering all of Greece," Morfeo said. He gave Korinna one long, appreciative look. "With the help of the new sibyl, of course. It ends here!" Morfeo bellowed into the darkness. "A prince of Sparta will betray the other," Morfeo said, his voice low and deadly. "When the dust of war settles over Sparta, the ephors will tell the Assembly how the treacherous Nikolas allied with the helotry to bring about a rebellion, betraying the noble Acayo in the process. The sibyl's prophecy will have come true in every regard, and the ascension of the Agiads will seem…" Morfeo stopped, his eyes turned to the dark sky as he thought of the right word. "Fated," he said. "No one will question the will of the gods."

"You said you don't believe in prophecies," Galen shouted, then thought, clearly enough for Korinna to hear: *But I do.*

"You are right," said Morfeo. "I just like it when things work out according to plan," he said, and sighed, pleased. Then, he turned dark, watery eyes to Galen and said, "Your deaths will pave the way for a new Sparta."

"We won't go easily," Galen said.

Morfeo squeezed the bridge of his nose and sighed in frustration. "Lamia is going to have you for dinner the hard way then." Morfeo was mad, that was clear now.

Lamia bent low and nuzzled Morfeo's neck. "How I've missed you," she said. "Seeing you now quells my hunger." Korinna struggled against Lamia, and each time her legs brushed against the drakhaina's body, she drew more blood.

"If your stomach is full, satisfy your vengeance instead," Morfeo said. "Start with that boy over there, Nikolas, so-called prince of the Eurypontids. His birth was welcomed, cheered, considered a blessing. Picture his mother, an Ithacan of all things, lounging about, peering into his eyes and squeezing his pudgy legs. Then think of what was taken from you." Lamia's tongue flickered moistly. "Then, move on to the parentless slave and take him out of his misery," Morfeo said.

"We won't run, no matter what," Nikolas whispered to Galen. Korinna fought on, while Zoi had begun tugging on her mother's arms, trying to loosen her hold on Korinna.

Galen's feeling of pride in his friends strengthened his will, and so his feet did not budge from the spot. Come glory or Hades, he would fight.

Lamia's huge eyes latched onto Morfeo as if he were the only other creature in the world. She seemed to settle into her massive, coiled tail. Her scales made a rattling sound. Zoi wrapped her arms around her mother's body, weeping openly. "Don't listen to him, mother. Don't. We can go away, the two of us," she begged.

Galen's heart beat with pity. It was all Zoi wanted, after all, to get away, to start a new life. It was what he had wanted once, too. Galen looked at Korinna, and saw that she, too, was weeping.

Morfeo pressed on ruthlessly. "What did you have, but a dark cave and a dim memory of your own baby boy? Take the prince now, as well as his slave, and settle the score the Fates have laid out for you. For us."

Zoi stared at Morfeo. "How dare you? You allowed Cyteria to kill Thanos."

At the sound of her baby boy's name, Lamia stiffened. Then, a shiver ran down her body, ending with a whip of her tail. She looked at Morfeo again, and a horrible grimace came to her face, her mouth opening with a hiss. Galen had expected fangs. Her grin was somehow more dreadful with a mouth full of blunt, human teeth. She stared intensely at Morfeo.

255

"Thanos lives!" Morfeo said, his voice shrill. "If only you'll help me now, Lamia, I promise you will see him again! Destroy the Eurypontids, once and for all!"

"Lies, Mother!" Zoi shouted. "He changes the story to suit the moment!" But already, Lamia's will had softened. Her great, unblinking eyes shone with tears.

"My baby, you say?" Lamia asked.

"For your assistance." He looked towards Nikolas again. "An exchange," Morfeo said. "Kill the boys, allow a new sibyl into the Temple of Artemis Orthia, and you will see Thanos again."

Lamia shook her head. She uncoiled herself. Then, she looked beyond Galen and Nikolas, each of them holding the sharpest edged stone they could find. Her eyes fell on Acayo, slumped over on the ground, still asleep. The drakaina seemed to swoon. Korinna slipped from her arms and tumbled to the ground.

"Look at me, Lamia!" Morfeo shouted. "The Eurypontids are our enemies! Wipe them from the earth!"

But Lamia's focus was elsewhere. "Thanos," they heard her say, and she swept past Morfeo towards Acayo. The length of her body took up the entire space between the cave and the rock where Acayo lay snoring.

They watched in horror as Lamia turned Acayo over. She grazed his cheek with her yellowed fingernails, shouting, "By the gods, Morfeo, our son looks just like you!" She sniffed Acayo as if he were a meal.

They heard Lamia calling, "Thanos? Thanos?" It sounded as if she were waking the boy up from a long nap.

"That is not Thanos," Morfeo screamed. "I'll bring Thanos to you later, if you do as I say."

"I have made no mistake," Lamia said, purring now in Acayo's ear. "My boy. You take after your father so. Lucky, lucky child," she said. Acayo's eyes fluttered open, and when they focused on the being hovering over him, he screamed.

256

Lamia jerked up, her hands clutched over her ears. "Ah, this curse! My own blood despises me!" she cried. At this, Zoi ran towards her mother.

"I love you, Mother, remember? Please. Thanos is gone. This is not your son," she said, tugging at Lamia's body with all her might. Stopping, Zoi looked around, but there was nothing she could do to help, nothing she could manipulate. Dead things—a parched earth and a dried tree—were all that surrounded them. Even the bees had fled. Nothing pulsed with life here. There was nothing she could move or will into being.

"This is your brother, I know it. Look," Lamia said, and she lifted the terrified Acayo's left leg, baring his ankle for all to see, revealing a small birthmark there, which was barely noticeable. Lamia looked at her daughter anxiously.

Zoi gasped, for she had a similar birthmark in the same place. "He is my brother, yes," Zoi said, covering her face.

"I knew--" Lamia began, but faltered. She glanced at Acayo, then at Morfeo. Realization dawned on her face. "Cyteria's son," she seethed. "She, the one who murdered my baby, had a baby of her own. A child for a child!" she roared. Then, she began to drag Acayo back towards her cave home.

A garbled, anguished noise erupted from Morfeo's throat, and he lunged towards Lamia with the spear, his right hand clutching the shaft tightly, his left extended for balance. But Lamia was fast, and she dodged him artfully. In her clutches, Acayo wailed.

Zoi crouched between Lamia and Morfeo, her arms reaching out to both of them. "Leave her alone!" Zoi shouted at Morfeo. Lamia swayed, her eyes black coals that raked over Acayo's body. Twice, she licked her teeth.

"Release my boy!" Morfeo screamed in return. Acayo moaned once, his eyes fluttering open, just long enough to see the blood on his chiton, covering the flesh that had been torn by Lamia's claws, and then he blacked out again.

"You loved me once, Morfeo," Lamia said, and it was not a request or a question. "I listened for your returning feet each night. And Zoi brought your messages. How you missed me. How you longed to join me. But it was a trick." Thick tears wet her face.

With a cry, Morfeo flung himself towards Lamia, the spear hefted over his head. It happened fast. With a thrust of her huge tail, Lamia wrapped herself around Morfeo once, twice, and squeezed. She'd struck hard, the way vipers did in the wild, catching unsuspecting travelers in the ankle and bringing them down within minutes. "My love," she said. "I've spent my life longing for you. But I am strong. I can go on this way forever." Morfeo's face went purple, then they all heard a loud crack, the sound of bones snapping, and Morfeo went limp.

Galen was overcome with sickening, cold, creeping fear. It was such a strong feeling, and so tempted was he to run, that Korinna, hearing his thoughts, cringed. But he knew now that there was no running from this. Lamia had to be destroyed, for to unleash her on Sparta would be unspeakable. She had murdered the one she claimed to love. What would she do to people she didn't even know? Sparta was in great danger, and Galen knew he had to do something.

"Now you are thinking like a king," Korinna whispered. But there was something else besides the fear in Galen's chest, and that was anger at the ephors' pact with Morfeo, and despair over Lamia's cruel and broken heart. The emotions fueled him, made him feel strong.

Lamia loosened her grip on Morfeo. Zoi stumbled to his body. Her fingers hovered over his form, and she strained the muscles in her arms, searching for the rush of life in him, but found none. She turned wet, unblinking eyes to her mother, but said nothing.

"Thanos would understand," Lamia said acidly. Zoi dropped her head on Morfeo's chest, and sobbed.

"But she hated him," Galen said, confused.

"Yes, but she loved him, too," Korinna said. "What else did she have?"

Lamia watched interestedly for only a moment before turning to Acayo again. Galen moved. He picked up the spear that had fallen from Morfeo's hand and dove at Lamia, the spear gripped in both hands and held high over his head. He would have stuck her in the back, directly between her shoulder blades, had not Acayo woken again and screamed. The drakaina swirled around at the sound, her eyes landing on the spear again, the weapon come to life in another's hand.

"What manner of slave are you?" she asked Galen, holding Acayo by the arm. The boy's body dangled like an autumn leaf just before it drops.

"I am no slave!" Galen said, rushing Lamia again. Once more she avoided the blow. Galen breathed hard, deciding his next move. Suddenly, Lamia turned away. A rock had struck her cheek, and she faced Nikolas, who raised his arm for another toss.

Lamia whipped around to face Nikolas.

With a quick movement, Korinna stepped into the fray, saying, "Do you remember me, Aunt Lamia? Do you see Meroe's face echoed in my own?"

Again, Lamia faced a new opponent, and now the fire in her eyes dimmed, betraying confusion and a touch of fear. "Meroe?" she asked as if she'd just heard it spoken that night. The name alone seemed to shock her for a moment. Thanos, Meroe, the ghosts of her past were upon her. Lamia had seldom faced a crowd. It had always been the monster versus the stray child here or there. There had been, too, the sibyls brought in by the ephors in the hopes that Lamia might let one of them live and work in the Temple of Artemis Orthia, the only place in all of Sparta where the earth poured out its fumes blessed by the gods. The sibyls saw their visions more clearly within the fumes, their lungs filling with godly purpose. Those weak girls had been bound in rope and gagged with cloth. They'd all died so easily, satisfying Lamia's thirst for vengeance, and the ephors had run away in horror, screaming like children.

Now Galen, watching Lamia sway in confusion, understood that for once she faced opponents she feared, and he called to her, "You can't fight us all!"

Lamia smiled. "No, slave. But I can begin with this one," she said, regaining her composure. She bent over Acayo, her back curving, the scales glinting.

Galen sprang beside her, stooped, drove his spear point into her back, leaving a gaping, glistening wound in her skin. Lamia bellowed, dropped Acayo, whipped around, and picked Galen up by his chiton. She pinned him to the side of the mountain, her great forearm against his throat. Jagged rock broke the skin on his back. Scales like shards of glass scraped his neck. Wincing, Galen watched as Acayo began to crawl away, his left leg dragging lifeless behind him, and disappeared over the crest of the hill. *You will save the one you hate*, he thought, remembering Korinna's prediction upon meeting her.

Lamia began to press her weight against Galen's throat, and Galen's world grew darker. He clung to his spear, but his strength had left him, and there was no way to maneuver the weapon into a striking position. "You will make a tasty morsel, slave," Lamia said, her breath rank on his face.

Behind her, Nikolas and Korinna were throwing stones. "For Sparta!" Nikolas was shouting, as stone upon stone rained on the drakaina, though nothing seemed to pierce her hide. As for Zoi, she lingered by Morfeo's body, going through the motions Galen had seen when Brygus had died—the laying of dried leaves, the chanting, the strange funeral rites. Then, she rose.

"You have a choice, Mother," Zoi said. "We can go now. Together, you and I, and leave Sparta."

"They have not paid the price for killing my Thanos!" Lamia shouted, pressing harder against Galen as she spoke.

"Or you can make me an orphan today!" Zoi went on, shaking with rage. "Choose! It is the only thing we can control in life, the only power we have. Choose!"

Lamia looked at her daughter. A shudder went through her. Galen watched in horror as a long line of spittle hung from the corner of Lamia's mouth. "You are mistaken, Zoi. Our true power is vengeance," she said, licking her lips.

At the sight of her forked tongue, the rest leapt into action. Nikolas drove his shoulder into Lamia's hardened back again and again, then set off a series of punches that thumped loudly against her ribs, sounding like a drum being struck— *boom, boom, boom.* Beside Morfeo's body, Zoi's arms rose in the air, and her eyes closed. Tears sprang from her eyelids. Korinna wrapped her body around Lamia's tail, intent on pulling her away from Galen, still pinned to the side of the mountain. But Lamia was strong, and her first instinct was to shake her tail to dislodge Korinna. She whipped the scaly appendage and sent Korinna flying, so that she landed on her stomach with a thud, and lay there in silence.

"Korinna!" Galen shouted, but Lamia pressed a cold, scaly palm against his mouth.

She considered him with a slight tip of her head. Up close, Galen could see that once Lamia had been beautiful. There was something of Zoi and Korinna in her face—the pointy chin, the square shape of her cheekbones. Her face was shaped like an upside-down teardrop. But her expression was like that of a statue. Her eyes would not close, nor did her mouth. The thin lips would not cover the dingy, sharp-edged teeth. Her lower jaw jutted out. Her breath smelled of iron. Galen's eyes darted towards Korinna, still on the ground. *Wake up. Please*, he thought hard.

"I loved once, too," Lamia said, having noticed Galen's concern for Korinna.

Galen banged the spear weakly against Lamia's side, and the drakaina cackled at the attempt. Then, she opened her mouth, her jaw seemed to unhinge, and she neared Galen's throat. His vision darkening, Galen felt that he hovered upon the edge of death. He braced himself against the pain. A rush of Lamia's hot breath washed over his face, and then, he heard Lamia scream. The smell of burning flesh filled his nostrils. Galen fell to the ground, landing awkwardly on his side.

Behind Lamia stood Korinna, and in her grip was a gnarled branch from the olive tree, its end burning brightly with the fire the ephors had started. Galen could see how the beeswax she'd gathered from the hive dripped down the limb and onto her forearm. It was a makeshift torch, and Galen felt a sudden surge of joy at the sight of it as he remembered the night they'd spent in the forest when he'd first taught her how to feed fire with beeswax. The red scales of Lamia's tail had been burned away in patches in the places where Korinna had applied the torch.

Enraged, Lamia raised herself to her full height, and struck swiftly at Korinna, clamping her cruel mouth down where the girl's shoulder met her neck, lifting her off her feet, and shaking her as a dog does a rabbit. When she let her go, Korinna collapsed in a heap. The torch rolled to the ground and was extinguished. Korinna tried to stand, but the ground was slick with her own blood, and she slipped, and did not move again.

The certainty of Korinna's looming death was searing. Galen's eyes stung. His stomach rolled over. The chaos around him was cloaked in silence. It was as if his ears had stopped working. *Don't be dead*, he thought, again and again, and watched as Nikolas danced around Lamia, pitching stones, dodging her strikes. Zoi worked the air, still, calling forth some power with twitching fingers. And Galen knew he had to act.

He roused himself. The spear in his hands felt like a living thing now, with a will to match Galen's own. He separated the halves, gripped them tightly, and with a shout of anguish, he buried the two points of the spear deep into Lamia's

262

chest. Her eyes grew big, as if she were bewildered by this turn of events. The drakaina whipped to and fro, snapping at the air with her mouth, her teeth clacking together. There was life in her still. Galen readied another thrust, but he stopped at the drone that now filled the air.

The bees were back, summoned by Zoi, and they swarmed around Lamia. Mad with agony, Lamia dropped to her hands and dragged herself into the cave. Her screams diminished as the swarm satisfied itself. And then there was silence.

Crying hard, unashamed that Nikolas and Zoi were watching, Galen crawled towards Korinna.

Her eyelids were partly open. The whites of her eyes were visible, looking like a pair of crescent moons. "Don't be dead," Galen said. His palms were rough from years of slavery, but he cupped her face anyway and squeezed, as if through resolve alone he could bring her back.

She coughed then, a weak cough. "Don't move, don't move," Galen urged, trying not to look at the giant wound on her shoulder, the blood that had soaked the earth beneath her, or the paleness of her skin.

"Fate has brought me here and I will see it through," Korinna said.

"We make our own fate, Korinna," Galen said. But she smiled at him, a sad, crooked smile.

They stared at each other for what seemed like a long time. The others moved out of Galen's line of sight, though he could hear Zoi's exhausted sobs and Nikolas trying to console her. Slowly, the bees began to make their way out of the cave, cutting a wobbly path through the air towards the hive. One rogue creature broke off from the group and landed on Galen's shoulder.

"You again," Korinna whispered to the bee. "You've come to lead me to the Underworld."

263

Galen shook his head. He swatted at the bee, but it only circled his head and landed again. "Get out," he said, choking on tears still. Once more, he swiped at the bee, and this time, it stayed in the air a little longer, then landed on one of Korinna's fingers.

She smiled again, more weakly this time, and lifted her arm to look at the bee more closely.

"You saw this," Galen said angrily, pressing the heels of his hands to his eyes. "You saw this in your future."

Korinna said nothing, but now her eyes filled with tears, too. "I will miss you," she said. "Be at peace. Become the kind of king your destiny asks you to be. For me."

"I don't want to sit on a throne."

Korinna moaned.

"Stay," Galen urged. She gave no answer. She'd closed her eyes, but her breathing had become softer and less labored. *Stay*, he thought this time.

"I'll miss that, too," she murmured.

"My Spartan bee," he said quietly, and thought, *I do love you, no matter what you think.* He ran the back of his hand against her cheek, then bent over her, closed his eyes and pressed his lips against hers. His mouth was parched from the yelling, from the dryness of this place, and he hoped she didn't care. Korinna's lips moved a little against his, then they were still.

The bee rose in the air again. It circled Korinna's head twice, and finally flew off into the dark cave.

264

36

Galen's memories of Korinna sharpened in the days following her death. He would be busy cleaning his father's spear, or listening to one of Nestor's lectures at the agoge, and suddenly would remember the way Korinna had spoken, clearing her throat softly every so often. He recalled, piercingly, the way Korinna's eyes turned up at the edges, as if she were always on the verge of a smile. Galen remembered observing her breathing once, how it matched his. He did not realize that he had noticed any of these things until after she had died.

Galen realized something else, too—he'd never known grief before.

It was in the midst of Galen's sadness that the Assembly met for the first time since the earthquake. Isaura had been allowed to speak to the senators, creating anticipation among the Spartans since a woman, even a queen, was rarely given the

265

floor at the Assembly House. Once before the Gerousia, Isaura had spoken of Morfeo's betrayal, of Lamia, and the heroism of Nikolas, Galen, Zoi, and Korinna. "Spartan children saved us from destruction. Let us remember that and be grateful," she'd said, and the murmurs among the senators grew until, one after another, they broke out in applause. In the end, all of senators had stood, cheering loudly.

Galen, Nikolas, and Zoi had watched the proceedings from the back of the room. Zoi had held both boys' hands and squeezed them anxiously throughout. Finally, Isaura had proclaimed Galen's freedom and pardoned Zoi, without betraying either one's true identity. Nikolas had lifted Zoi in a hug, then clapped Galen on the back, thrusting his fist in the air.

Galen had only managed a weak smile. He had longed for his freedom for so long, and yet at that moment, the only thing Galen could think about was the way Korinna had looked at him the last time.

Isaura ordered a tholos to be built for Korinna, and Galen oversaw the construction of the hive-shaped tomb brick by brick. All he wanted was to stand in the sun, feel it heavy and hot on his bare back, and watch as the tomb took shape. Sometimes, he scanned the air, hoping that another bee might perch on him with a message from Korinna, but none did.

In the main, Galen kept his watch alone. Sometimes, Zoi appeared behind him, like a shadow. She'd say nothing, but Galen knew her from the sound that her long, heavily draped, sleeved chiton made. Zoi had taken to wearing them, though the scales on her body had smoothed away. Once, Galen asked if she could still move the earth, and Zoi had said, "It comes and goes."

"Does it make you sad?" Galen asked without tearing his eyes off the growing tomb.

"Everything makes me sad these days," she'd answered, leaving the burial site.

When he wasn't at the tomb, Galen was at the agoge. He'd been given a bed in the barracks, with the other Spartan boys, but he hadn't used it yet. His cot in the helot quarters felt more like home. Most days, he helped with dinner. Galen found the skinning of an animal mindless work, and he relished those moments when his mind was blessedly blank.

When Queen Isaura learned of it, she summoned Galen to her private home, her little Ithaca, asking him angrily, "Why can't you accept your place?" Her eyes were full of tears and she twisted the fabric of her dress as she spoke. "I await your choice, Galenos," she said. "The right to the crown is yours, but if you mean to take it, this delay is cruel. Either Nikolas will be king or he won't."

"I know it," Galen said, frustrated, touching his hair that was growing long now for the first time. He was shocked to see it curl, to feel the softness of his hair under his fingertips. He thought of Korinna's urging him to fulfill his destiny, and it paralyzed him. Nikolas was the perfect royal. *I will only make a mess of things*, he thought. "After the funeral, I'll decide," Galen assured his mother, but her mouth was turned in a deep frown.

"You're all but grown, Galenos. The choice you make will determine the man you will be. King or citizen, you must decide," she said.

Galen glanced around the room. There stood Nilos, Nikolas' true father, at the doorway. He held a sword and looked like any other soldier. And yet he was a helot. Just another helot. Galen glanced at the finely appointed room, at the embroidered cloths on the floor, and the gleaming shield over the hearth, at Astron, the mynah bird that watched Galen with dark, glossy eyes, and he thought: *I don't belong anywhere.*

"Mother," he began, "You say I am nearly a man."

"You are, Galenos, you…"

267

"But I am not the man I was born to be," he said, deciding his fate even as he spoke the words. He didn't need to wait until after the funeral to make the choice. He would not be the Eurypontid king. But he wasn't a helot either. With Korinna gone, Galen felt unmoored, and strangely, free to decide what he was meant to do with his life.

The queen looked away, a melancholy look on her face. "I accept it. I love you both, you and Nikolas," she said, and Astron squawked quietly in his cage.

In the days that followed, Isaura gave Galen a red cloak of his own, and he was formally initiated into the Spartan citizenry. He would become a warrior and landowner when he completed his training at the agoge. He was expected to find a wife, and soon thereafter, join one of the Persian campaigns.

But Galen's heart wasn't in any of that. The wife he would have chosen had gone forever. He rarely wore the crimson cloak.

Nikolas spent most of his time studying with a council of senators composed of those who had not supported Morfeo's bid to eliminate the Eurypontids. He was learning the intricacies of Spartan politics and training to fully take up the reins of the Eurypontid kingship as soon as his agoge training was complete at his eighteenth birthday. For now, their tasks were numerous. The first was to select a new set of ephors since the five that had betrayed Sparta had fled over land towards the Persian border. Every soldier in the Spartan command now sought the traitors, and their death at the hands of one or more furious Spartans seemed inevitable.

As for Acayo, he had gone missing. There had been search parties, but they'd returned empty-handed. When Morfeo's body was burned on a pyre like a common helot, there was no son to grieve for him. In the end, Timios' father, Tymos, a storied warrior, senator, and a member of the Agiad family line, was selected to wear the crown in Morfeo's place.

So, the prophecy had come true. Sparta had only one king, one true king by blood, and that was Tymos, not Nikolas.

The question of the sibyl remained. Once again, the Rock of the Sibyl sat empty. "There's talk of a little girl with some talent out in Messenia," Nikolas told Galen on the eve of Korinna's funeral. It was the day before the first of spring, and the nights had grown warm again.

Galen rubbed his hair, a habit now, before saying, "So what now? You go to Messenia and kidnap a child and take her to that forsaken Rock?" he said, anger in his voice. He thought of Korinna, who had been taken to Persia by force.

"We need a sibyl, Galenos," Nikolas said, using that senator's tone he'd acquired since he began studying with them.

"No, we don't," Galen said.

"It's tradition. And besides, without the prophecies of the sibyls we…"

"The prophecies come true or they don't! Why can't you Spartans rely on your own instincts? Why can't you rule from here?" he said, thumping Nikolas' forehead with his fingers, "Or here?" then punching him lightly in the chest.

Nikolas glared at Galen. "'We Spartans?' You're a Spartan, too, you know," Nikolas said. His voice sounded hurt, but his jaw was set tightly.

They were in the mess hall of the agoge, which was empty of students. Galen sat down hard on a bench and drummed his fingers on the table. "The Rock should remain unoccupied. It is time Spartans started thinking for themselves, as they do in other Greek city-states, and stopped relying on the visions of slaves."

"Sibyls are not slaves," Nikolas growled.

"Aren't they?" Galen answered, thinking of Meroe, whose life was forfeit to the whims of the ephors and Morfeo, and of Korinna, wracked by visions. Galen felt himself growing angrier. "You know what it means to be a slave, do you, Your Highness? Your full belly, your fancy armor, all that pretty hair—you're as empathethic as they come," he said without looking at Nikolas. It was a mean thing to say, he knew. Nikolas was kind to the helots, as if he were one of them. *He IS one of them*, Galen thought miserably.

From the corner of his eye, Galen saw a chair flying in the air, and heard the crash of it against the wall. He looked up, startled. Nikolas was standing there, huffing from exertion. "This isn't about you, Galen! This is about something bigger than you. Sparta is bigger than you!" he yelled. Then, breathing hard, he said, "I know you miss her. But don't take it out on me. I'm doing the best I can here." Nikolas waited a moment, but Galen didn't respond. At last, Nikolas stomped off, kicking another wooden chair out of his way and sending that one to the floor, before leaving the mess hall.

37

The morning she was entombed, Korinna's body was wrapped in linens. She'd been embalmed in honey, as was the Spartan custom. When Galen learned of it, he couldn't help but wonder about the bees again and how they seemed to play a role in every aspect of death. Two servants carried her white form into the tholos. Galen did not enter the tomb. He was not her husband, no more than a friend, really, and so he had no right to enter. The tholos was sealed once the helots stepped out. Her name would not be carved on the entrance to the tomb. Bitterly, Galen thought of it as a slight. He'd wanted to see how the scribes would write out her name. He imagined the letters would be beautiful, coming together to form a picture of her, something he could revisit, and maybe even learn to write, too.

King Tymos was at the funeral, paying his respects to the sibyl. Nikolas stood near the king, and did not look in Galen's direction. Galen sat alone, away from the crowd that had come to pay respects to the young sibyl who had helped to save Sparta. The stars began to blink in the bluish sky. With the dusk, came the chorus of crickets in the high grasses surrounding the tholos. And with the crickets, came the singer.

He sat down before the tomb, so slowly that it seemed his body must have been tender in spots. The gathering hushed, ready to listen to the story the singer would tell. He strummed his lyre, and began the tale of Orpheus and Eurydice. The listeners settled in. It was a common choice of song for a funeral. Sitting with her two attendants, Helena and Diantha, the queen spun a bronze ring around her thumb. This would be the singer's payment, given only if his song was beautiful and stirring. Though Spartans did not cry at funerals, or rend clothes, they still wanted to feel their hearts banging in their chests in sadness.

The singer spoke of Orpheus' love for the beautiful Eurydice, how she walked into a nest of vipers on her wedding day, and was killed. Orpheus, who fathered music, plucking notes out of the air with skill, was overcome. He played such mournful songs that the gods' marble hearts broke. They urged him to go down to Hades, to beg for Eurydice's return.

Zoi sat down next to Galen, and as the singer finished his song, she touched his arm for a moment. Galen did not move, but he felt warmth there, and the faint beat of her pulse. Lamia had taken the curse of the viper with her.

"I hate this song," Galen said.

"It gets worse," Zoi responded.

Then the singer told of Orpheus in the Underworld, how he played his lyre, and for once, old Hades cracked, his will softened, and he allowed Orpheus to lead Eurydice out. But the musician turned at the last minute, despite Hades' warnings, and Eurydice disappeared in a wisp of smoke.

The message was clear. The dead did not return. And with the last twang of the lyre, the singer ended his song. Isaura handed the ring to Helena, who placed it in the singer's palm, and he closed his fingers around it. The singer was nearly blind, as many of the singers were. Storytelling was their only vocation. What else could a blind man do in Greece except memorize stories and learn to play an instrument? Galen felt pity for the singer.

Then, just as people began to stir and murmur, the singer struck the lyre again. "One more song," he said, and his voice was stronger now, the mood shifting with each vibrating string, the melodies recalling the songs of heroes.

The singer's eyes were dark pearls. Despite his blindness, he ran his third finger along the strings deftly. There was delight in his voice as he sang the song of the red cloak—the story of Galenos, who slew the drakhaina.

People listened, rapt. They furtively glanced at Galen, and he had to keep himself from concealing his face in his cloak. He had practiced the art of hiding his feelings and his grief for Korinna. He always appeared stoic and controlled, giving no one reason to doubt whether or not he deserved to wear the Spartan cloak. But hearing this new song made it difficult to keep up appearances. When the singer first uttered Korinna's name, Galen felt his throat clench. He rubbed his arm where his tattoo was, and it calmed him. Nikolas had offered to carve out Galen's captive tattoo for him, but he'd refused. He bore it with pride now, and often arranged his chiton so that it could be seen. Galen felt as if he might be sick. *This isn't what I wanted*, he thought fiercely. *Who am I to be in the songs? The songs should be all about her, Korinna.*

The song was nearing its end when Zoi reached out and loosened the fingers of his right hand.

"Don't," Galen whispered.

"I'm not doing anything. I just thought you needed a hand to hold," Zoi said. Galen didn't respond. He listened as the song came to an end, stood and nodded at the Queen, who had surely commissioned this particular song. Everyone was looking at him with such sympathy now. *Do they all know I loved her? Is it so obvious?* he asked himself.

Galen and Zoi sat quietly for a long time. When Galen spoke, he said, "I miss her," but his voice was croaky. When the singer rose, tapping his way back from where he came with a walking stick, Galen spoke again, saying, "I wish he wouldn't go. The songs are welcome distractions," he said, then added, "When they aren't about us, I mean."

Clearing her throat, Zoi said, "Allow me, then." She strummed an invisible lyre, uttering a high note. "When Thanos was killed, my mother tried to retrieve his shade. She carried me on her back, strapped to her body with rags and oiled cloths. Down through the tunnels of the Rock of the Sibyl we went. For days she travelled, deep into the earth. There were fiendish creatures in those caves, and strange vapors that could make a person mad, and other things I think I remember, though they might just be memories of nightmares. The pressure built in our ears and they made popping sounds in our heads. At last, when the smell of sulfur became unbearable, Lamia heard the rippling of water. A few paces down, a vast, underground ocean came to view. The water was dark, for there was no sun or sky to reflect the light. But Lamia had forgotten a sacrifice with which to feed the spirits and call Thanos back to her. She considered offering me. My tender flesh would appeal to the shades, but she thought better of it. Lamia was not yet a monster."

Zoi paused, and when she spoke again, her voice was strained, and she sounded a little like an old woman. "We waited there for three nights. Lamia hoped that the spirits would come without a sacrifice. It was so long, that Lamia grew weak with hunger, and she was forced to return to the mouth of the cave. But when we rose to the world above, an unfortunate child was there to greet us, and Lamia asked her, 'Does your mother love you?'

"'Of course,' the girl said. 'We are helots, but we have each another.'

"'How fortunate for you,' Lamia said to the girl, and out of rage, frustration, and jealousy, killed her. The next night, we tried to reach the Underworld again. But the path was blocked to us. Whatever mercy Hades had given, allowing us to get so close to the waters of the dead, had been taken away."

Zoi pretended to pluck the strings of a lyre again. "The end," she said, closed her eyes in mock blindness, and lifted her hand, palm up, as if she were ready to receive her payment.

"That isn't funny," Galen said.

"No, but it is true," Zoi answered.

Galen looked up at once, his eyes bright with an idea. "How can you know this story?" he asked, trying to sound measured, though his foot tapped wildly on the ground. "You were a baby."

"Lamia told me." When Galen arched an eyebrow, Zoi said, "She may have been a monster, but she never lied to me. Not once."

"Can you point the way to the Underworld?" Galen whispered. The people were dispersing, and he had a clear view of the tholos from where he sat.

"The dead can't come back," Zoi said.

"Just point the way."

Zoi got to her feet. "They don't come back," she repeated.

Galen rested his elbows on his knees and stared at the tholos. Zoi left him there, brooding. She wiped her cheeks with the end of her long robe, and wrapping the cloth around her head like a hood, walked away.

Though the palace had its own places of worship, Nikolas still preferred the small temple to Ares behind the agoge. That night, while the agoge was quiet, Galen found Nikolas there, pouring out libations and saying a prayer to the god of war.

275

"Send a prayer down to Hades, next," Galen said at the entrance to the temple, startling Nikolas.

"What are you doing here?" Nikolas asked.

Galen pushed a little mound of earth around with his foot before speaking. "I wanted to apologize," he said.

Nikolas said nothing for a long while. He arranged the figures on the altar, mumbling to the gods as he did so. Finally, he turned to Galen and said, "So, what did you think of that song?"

"The one about us?"

"Mainly it was about you," Nikolas said with a little laugh. Galen felt the last of his anger fade. The song *had* featured Galen, and yet Nikolas wasn't angry. Or even a little jealous. Galen had been ignoring Nikolas these last few days. It felt good now to be in this place with him again. It had been here, in the modest temple of Ares that they'd planned jokes and strategies for winning wrestling matches, where they'd decided on a course of action regarding the Crypteia, and where they'd begun to unravel Morfeo's plot. The little temple felt more like home than any place Galen had ever known.

"It was the other song, the one about the Underworld, that interested me more," Galen said. "You may want to take a seat." Then, he told Nikolas about Zoi's tale and the path she and Lamia had taken trying to get to Hades.

"Those are just stories," Nikolas said, after hearing it all.

"Lamia was just a story, too." Nikolas shook his head.

Galen changed the subject. "I've got some ideas about the helots. We can make things better for them. Let them join the army," Galen said quietly.

Nikolas nodded slowly. "The Assembly will take some convincing," he said. "But we'll whip the helots into shape, you'll see. They'll join the finest army in the world." He was so eager to agree, that Galen knew he was trying to make up for their fight in the mess hall.

276

They were quiet for some time after that. Galen was aware of the ordinary peacefulness of the moment, so much like those days when he and Nikolas chatted in the small temple. Galen laughed, and it felt good and strange after so many days of grieving. Nikolas laughed, too, a look of delight in his eyes.

They talked a bit about recent wrestling matches, about Persia, and King Tymos, who had a broad face and towered over nearly every man in Sparta. "He's built like a bear," Nikolas said.

"And yet his son Timios looks like a little mouse, big ears and all," Galen said, chuckling.

They joked for some time, until their laughter died down to silence. "You know you can't bring her back," Nikolas said suddenly. Surprised, Galen looked away, his eyes stinging. "The dead are where they belong, Galen, and we do them honor by remembering to live."

Galen was about to say something more, when he heard a melody drifting in the air. Nikolas heard it too, and got to his feet. In the distance, they could make out flickering flames that left trails of light in the darkness. The sound came from someone singing. "What the--?" Galen started to say, and stepped outside, heading towards the glow. Nikolas followed close behind.

There, near the stream that had once flooded and nearly drowned Galen, was a group of girls and women from the village. The crowd that stood to watch the girls parted for Nikolas, people here and there smiling at the prince. Galen followed Nikolas closely, so that they stood very near to Zoi and her performers. The girls were dancing in a circle, holding candles, which they moved about in intricate patterns. In the center of the circle danced Zoi, singing a song about Persephone, Hades' queen, who returns from the Underworld in the springtime. Zoi was spinning, and at her feet, flower petals swirled, casting their sweet fragrance everywhere.

"It's a rite, in honor of the first of spring, and of Persephone," Nikolas said. "I'd forgotten all about spring. Listen."

Zoi sang boldly, loudly, so that everyone in the village near the agoge must have heard: "Praise to Persephone, Queen of the Underworld," she sang. "Persephone, the Queen Bee, who travels to and fro. Persephone, Death's Conquerer," she said, and with that last note, stopped her spinning and looked directly at Galen. With a flick of her wrist, the petals rose through the air, and landed in her cupped hand, which she clenched closed, eyes still locked on Galen. "Women of Sparta!" she shouted then, finally breaking her gaze. "Hail our Spartan heroes, Nikolas of the Eurypontids, and Galenos, destroyer of monsters!" Her voice broke a little on that last word, but her face betrayed no sadness, no regrets.

The women and girls broke formation, wreathed Galen and Nikolas with flowers, and danced around them. Galen felt his spirits lift, and he searched the circle for Zoi, finding her at last outside the dancing ring, staring at him with a smile on her face, her eyes watery. She strode over to him. When she drew near enough to whisper in his ear, she said, "It won't be easy, you know, getting to the Underworld. But we can try."

Galen took a deep breath, a breath he felt he'd been holding since the moment Korinna had died in his arms. His lungs filled and he felt heady. He gave a fleeting look towards Nikolas, who was watching him with narrowed eyes. Galen turned away.

He'd made another decision, sure as the fact that spring had arrived and summer would follow—he would travel under the earth and retrieve what he'd lost. The song of the red cloak, Galen knew, was not yet finished.

READ ON FOR AN EXCERPT FROM
SONG OF GLASS AND DUST

By the time the three of them reached the Rock of the Sibyl, the sun was high in the sky. The lamb that Nikolas carried bleated weakly. The sun was hot, and Galen didn't blame the creature for voicing its discomfort. Nikolas shushed the animal, while Zoi lifted a hand to pat its head.

Though the mouth of Lamia's cave was broad, the space tapered into a tunnel after only a few spaces. Galen lit a torch. Zoi led the way. The boys followed her, careful where they put their feet. Here and there, crinkled, old snake's skins littered the ground, and Galen felt his stomach jolt at the sight of them. As for Zoi, she kept her head held high, her eyes pinned to the farthest reaches of the tunnel.

They walked in silence. Now and again the fleecy lamb cried out, and then Nikolas muttered over its head, calming it. "It goes willingly. The sacrifice will be good," Nikolas said, trying to ease everyone's anxieties. It was said that sacrificial beasts had to display a readiness to die, or else the offering was tainted. Galen's experience butchering animals was different. It didn't matter if a goat or pig struggled. Food was food.

Now, looking upon the lamb, its white fleece reflecting the torchlight like a beacon, the idea that the lamb was so willing to die made Galen feel uneasy. It reminded him of Korinna, who'd foreseen her death at the Rock of the Sibyl. It had been laid out like map in her vision, and she followed it faithfully. For what? To save Galen's life? So that Galen could thwart a prophecy? Take his place as a Spartan king? It didn't make sense to him. More than once, he wished the Lamia had destroyed him instead. Nikolas could have finished the monster off, and Korinna would be breathing on the surface of the world still. His real destiny, as Galen saw it, had been to tumble off the face of Mount Taygetos as an infant. That's where Leandros had faltered. And nothing had gone right since.

These dark thoughts dogged Galen as they walked, ponderously slow, down the tunnel. None of them voiced the fear that Lamia's story about the underworld was only legend. There was no point in it. They drank goats' milk that Zoi carried in a lambskin bag slung across her chest, pouring the drink into clay cups that Galen had in a bag of his own. They'd brought no weapons, though there were legends about the beasts that lived in the underworld—creatures like the Furies, snake-haired women who tortured unfaithful men, or Cerebrus, the three-headed dog.

"What's the point?" Galen had said regarding weapons. "Spears will slow us down as we walk. And everything in Hades is dead already. What damage can a sword do to a spirit?" He did carry a short knife in his chiton, and he urged Zoi and Nikols to do the same. They had agreed, and by the third day of walking in near silence, they were glad to have brought plenty of food instead of cumbersome weapons. By then, Nikolas had stopped carrying the lamb. It followed them like a little dog, ate scraps of food they left behind, and lapped up goat's milk with a flick of its pink, wet tongue.

By then, their feet were throbbing, and the going was slower. Just when they thought they could go on no longer, they heard the slap of water against a shore, and were soon upon the vast lake. It might have been an ocean for all they knew, for it seemed to have no end.

"Now what?" Galen asked, suddenly wishing he had brought the spear after all. The water at his feet churned. Tendrils of smoke rose off its surface, and here and there, bubbles popped thickly.

"This is as far as we got last time," Zoi said. "When I came with my mother." She'd gone pale, and her fingers twitched. Galen could tell she was wishing she had her old powers back, faced with this ominous, massive body of water.

"Hades must be on the other side," Nikolas said. "But I'm not swimming."

Galen's eyes fell on the lamb. It was sniffing the water, jumping back as the water rolled in and out of the shore. "Come here," he said to it, and the lamb trotted over. He'd never spoken to an animal. Not once in all the years he'd worked in the agoge kitchens. But now felt like a good time to start. Galen rubbed the lamb's long snout and its knobby head. "If there are fields of asphodel, as the singers claim, may you find yourself there, little one, keeping the grasses trim." From his chiton he pulled the knife. The lamb settled itself on Galen's lap. He tried hard not to think of Korinna, but her face filled his mind. Fighting against it, he positioned the knife against the lamb's throat, closed his eyes, and moved his hand in one, quick, slicing motion.

The creature fell limp at once, and Galen felt the warmth of the lamb's blood over his hands. "It's done," he said, but the others weren't listening. The vapors rising from the water were coming together before them, swirling dark and gray, and forming the shape of a man with a thick, bulbous nose and long hair and beard. He wore no shirt, and his ribs could be counted. When the shade spoke, his voice was husky, like that of men who worked as blacksmiths and spent their day inhaling the smoke.

"Charon hungers," the shade said, descending upon the lamb and drinking the blood there. When it was done, it said, "The offering is good. Charon will take you across." His eyes looked feverish, as if the shade were sick. Behind him, a great gurgling of water began, and soon, a boat rose from the depths. Charon indicated that the three should step inside, which they did.

Then, they were off, skimming over the dark waters towards a distant shore. When Charon turned to face them, that look of sickness had gone from his eyes, and the smoky texture of his body took on a rosy tint. The lamb's blood had seemed to strengthen him. Nevertheless, the smoke wafting from his body smelled like something rotten, as if he spent his time lying in the muck at the bottom of the waters.

"The boat only takes passengers one way," Charon said. "But Charon can make an exception." With a toothless smile, he eyed Zoi.

"What?" she asked.

"Nothing," Charon said, then hummed a little, funereal sounding song.

"How will we find the shades we seek?" Galen asked.

"What a question," Charon said, laughing.

"Answer us, please," Galen pressed on.

Charon smiled again. He cut as unpleasant a figure as could be imagined. Wide-eyed, Nikolas watched the boatman, while Zoi sat motionless, her face drawn. Galen observed her a moment, and thought she almost seemed as filmy and translucent as Charon.

"The shades never get visitors. They'll find you, mark Charon's words," he said. Then: "Look there, the shores of the underworld. The Fields of Asphodel."

"I don't see any *fields*," Nikolas said.

In the distance, they saw the fuzzy outlines of a city. There were temples and homes, forests and palaces. The silhouettes were trembling, diaphanous things. Everything was made of the same, dark smoke—the water, Charon, all of Hades. They de-boarded the little vessel, and Charon said, "Charon'll give you an hour. If you miss the boat, consider this your new home," he said, then plopped down into the belly of the boat and closed his eyes.

"Good-humored, isn't he?" Nikolas said, but Galen and Zoi ignored the joke. The ground beneath their feet was spongy, and every so often, the surface of it sunk to their ankles, and they had to tug at their legs to release them from the smoke-thick earth. Around them, shades walked, some displaying earthly injuries still. They saw hanged men with necks bent at awkward angles, and war heroes carrying their heads in their arms. The shades chatted with one another. Some sat at the edge of the water washing linens. Smoke blended into smoke, but the shades seemed satisfied with the "clean" clothes. In the distance, a woman led a few children in a dance, and their squeals echoed in the air.

"Where could Korinna be?" Galen asked, but his friends were off in different directions, their heads swiveling side to side, taking in the wondrous horrors of Hades. "We've only an hour!" Galen shouted after them, took a deep breath, and plunged into the thick of the underworld city.

He walked for a long time, in and out of markets, where the shades bartered for food made of the same foggy material they were made of; he passed through temples, though these were all dedicated to Hades, his severe demeanor captured in gray statues. Twice, Galen blew air at the back of a man's head walking before him. The hair, skull, everything, seemed to blow away, dissipating in the air for a moment before reforming. The shade in question, an old man, turned around and tried smacking Galen's upper arm, but his hand went right through it. "Insolent little flesh-bag," the man said, and teetered off.

Soon, the novelty of the place wore out, and Galen began to feel real panic. Surely, there wasn't much time left, and he needed to find Korinna soon. But this city seemed vast, and the shades were too numerous. Then, he remembered Korinna's gifts, closed his eyes and thought as clearly as he could, *I'm here, Korinna. I want to speak with you.*

"You can do that without coming all the way to the underworld," Korinna said, standing now before him and smiling. "I'm always listening for your voice."

Galen tried wrapping his arms around her, but he could not hold her. He tried twice, and failed. He blinked away the pricking in his eyes. "I had them build you a tholos," was all he could think to say.

"Thank you."

"Spartan bee," Galen said with a sigh.

"You've come all this way," she said.

"Only to disappoint you. I will not be the Eurypontid prince, or the king. That's Nikolas' destiny." Galen cast his eyes downward, noticing for the first time that shades didn't quite touch the ground. Korinna's sandaled feet hovered just over the earth.

"Why would I be disappointed?" she asked.

Galen stepped back, shocked. "You said I was to fulfill my destiny. It's what you wanted me to do."

"And so you have. Nearly, anyway." She cocked her head, saying, "Follow me. There's someone I want you to meet."

She floated away, leading Galen down an alley between two buildings. He extended his arms and let his fingers trail against the walls, disturbing the smoke. The sounds of angry shades inside shouted, "Watch it!" as Galen cut through their homes.

Korinna turned around, smiling. "Troublemaker," she reprimanded, and went on.

Now Galen gazed at her, getting his fill. Oh, how he'd missed Korinna. It was like a wound that wouldn't heal up. Even now, staring at her, he missed her. Feeling wretched, he thought, *I have half an hour, maybe less.* Korinna did not indicate that she'd heard his thoughts. She only pressed on through the city, until she arrived at a modest home, with gauzy curtains for a door. These Korinna parted with a touch, and led Galen inside.

There, seated on a rug, were two beautiful women. The first resembled Korinna so much that Galen felt a pang of sorrow again. *This is what you would have looked like, had you lived*, he thought miserably, and Korinna nodded at him. The other was a heavy woman, with fine, dark eyes, and broad mouth. She resembled a horse more than anything, but there was still something beautiful about her. Galen thought that perhaps her beauty was in her hair, which was done in long braids that grazed the floor.

"My mother, Meroe," Korinna said, motioning the woman on the left. "And Sambethe, my second mother."

The heavier, horse-like woman nodded. Then, she said, "Greetings, king."

"I am no king," Galen said. "It's what I've come to explain. To beg Korinna forgiveness for breaking my promise."

The Persian sibyl rose, and though she was a shade, she seemed to move with great effort. She even grunted a little. "You are a king forever," she said. "I saw you in my dreams. You, the king who is not king, will make men free..." Her eyes were clear and blue, as if she were looking at him through water and not smoke. It was the only color in the room.

"You're mistaken, Sambethe," Galen started to say.

"Hush now, and listen to me. Sit."

Galen did as he was told. He crossed his legs, feeling himself sinking a little into the earth. Sambethe sat too, arranged her smoky robes about her. Korinna sat by her mother, who ran her fingers through Korinna's short hair, rubbing the girl's scalp.

"It was the custom in Parsa, the city you Greeks call Persepolis, for men captured in war to be brought to the sibyl so that their fates might be read. The Persians feared gods in disguise, and it was the sibyl's duty to make sure that the prisoners were who they claimed to be. I was that sibyl, the one they called Sambethe." The woman stopped speaking, put her hands on her hips, and said to Galen, "Now you wipe that look off your face. Persians are people like Greeks are people, and that's a truth you need to understand."

Galen did understand it. It's what he had always thought concerning helots and citizens. There was no difference between them. And yet, the Persians killed Leandros. Maybe Sambethe was right. They didn't seem like people at all to Galen.

Sambethe did not appear satisfied with the "look" on Galen's face, but she began to weave her story again in spite of it. "On the day I met Leandros, your father," she began, and Galen perked up as she continued: "the Persians had captured so many Greeks that I was brought to them. A tent had been set up, and the wounded and dying Greeks were laid on the ground, writhing in their agony. The men that were still sound of body were bound, gagged, and guarded by sullen-faced Persians. I walked among them all, trying to sense whether our gods, like Mithra or Atar, stirred in the captives, trying to trap the Persians in some misdeed.

"When I reached Leandros, I knew at once that he was a king. The soldiers knew it, too, for the campaign had been won thanks to Spartan traitors."

"The ephors," Galen said, his stomach roiling in disgust at the thought of them.

"Indeed. Leandros was handsome, even as he lay dying. His body bore the scars of many wars, yet there was a softness in his face I have not forgotten, as well as a sadness carried long in his heart. He was wincing against pain. An arrow had pierced his breast, and he'd pulled it free. Out went the arrow, as did his life's blood. So, Leandros breathed his last in a tent in Parsa, his hand in mine."

Galen had looked away as Sambethe told the story. Maybe there was something about this place that made the imagination more vivid. But as she told the tale, Galen swore he saw his father's last moments in his mind, as crisp and alive as if it were his own memory.

"We can only live in our minds here," Korinna said, interrupting the story. "Our memories are the only things that are real, Galen." She drew her hand across her face, and her features became a blur for a moment before once again taking their familiar shape. Galen shuddered.

"I could never see in the minds of men and women," Sambethe said. "But when Leandros was dying, he looked into my eyes and I into his, and I saw you, Galenos, in his arms. You, his only true child, spared the deadly ridges of your Spartan mountain, but made a slave in exchange. I saw you in the kitchens. You, befriending the imitation prince, Nikolas. You, wielding a spear like a king. And further still, I saw Leandros' dream of a Sparta ruled in fairness. It would be, I knew, a place for my Korinna to finally know freedom and joy.

"I whispered in Leandros' ear what I had the mind to do. I would take Korinna to Sparta. I would offer my services as a sibyl and a mentor to Isaura, and we would reestablish the Eurypontids with you as their leader. But it was not to be. A wounded soldier had just enough strength to rise from the ground and pierce my breast with a short sword. The Persians carried me back to my home with Korinna, and with what little strength I had left, I gave her the gift of Leandros' memory, which was the story of you, in the hopes that she'd find you and set things aright."

"Then the visions began," Korinna said. "And, you know the rest."

Galen shook his head. "The prophecy," he began, then shifted a little to face Meroe, "Your prophecy stated that Sparta would have no king. That's what I've come here to say. You were right, Meroe. I won't take the kingship away from Nikolas. My father's wishes won't come true. The prophecy was like a map, and as hard as we tried to carve out other routes, we followed it, down to the last detail, and ended up in the same place. Sparta will have no king, as you predicted."

"Is that a bad thing?" Meroe asked.

Galen looked at her hard. "I'd say so, yes," he answered. Korinna was dead. Leandros was dead. Sparta was a city still on the edge of panic. Galen looked at Korinna, and she turned away from the force of his stare. Then, he felt the same ache that struck him as he'd watched her tholos being built. "I don't want to disappoint you again, Korinna."

"You haven't."

"But you wanted me to be king. I won't do it, Korinna. I can't--"

"I said no such thing," Korinna said. "I wanted you to fulfill your destiny, to wear the red cloak you saw in your dream, to wear it proudly and rightly."

"I can't bear to wear it. When I put it on, all I can think about is my freedom, and what follows is a terrible guilt. I can't eat. I can't sleep," he said. He swirled his finger over the earth, creating a little twist of smoke that spun slowly before him. "I miss you," he said again, feeling like a child.

"Then fix it. You have Isaura's ear. The gods know you have Nikolas'. Do something about the helots. That's your destiny, Galen. That's my hope for you. It has nothing to do with a crown," Korinna said. She'd risen as she spoke, leaving her mother's side and floating over towards him. Tracing his face with her finger first, she then rose a few inches from the ground and brushed her lips against his.

288

It felt like a breeze against Galen's skin. There was nothing more to the sensation. "I have to go," he said softly, aware, in spite of his sadness, that he'd lingered in Hades close to an hour.

"I'll lead you to the shore," Korinna said, embraced her mothers and left the small house, prompting Galen to follow.

Galen turned to Meroe and Sambethe for one last look. The women were smiling, and it seemed to him, for a moment, that they were suppressing something more, as if they were on the verge of erupting in great laughter.

The sky, if it could be called a sky, had darkened over Hades. But there were no stars in it. Korinna and Galen rushed down the narrow streets, Galen glancing here and there, seeking Nikolas and Zoi. "Perhaps they're already at the boat," Galen said.

"No. Look." Korinna pointed towards a small plaza, fitted with a stone bench, and a great, gray laurel tree. Nikolas sat with a man wearing a bronze breastplate, a plumed helmet on his lap. The man had dark hair and eyes, and his lips were full. His arms and legs bore old scars, and the breastplate had a jagged hole in it, right over the man's heart.

"Leandros," Galen said, and the man looked up as if he'd heard his name. Leandros' face contorted a little and he grew tearful in that smoky way of the shades. Then, Leandros faced Nikolas, put his large hand on Nikolas' shoulder, and nodded a few times. Nikolas nodded in return, then swiped his eyes with the back of his hand. They rose together, and Nikolas saluted Leandros the formal way, extending his hand before him, palm down, then bringing a closed fist over his heart. Leandros smiled, turned, and saluted Galen from a distance.

"There isn't time," Korinna said, when Galen found he could not tear his eyes away from the father he'd not known. He moved only when Nikolas did, approaching them with his head down.

"Are you well?" Galen asked Nikolas in a whisper.

"No," Nikolas said, his hands shaking. Galen clasped Nikolas' shoulder and squeezed. Then, Nikolas said, "Let's find Zoi and go home."

They rushed on, breaking apart a number of shades that were sitting on the ground, listening to a man giving a speech. Their solid feet pounded the earth and clouds formed beneath them, so that it seemed as if they were floating like the shades. But they weren't. They were running hard, passing by Charon twice, who held up two fingers and scowled at them.

"Where is she?" Galen yelled. Nikolas paced in panic.

"I think I might know," Korinna said. She hurried inland again, towards a massive pair of gates high on a hill. They seemed to be made of cedar, and solid, as opposed to everything else in the underworld.

"What are those?"

"The gates to Tartarus," she said breathily as she moved. Even her voice lacked any real form here.

"Where the evil are punished," Galen said, understanding whom Zoi had sought. His hands and feet had grown cold, and he didn't know if it was because he feared Tartarus, or because he'd been in the underworld too long.

"You have been here too long," Korinna said. "There are others at the gate, too."

Cerebrus, the Furies, Galen thought, remembering the monsters of the underworld. Now he wished he'd brought his spear.

"And Lamia," Korinna added to his thoughts. "That's where she resides here."

They pressed on until they reached the enormous gateway, hinged in bronze, and laced with hundreds of bolts. Chained to one of the posts was the three-headed dog, Cerebrus, and it gnawed on a massive bone, paying the visitors no mind.

"He's a bit ineffective," Nikolas mused.

"I hate dogs," Galen said in a whisper, hoping the thing would go on chewing his toy.

290

The Furies, women with ragged, blackbird wings, talons for feet, and snakes nesting in their hair, flew high over the gate. Their screeching could be heard, thin and tinny, down on the ground.

Then there was Lamia. She'd retained her form, though she was bigger now. Her scales no longer glistened, but burned red, as if on fire from within. She was coiled at the base of the post opposite the dog, her head bowed, listening to Zoi, and stroking her daughter's cheek with one long claw.

VISIT WWW.CHANTELACEVEDO.COM FOR UPDATES ABOUT
SONG OF THE RED CLOAK,
AUTHOR VISITS, AND MORE

SONG
of the
RED CLOAK

CHANTEL ACEVEDO

A READERS GUIDE

"AN EPIC AND MAGICAL TALE ABOUT LOYALTY, FRIENDSHIP AND LOVE. ACEVEDO HAS CREATED A RIPPING, FAST-PACED STORYLINE, OF HEROES AND VILLAINS, TWISTS AND TURNS."

JULIANNA BAGGOTT, AUTHOR OF PURE

QUESTIONS FOR DISCUSSION

1. Galen, Nikolas, Zoi and Korinna, have all grown up in a brutal environment. Yet, they make moral choices in the end. What elements of each character's personality help them do this? Faced with a similar situation, what sorts of choices might you make?

2. In what ways do you think Galen's definition of himself, beyond the labels "helot" and "prince," changes between the beginning and end of the book?

3. The Crypteia marks the transition for Spartan boys from childhood to adulthood. How do Nikolas and Galen make that transition over the course of the book?

4. Why do Galen's real parents choose to give him up? Was that a good choice?

5. Several characters in the book are caught between loyalties. How did they choose which "side" to be on? What sacrifices did they have to make in order to decide?

6. Sparta itself is a kind of character in the book. In fact, one might say Sparta is an *adolescent* character, on the verge of change. What kinds of changes does Galen wish for Sparta? If you were the Eurypontid leader, what new laws might you propose?

7. The helots outnumbered the Spartans nearly ten to one. Yet, few helot rebellions were recorded in history, despite the cruel treatment of the helots. Why do you

think this was so? How would Galen answer this question if asked?

8. Korinna accuses Galen of falling in love too easily. Meanwhile, Galen accuses Nikolas of the same thing. Do you think they are impulsive when it comes to matters of the heart?

9. In the end, Galen is adopted into the Spartan citizenry, leaving his helot status behind. What difficulties can you imagine he will face in the transition? What about guilt?

10. Galen keeps Nikolas' true identity secret at the end of the novel. Is this a good choice?

IDEAS FOR FURTHER RESEARCH

1. Compare and contrast Spartan society with Athenian society. How were these two groups essentially different? How were they similar?

2. Spartan women enjoyed rights that no other women had in the ancient world. Why was that so? What made the Spartans different from everyone else in this regard?

3. Research the living conditions of the helots in Ancient Sparta. Some historians wouldn't classify the helots as slaves, given their freedom of movement within the city. What do you think?

4. Consider the ways rebellions and revolutions throughout history have been organized. Were there any helot rebellions? Why might they have succeeded/failed?

5. The Spartans relied on "wise elders," like the ephors, to make crucial decisions. What other cultures/nations/societies in history depended on "wise elders"? How might such a structure be helpful, or damaging?

6. Research the battle at Thermopylae and King Leonidas. What particular Spartan qualities made that battle so memorable?

7. The Spartans studied wit in the agoge. Having an appropriate riposte at the ready was considered a particularly Spartan gift. Compare the method of argumentation used by the Spartans with that of the

Athenians. How was rhetoric used differently in each city state?

8. Compare modern day militaries to that of the Spartans. Do you recognize any of the ancient traditions in today's armies?

9. Sparta had no walls around its city. This was unheard of in Ancient Greece. What did this say about the Spartans as a people, geographically, and strategically?

10. Research historical sibyls. Who were these women? Where did they live? What were their lives like?

IDEAS FOR CREATIVE WRITING

1) Choose a Greek myth and write the story from another perspective. For example, tell the Orpheus myth from Eurydice's point of view.

2) The clothes make the man. Or so the adage goes. It certainly must have *felt* true in Ancient Sparta, where those with red cloaks were citizens, and enjoyed that society's full benefits. Write a character sketch or story in which an article of clothing defines your character.

3) Singers, who used a lyre to accompany their verses, sang the stories of the heroes in Ancient Greece. Write a song or poem in which you honor your own hero.

4) In *Song of the Red Cloak*, each of the characters makes a series of poor choices. Write a narrative in which your character chooses the wrong path. How will he or she find his or her way again?

5) The ancients could never have imagined the kinds of lives we live today. Write a letter to one of the characters in *Song of the Red Cloak*, describing your bedroom. How would you explain a computer? A telephone?

6) The Spartans believed they were descended from Hercules. If you could have one of the Greek gods or demi-gods as an ancestor, which one would it be? How might that change the way you view yourself? Write about it.

BOOKS FOR FURTHER READING

Cartledge, Paul. *The Spartans: The World of the Warrior Heroes of Ancient Greece*. Vintage, 2004.

Miller, Frank and Lynn Varley. *300*. Dark Horse, 1999.

Plutarch. *On Sparta*. Penguin Classics, 2005.

Pressfield, Steven. *Gates of Fire: An Epic Novel of the Battle of Thermopylae*. Bantam: 2005

Spivey, Nigel. *Songs on Bronze*: *The Greek Myths Made Real*. FSG, 2005.

Thucydides. *History of the Peloponnesian War*. Penguin Classics, 1972.

GLOSSARY

Agoge—the demanding schooling required of all Spartan males, beginning at age seven.

Agiad—one of two royal lines in Sparta. The Agiad line was considered older than the Eurypontid, and are said to have been descended from Eurysthenes, a great-great-great-grandson of Heracles' (Hercules).

Chiton—clothing worn by men, women and children in Ancient Greece. The Spartan chiton was cut shorter than was worn elsewhere, as the Spartans were proud of their physiques, acquired after rigorous training.

Crypteia—there are a number of disputes among historians regarding the Crypteia. As it is generally understood, the Crypteia was a secret tradition among the older students of the agoge. In the fall, the ephors would declare war on the helots, thereby making their murder legal. Agoge students would be required to kill a helot in order to prove their leadership ability.

Drakhaina—a giant serpent, with some features of a woman. Famous drakhainas in Greek myth include Lamia, Scylla, and Echidna.

Ephor—elected elder statesmen who served as advisors to the kings of Sparta. Ephors only served one term, but they were powerful players in Spartan politics and religion.

Eurypontid--one of two royal lines in Sparta. The Eurypontid are said to have descended from Procles, a great-great-great-grandson of Heracles' (Hercules), just like the Agiads.

Gerousia—the Spartan senate, made up of 30 male citizens, 60 years of age or older.

Helot—the slave population of Sparta. Their work was primarily agricultural, and their treatment at the hands of the Spartans was brutal.

Periokoi—free, non-citizens of Sparta. They could not participate in Spartan political affairs, nor could they marry Spartan men and women.

AUTHOR'S NOTE

A work of fiction makes no promises about factual truth. Girls who see the future or control the elements are, of course, my inventions in this book. Lamia, the half-snake, half-woman children-eater is a Greek myth, and so, someone else's fabrication long, long ago. But that doesn't mean this fiction is *all* untrue.

Here are some facts about the Spartans:

Two royal families and an assembly of male citizens led the Spartan government, advised by five ephors in some consultation with a sibyl, or other seer. Men lived in army barracks, not with their families. Young soldiers and older students were whipped to test their strength. There is some evidence that weak babies were discarded at birth. The citizens of Sparta depended on slaves, called helots, to farm, make weapons, weave, dig wells, build bridges, and on and on, because the Spartans were quite busy training for war. Spartan women stood in sharp contrast to their Greek peers because of their relative freedom. They were free to dress in short chitons like the men, proud as they were of their athletic builds. Young girls were sent to school, and they competed in the Olympics. Spartan women were allowed to own property. Women who died in childbirth were given burials of honor. They were encouraged to speak their minds. I can't help but love the Spartan women.

As for Spartan youth, well, high school is hard on everyone. But I think, in the history of humanity, no school was as difficult to attend as the Spartan agoge. Spartan boys entered at the age of seven, and did not leave the agoge until they were eighteen or so, and ready to fight for their city-state. They went hungry most of the time in order to toughen up. Students were publically whipped until they yielded, lost consciousness, or died, whichever came first. Furthermore, the Crypteia, the "hunting" of helots, was the job of promising agoge students, meant to control the helot population and strike terror in the hearts of the slaves. The Crypteia may not have been an annual event, though I've depicted it as such here.

This brings me to the helots.

In all my research, I couldn't find the names of any helots. Better scholars than I probably know where to access the names, but I was at a loss. The helotry outnumbered the Spartans by about 200,000 people. Some estimates are more conservative, but the bottom line is this: the Spartans were a tiny group compared to their slaves, and the Spartans' greatest fear was a helot revolt. Because they constituted the majority of the population, helots had a certain degree of mobility in Sparta. But they were a decided underclass, and events like the Crypteia served to keep them in check.

So many helots, and not one name easily accessible among them. Hence, Galen was born out of that wish to give names and faces to the unnamed thousands of Spartan slaves, the people who made Sparta Sparta, but who never got the chance to wear a red cloak.

The book you hold in your hands is an invention, but there are many historical truths in it. I've tried to be as accurate as possible regarding places and landmarks in Sparta, the city-state's governmental structure, and its cultural beliefs. But I've taken some liberties, too, for the sake of the story.

I set Galen's tale in the final years of the Persian War (which the Spartans won, thus paving the way for an explosion of Greek culture in the region), and well after the famous battle at Thermopylae, which happened in the summer of 480 BC. There, in the place where 300 Spartans fought against a massive Persian force, lies an epitaph for the fallen soldiers, one I like to imagine Galen and his friends would be proud of. It reads:

CHANTEL ACEVEDO

Stranger, go tell the Spartans
That we lie here
True, even to the death
To our Spartan way of life.

Greek stories and myths make up the root metaphors of Western culture, so in a way, the epitaph above is a reminder to all of us to remember the Spartans, who live on in our art, our culture, and even our language.

The Spartans, in particular, were a quick-witted, pious, sometimes cruel, often courageous people. Galen, Nikolas, Korinna and Zoi are all these things, too, in good measure, as we all are.

ACKNOWLEDGMENTS

Many thanks to Judith Weber, agent and editor of wonders. Thanks to Julie Stevenson and Kirsten White at Sobel Weber, too, for their enthusiasm and attention to this manuscript.

A grateful bow to Julianna Baggott, blazer of trails. Thank you.

I owe a huge debt to Andrea Cabrera, the first to meet Galen and his crew. This book exists, largely, because you wanted to read more, Sissy. Thanks.

A big, thankful hug to Rachel Hawkins, who loves reading about Boys with Swords as much as I do. Thanks for loving these characters, long lunches, and escandalo, in general.

Thanks to Guy Beckwith for his expertise, keen eye, and for knowing how heavy a spear should be.

To Jim and Marta Quinn, for your support in this, and all things. I love you.

Finally, I want to thank my husband and best friend, Orlando, who convinced me to write this in the first place, and my daughter Penelope, for asking me to tell her the story about the "snake lady" and the "boys who win" again and again. I love you guys.

ABOUT THE AUTHOR

Chantel Acevedo's first novel, *Love and Ghost Letters*, won the Latino International Book Award for Historical Fiction and was a finalist for the Connecticut Book of the Year. Having started her career as a high school English teacher, she holds an MFA from the University of Miami, and is currently an Associate Professor at Auburn University in Auburn, Alabama, where she lives with her husband and daughter. *Song of the Red Cloak* is her first novel for young adults.

SONG OF THE RED CLOAK

SONG OF THE RED CLOAK

SONG OF THE RED CLOAK

Made in the USA
Monee, IL
18 June 2020